TRANSFORMERS ANIMATED™

VOLUME 3

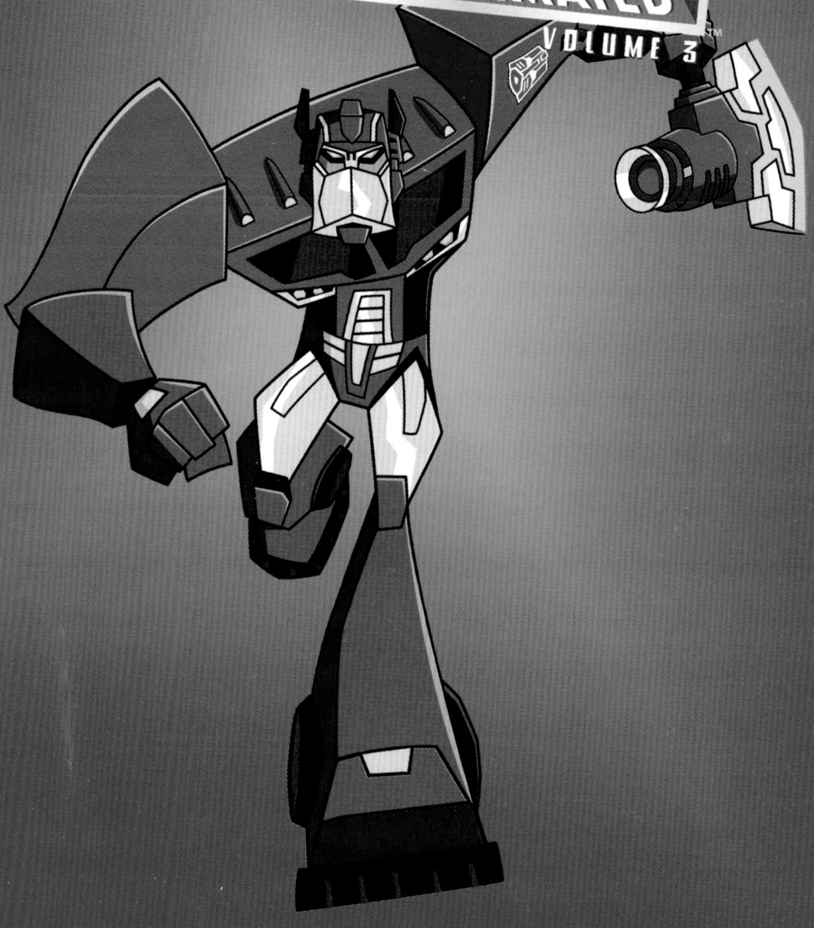

HOME IS WHERE THE SPARK IS
BASED ON THE SCREENPLAY BY: MARTY ISENBERG

WRITTEN BY: MICHAEL RYAN

TOTAL MELTDOWN

WRITTEN BY: RICH FOGEL

ADAPTATION BY: ZACHARY RAU

LETTERS AND DESIGN BY: TOM B. LONG

EDITS BY: JUSTIN EISINGER

ISBN: 978-1-60010-215-8
11 10 09 08   2 3 4 5 6

Licensed by:
Hasbro

Special thanks to Hasbro's Aaron Archer, Michael Kelly, Sheri Lucci, Richard Zambarano, Jared Jones, Michael Provost, Michael Richie, and Michael Verrecchia for their invaluable assistance.

IDW Publishing is:

Operations:
Moshe Berger, Chairman
Ted Adams, Chief Executive Officer
Greg Goldstein, Chief Operating Officer
Matthew Ruzicka, CPA, Chief Financial Officer

Alan Payne, VP of Sales
Lorelei Bunjes, Dir. of Digital Services
Marci Hubbard, Executive Assistant
Alonzo Simon, Shipping Manager

Editorial:
Chris Ryall, Publisher/Editor-in-Chief
Scott Dunbier, Editor, Special Projects
Andy Schmidt, Senior Editor
Justin Eisinger, Editor

Kris Oprisko, Editor/Foreign Lic.
Denton J. Tipton, Editor
Tom Waltz, Editor
Mariah Huehner, Assistant Editor

Design:
Robbie Robbins, EVP/Sr. Graphic Artist
Ben Templesmith, Artist/Designer
Neil Uyetake, Art Director

Chris Mowry, Graphic Artist
Amauri Osorio, Graphic Artist

To discuss this issue of *Transformers*, or join the IDW Insiders, or to check out exclusive Web offers, check out our site:

www.IDWPUBLISHING.com

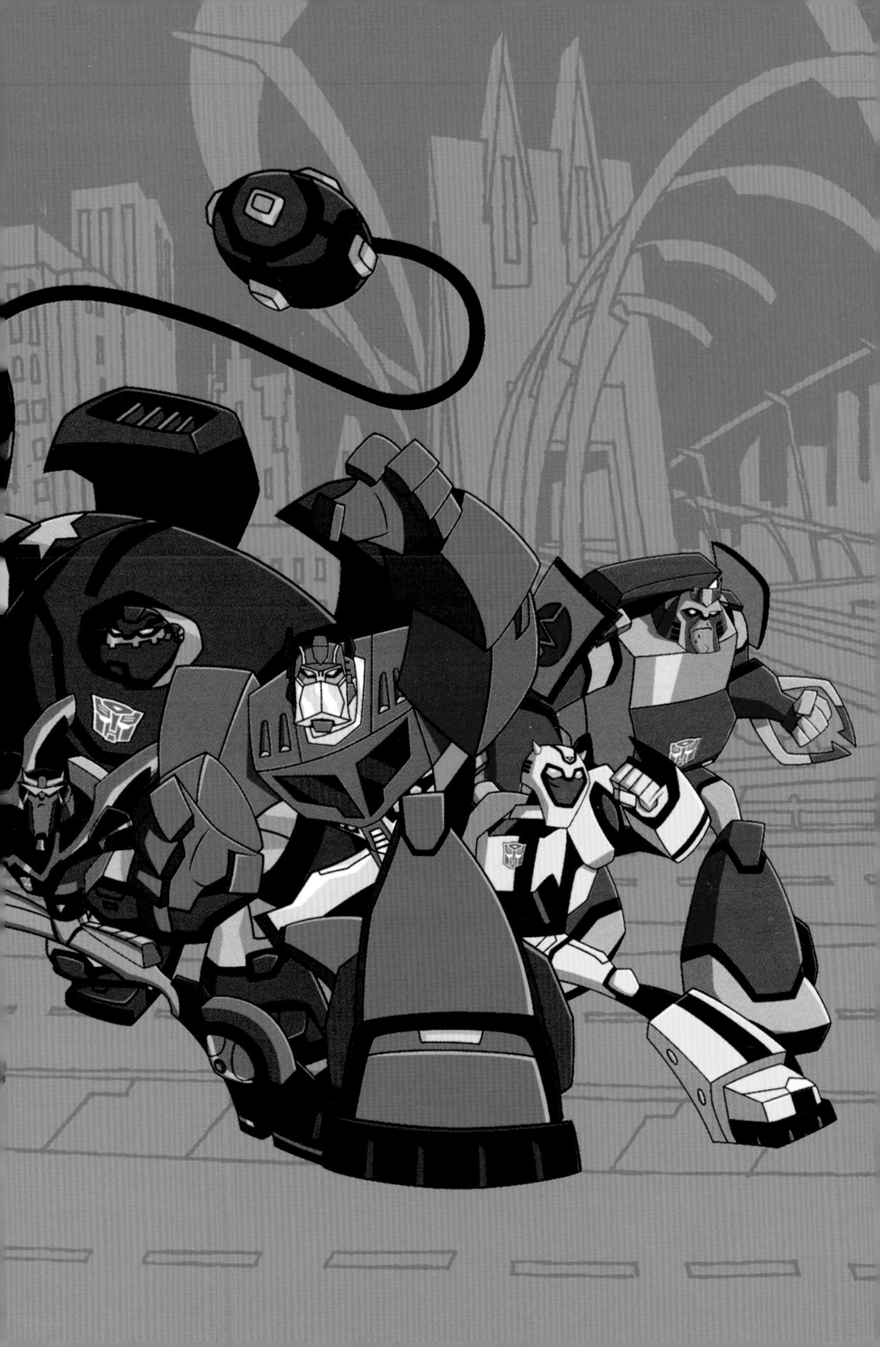

Roll Call

Optimus Prime

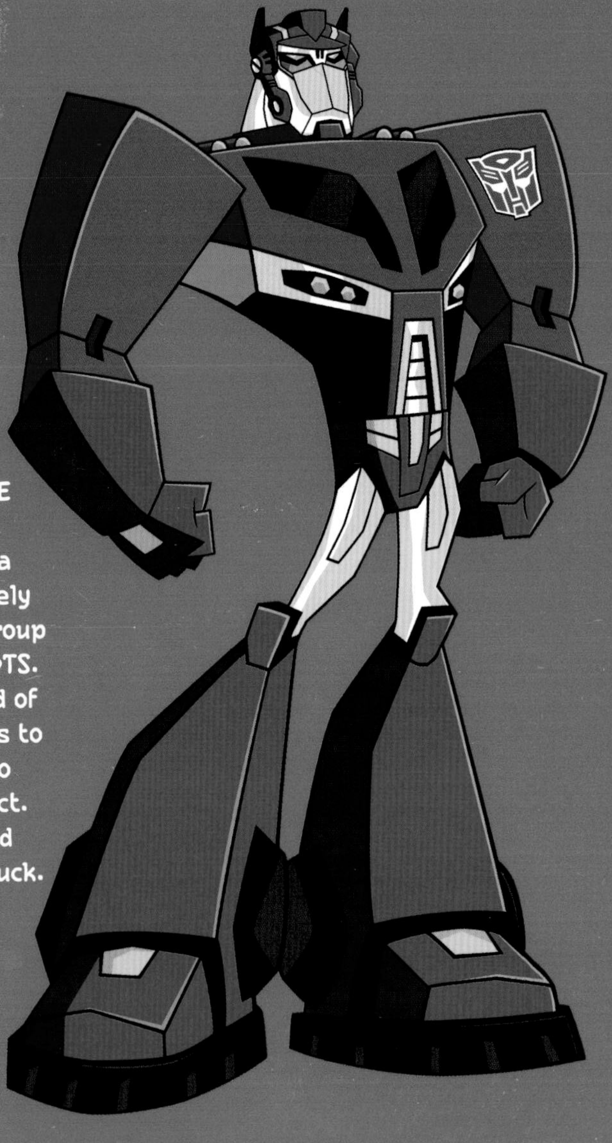

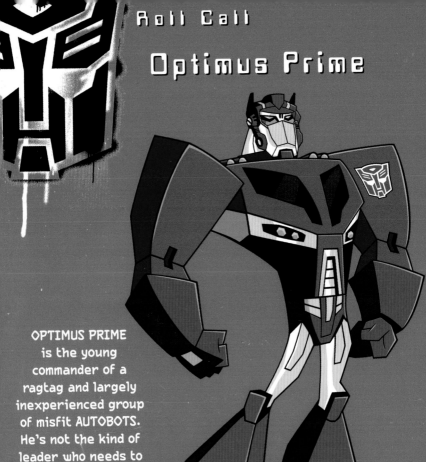

OPTIMUS PRIME is the young commander of a ragtag and largely inexperienced group of misfit AUTOBOTS. He's not the kind of leader who needs to bark orders to command respect. His mechanized form is a fire truck.

Ratchet

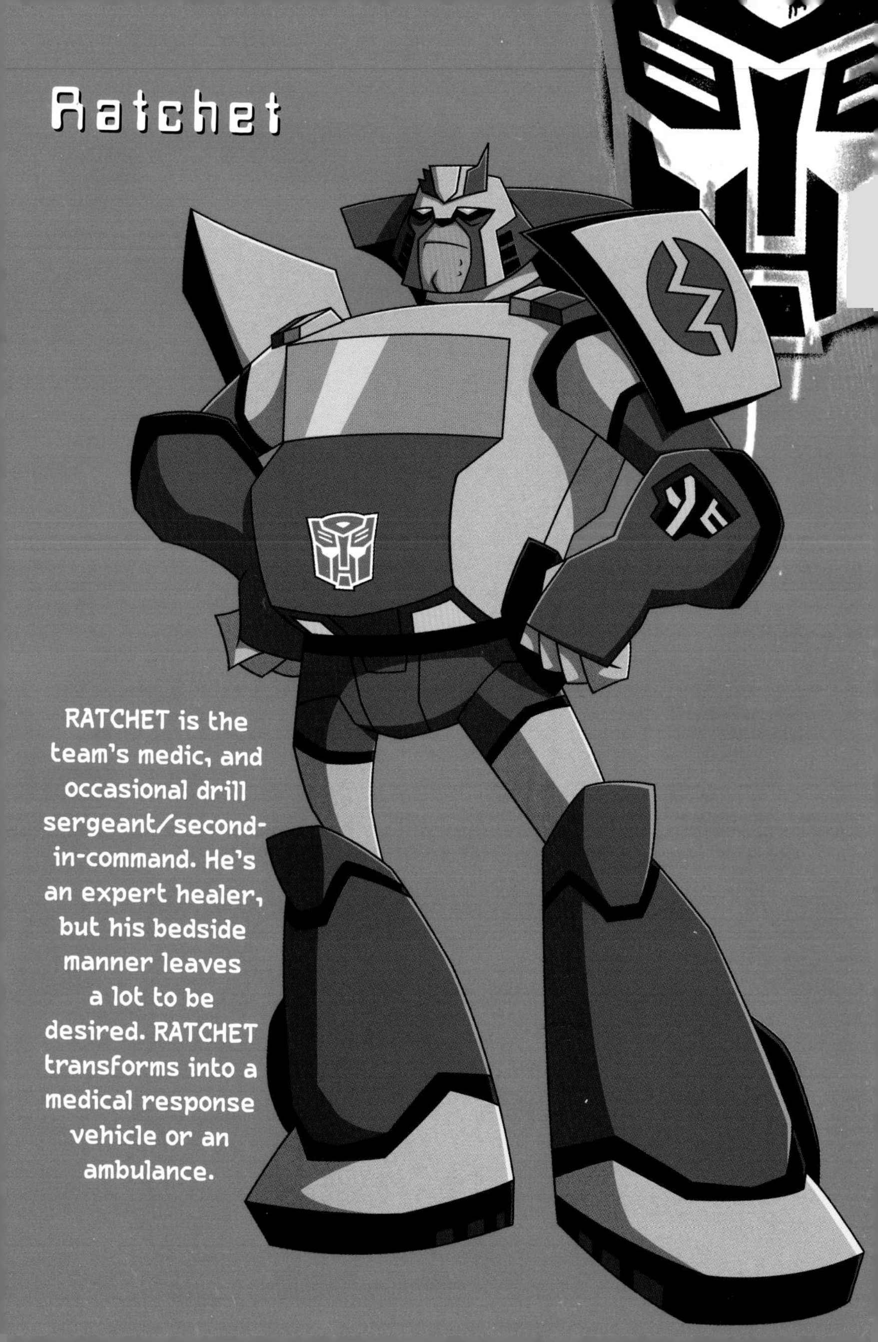

RATCHET is the team's medic, and occasional drill sergeant/second-in-command. He's an expert healer, but his bedside manner leaves a lot to be desired. RATCHET transforms into a medical response vehicle or an ambulance.

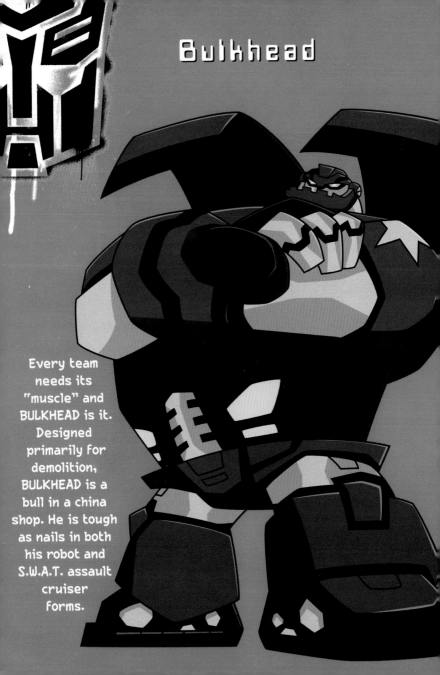

Bulkhead

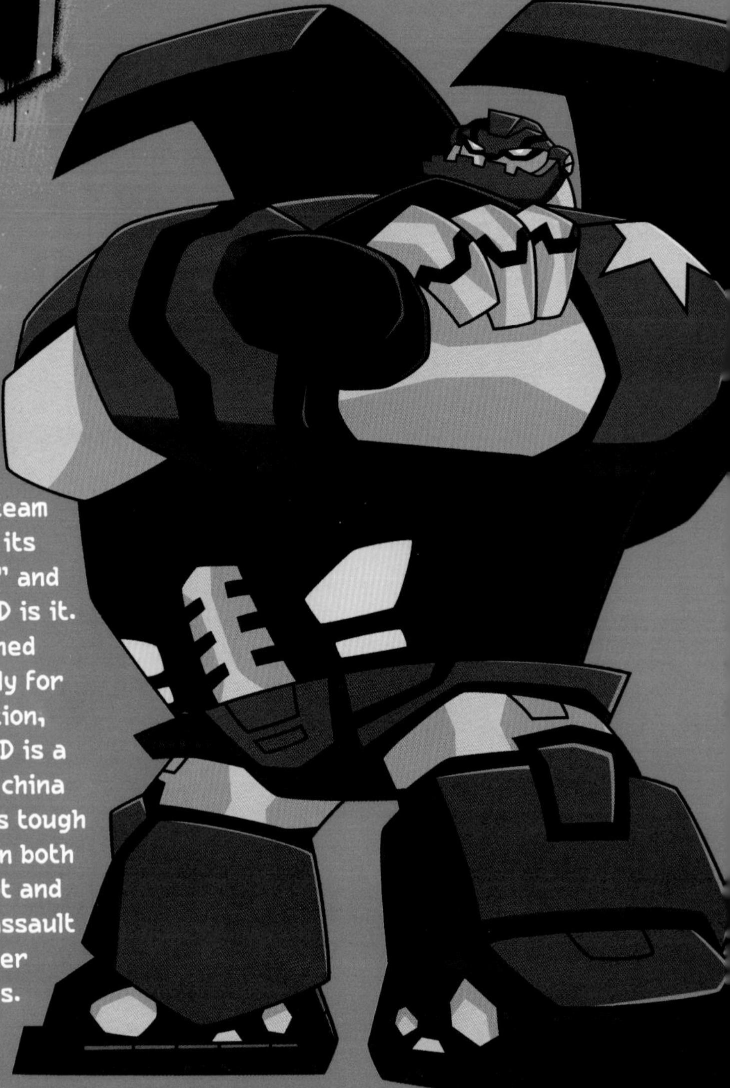

Every team needs its "muscle" and BULKHEAD is it. Designed primarily for demolition, BULKHEAD is a bull in a china shop. He is tough as nails in both his robot and S.W.A.T. assault cruiser forms.

Bumblebee

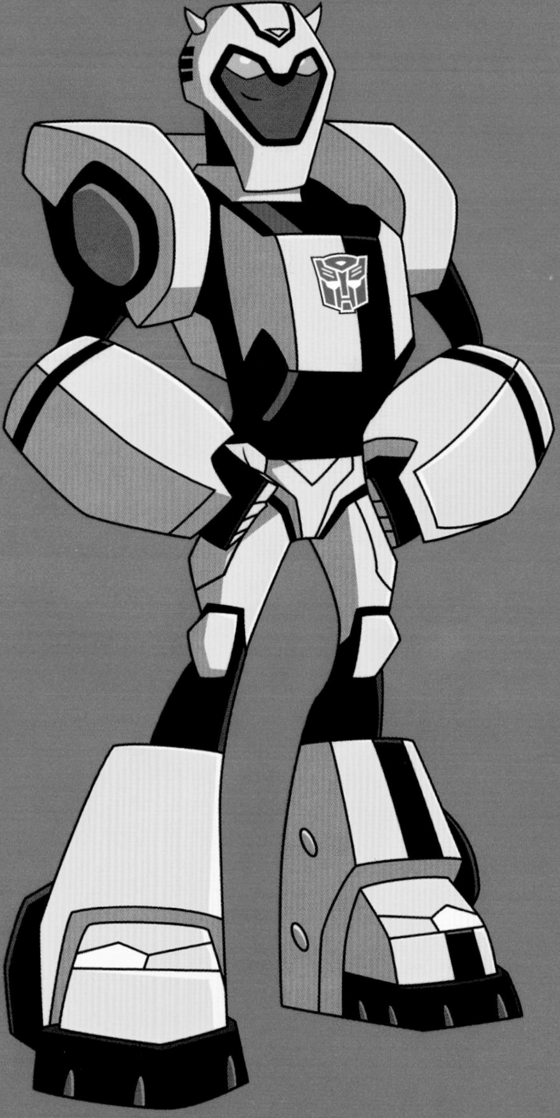

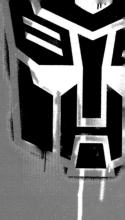

BUMBLEBEE
is the "kid" of
the team, easily
the youngest and
least mature of
the AUTOBOTS.
He's a bit of a
showoff, always
acting on impulse
and rarely
considering the
consequences.
But he looks
awesome in
his undercover
police cruiser
form.

Prowl

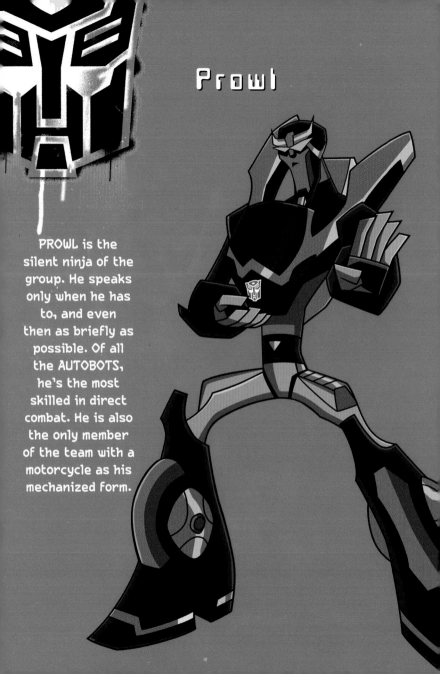

PROWL is the silent ninja of the group. He speaks only when he has to, and even then as briefly as possible. Of all the AUTOBOTS, he's the most skilled in direct combat. He is also the only member of the team with a motorcycle as his mechanized form.

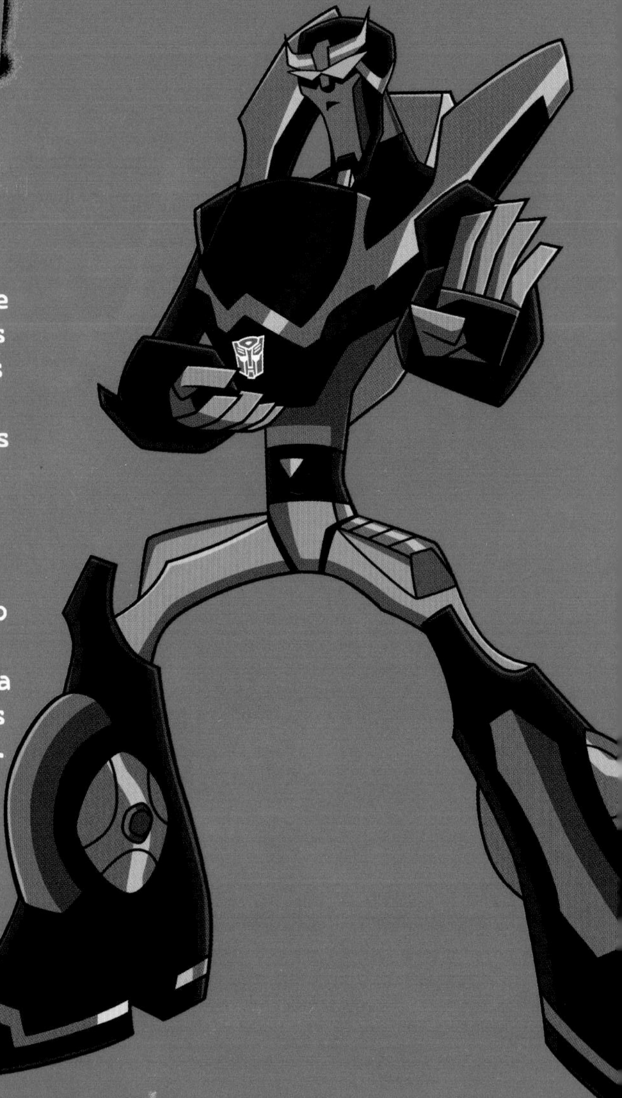

Megatron

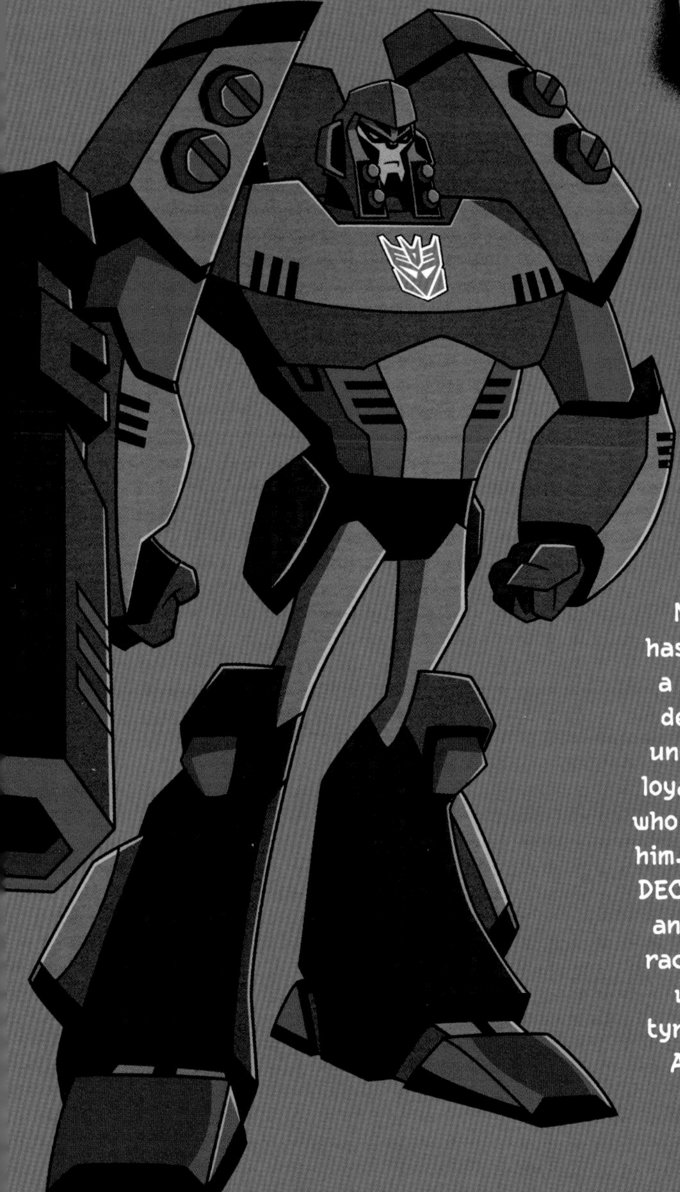

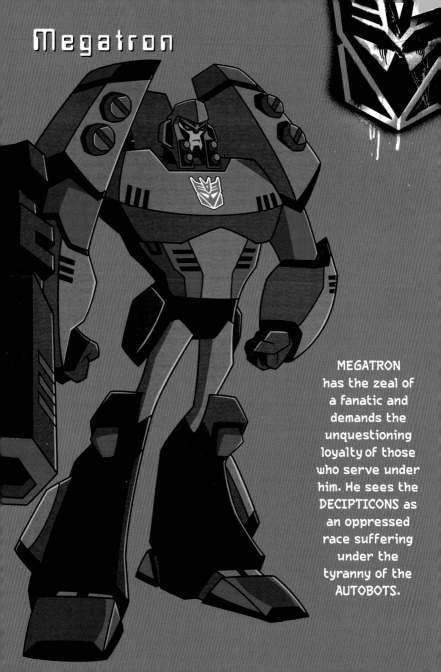

MEGATRON has the zeal of a fanatic and demands the unquestioning loyalty of those who serve under him. He sees the DECIPTICONS as an oppressed race suffering under the tyranny of the AUTOBOTS.

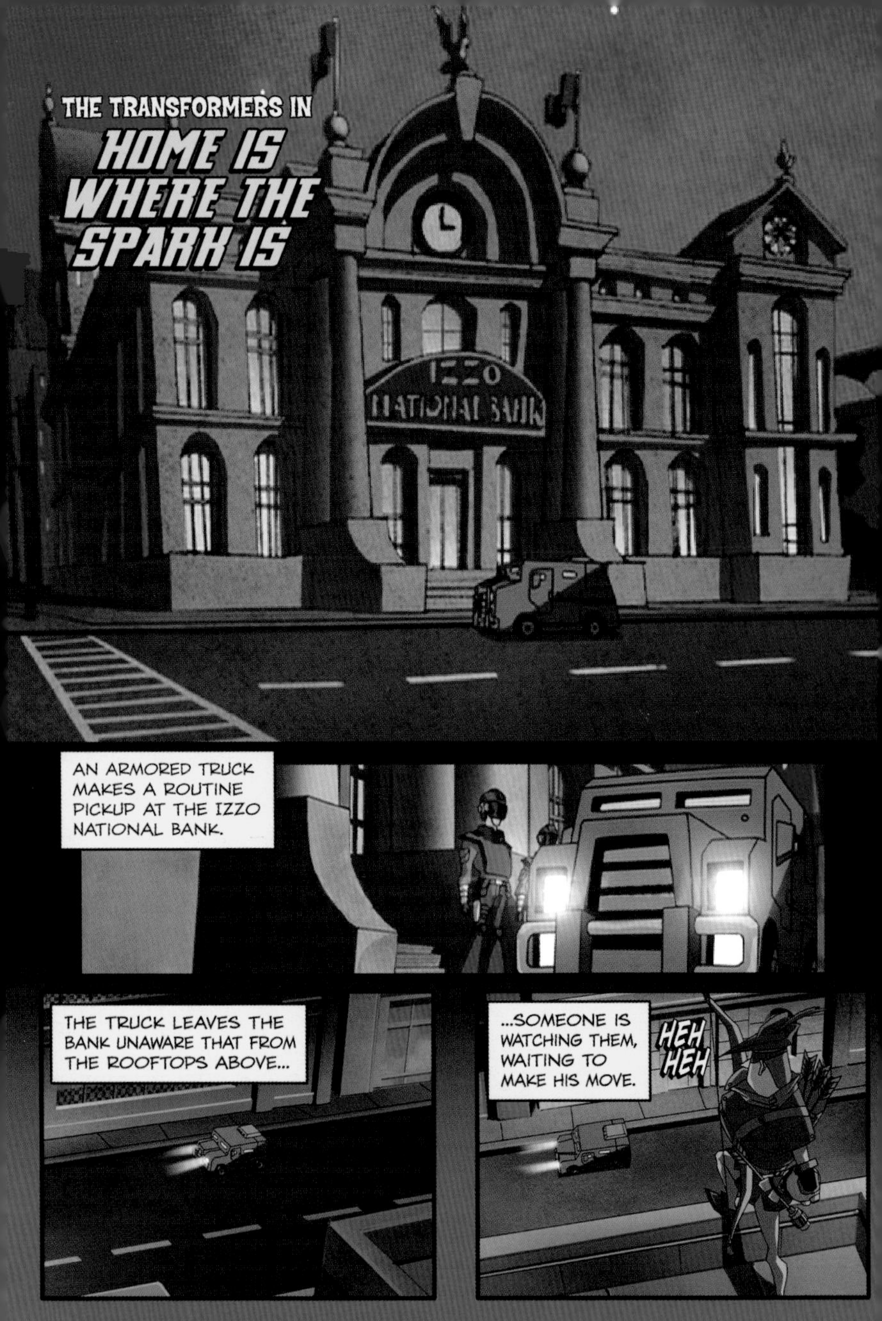
THE TRANSFORMERS IN
HOME IS WHERE THE SPARK IS
IZZO NATIONAL BANK
AN ARMORED TRUCK MAKES A ROUTINE PICKUP AT THE IZZO NATIONAL BANK.
THE TRUCK LEAVES THE BANK UNAWARE THAT FROM THE ROOFTOPS ABOVE...
...SOMEONE IS WATCHING THEM, WAITING TO MAKE HIS MOVE.
HEH HEH

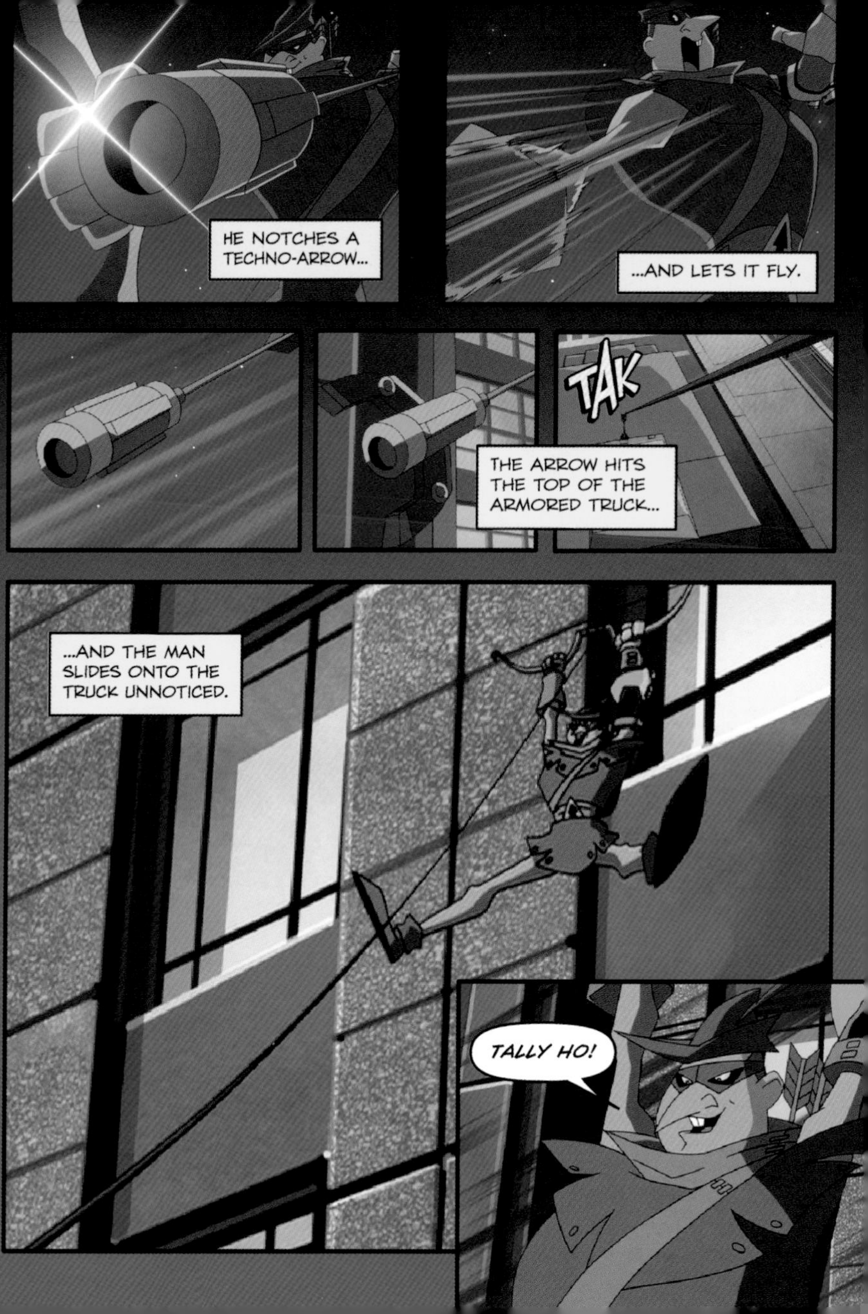
HE NOTCHES A TECHNO-ARROW...
...AND LETS IT FLY.
TAK
THE ARROW HITS THE TOP OF THE ARMORED TRUCK...
...AND THE MAN SLIDES ONTO THE TRUCK UNNOTICED.
TALLY HO!

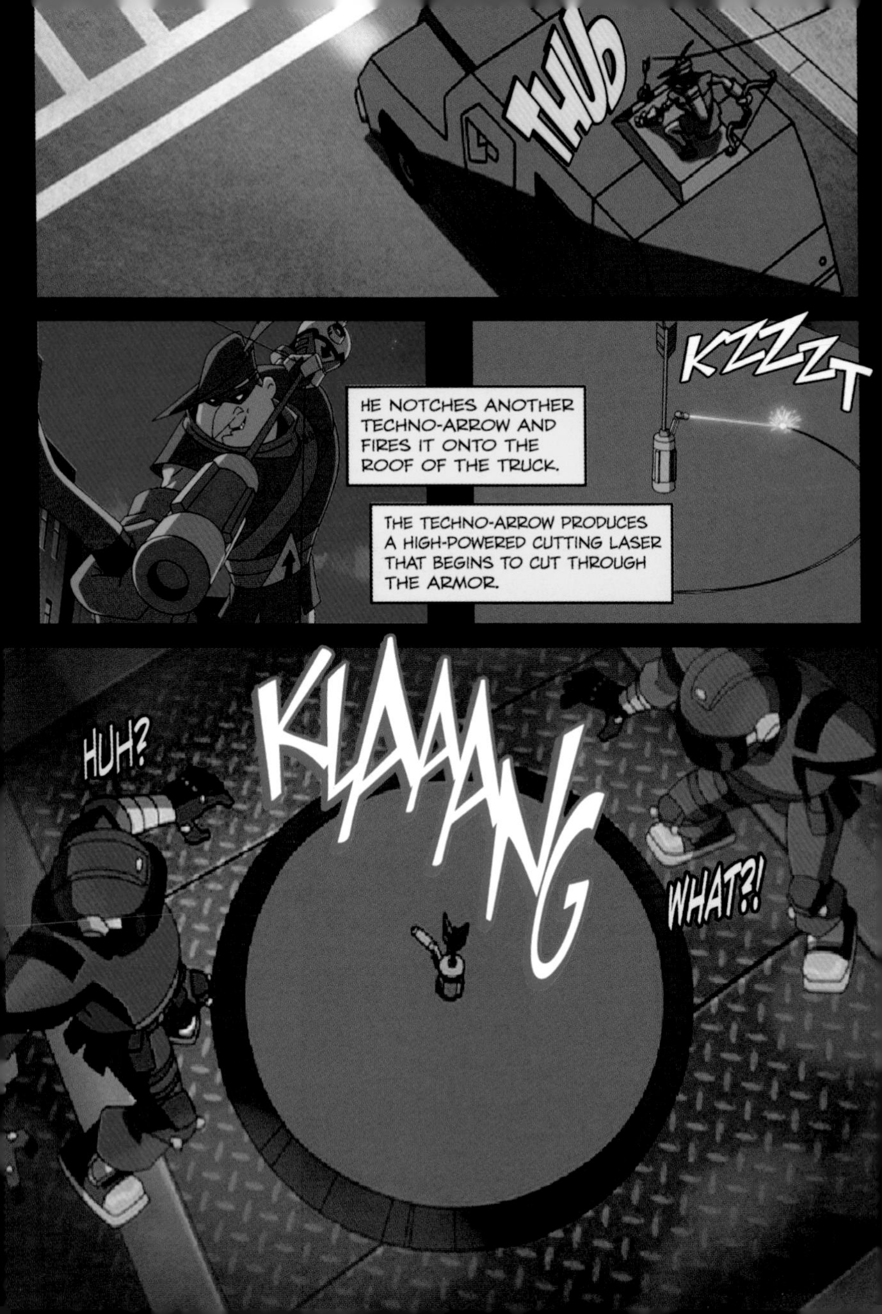
THUD
HE NOTCHES ANOTHER TECHNO-ARROW AND FIRES IT ONTO THE ROOF OF THE TRUCK.
KZZZZT
THE TECHNO-ARROW PRODUCES A HIGH-POWERED CUTTING LASER THAT BEGINS TO CUT THROUGH THE ARMOR.
HUH?
KLAAAANG
WHAT?!

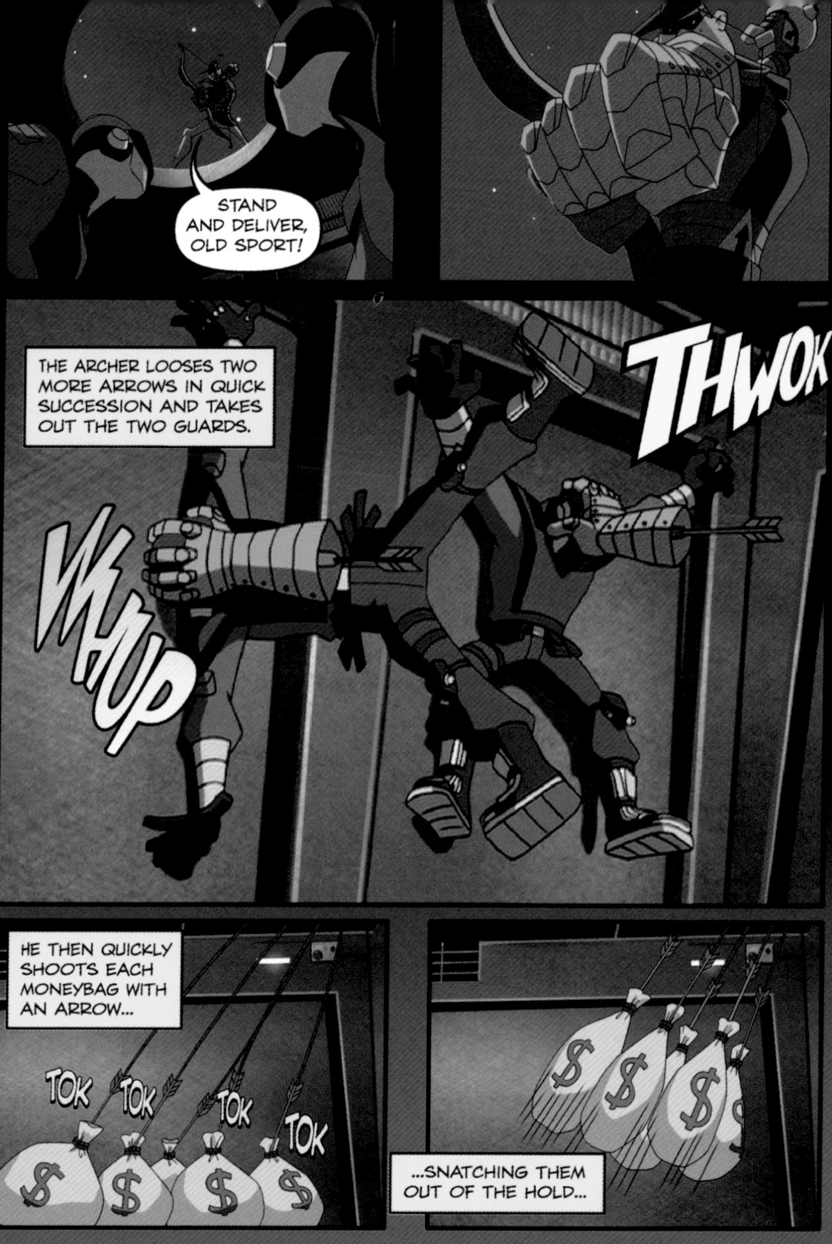
STAND AND DELIVER, OLD SPORT!
THE ARCHER LOOSES TWO MORE ARROWS IN QUICK SUCCESSION AND TAKES OUT THE TWO GUARDS.
THWOK
WHUP
HE THEN QUICKLY SHOOTS EACH MONEYBAG WITH AN ARROW...
TOK
TOK
TOK
TOK
...SNATCHING THEM OUT OF THE HOLD...

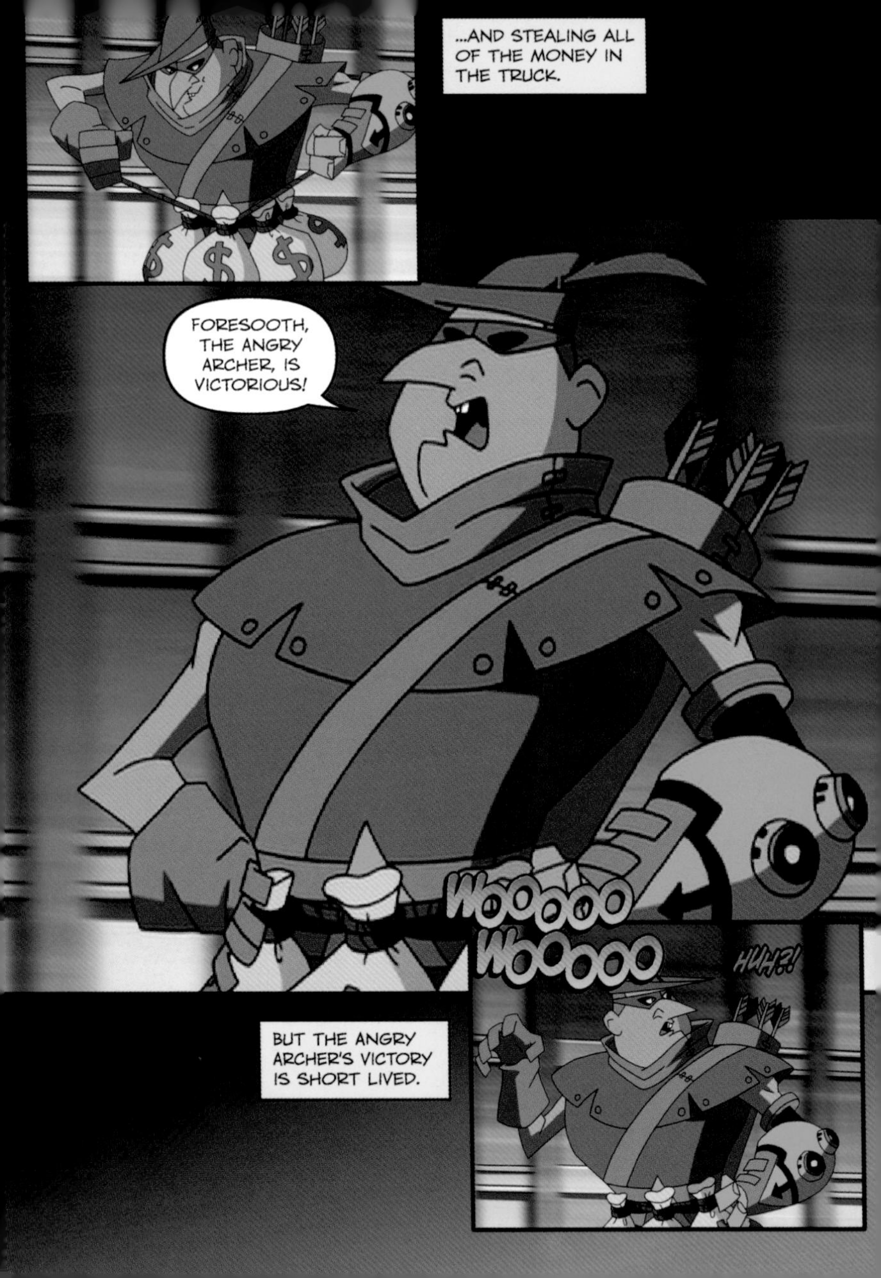
...AND STEALING ALL OF THE MONEY IN THE TRUCK.
FORESOOTH, THE ANGRY ARCHER, IS VICTORIOUS!
WOOOOO WOOOOO
HUH?!
BUT THE ANGRY ARCHER'S VICTORY IS SHORT LIVED.

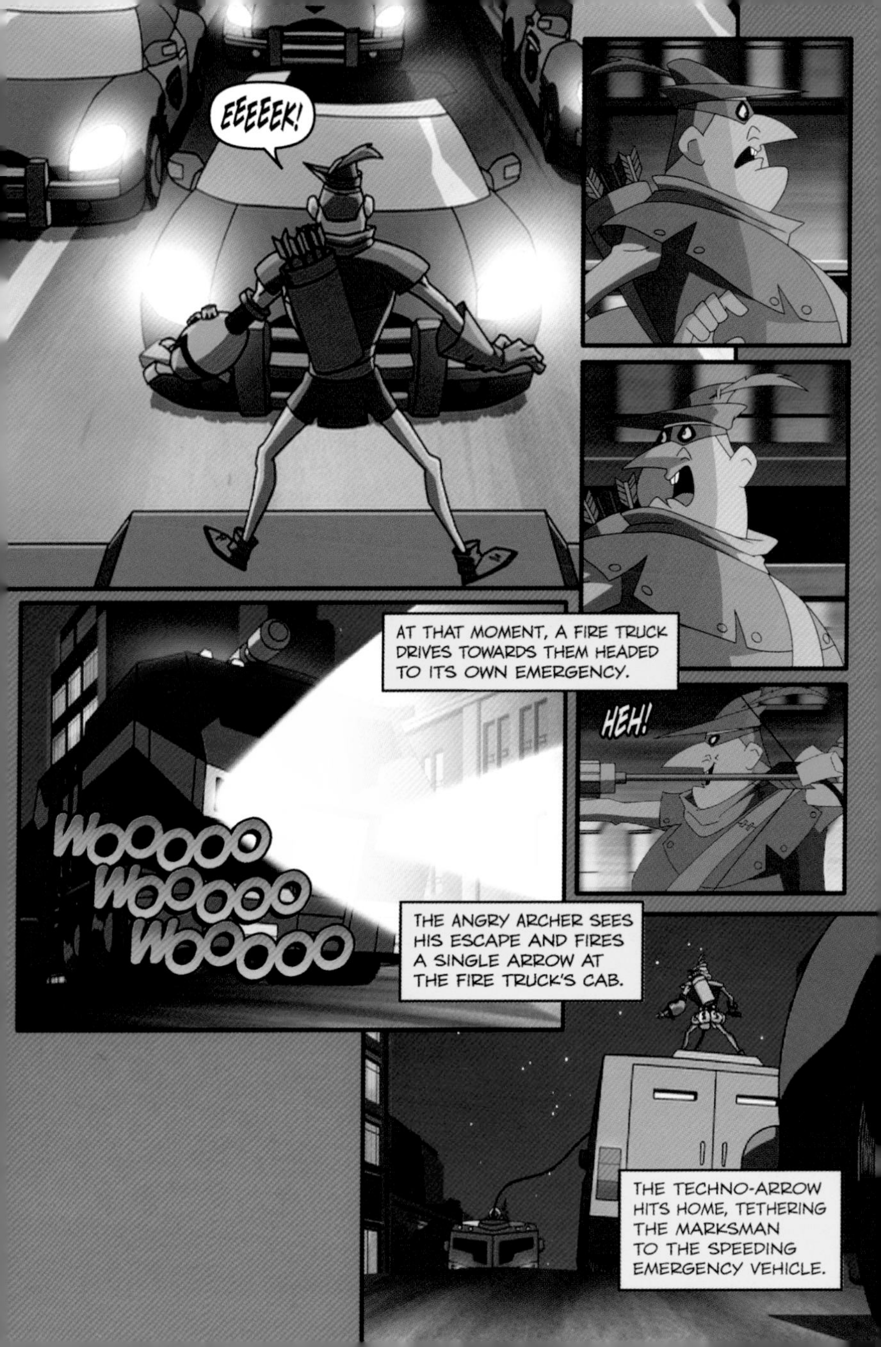
EEEEEK!
AT THAT MOMENT, A FIRE TRUCK DRIVES TOWARDS THEM HEADED TO ITS OWN EMERGENCY.
HEH!
WOOOOO WOOOOO WOOOOO
THE ANGRY ARCHER SEES HIS ESCAPE AND FIRES A SINGLE ARROW AT THE FIRE TRUCK'S CAB.
THE TECHNO-ARROW HITS HOME, TETHERING THE MARKSMAN TO THE SPEEDING EMERGENCY VEHICLE.

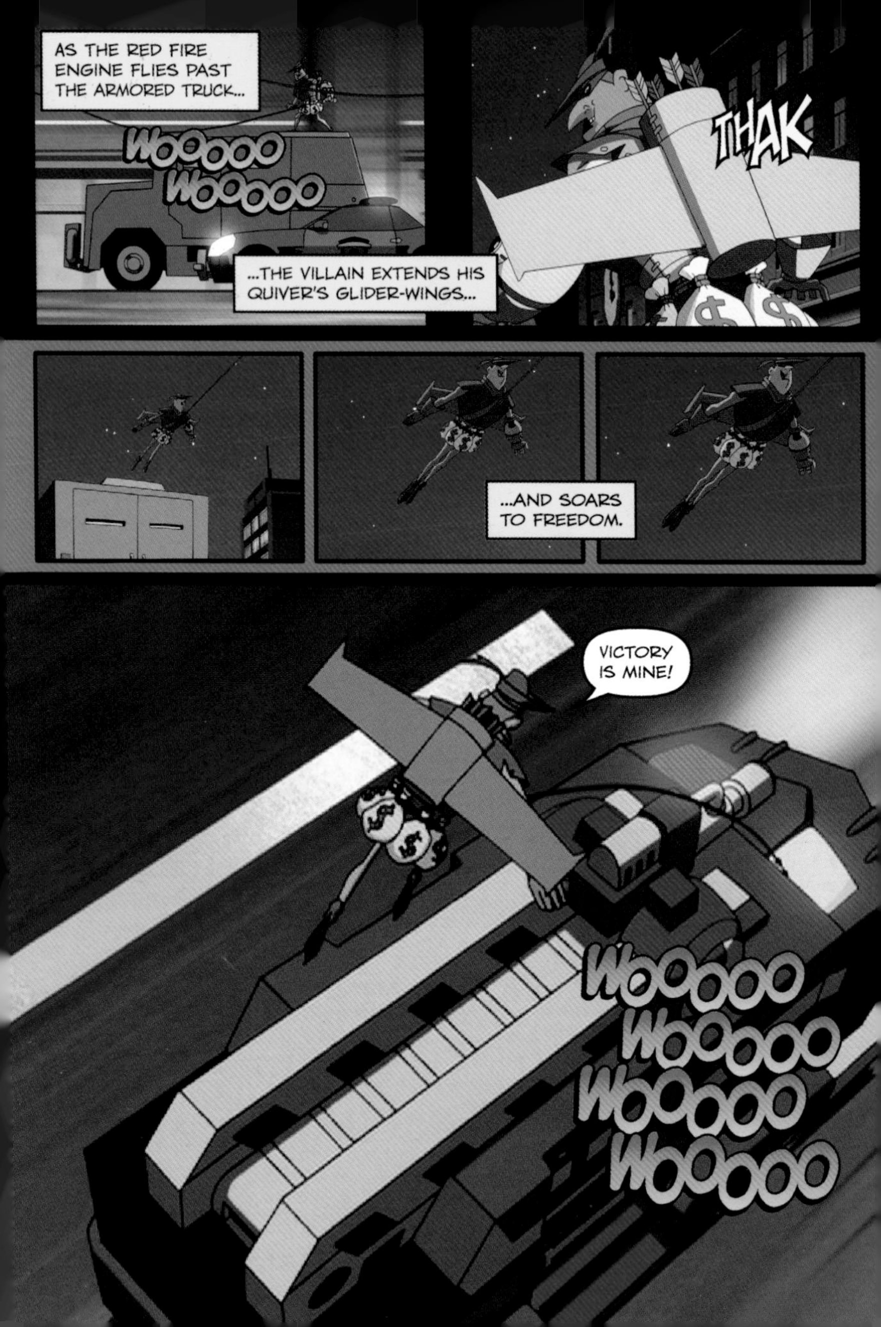

AS THE RED FIRE ENGINE FLIES PAST THE ARMORED TRUCK...
WOOOOO WOOOOO
...THE VILLAIN EXTENDS HIS QUIVER'S GLIDER-WINGS...
THAK
...AND SOARS TO FREEDOM.
VICTORY IS MINE!
WOOOOO WOOOOO WOOOOO WOOOOO

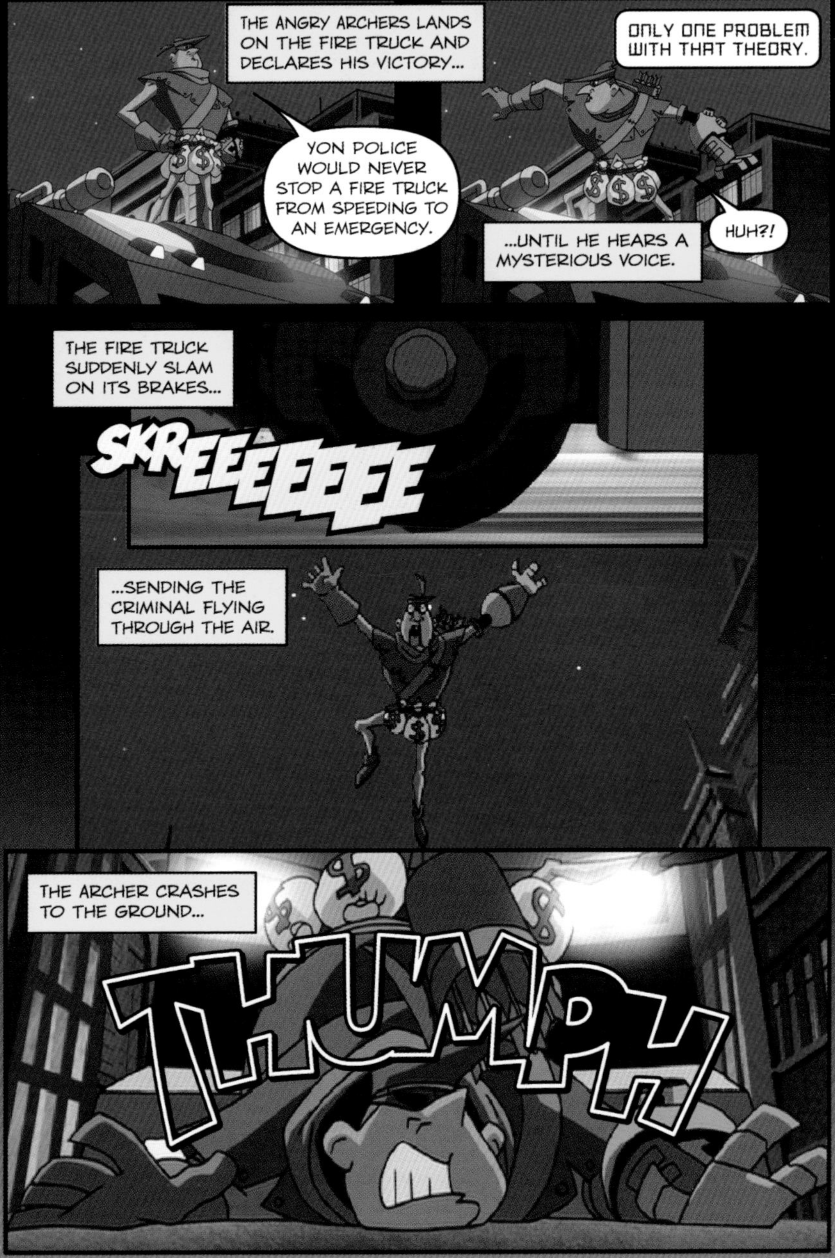
THE ANGRY ARCHERS LANDS ON THE FIRE TRUCK AND DECLARES HIS VICTORY...
YON POLICE WOULD NEVER STOP A FIRE TRUCK FROM SPEEDING TO AN EMERGENCY.
ONLY ONE PROBLEM WITH THAT THEORY.
...UNTIL HE HEARS A MYSTERIOUS VOICE.
HUH?!
THE FIRE TRUCK SUDDENLY SLAM ON ITS BRAKES...
SKREEEEEEE
...SENDING THE CRIMINAL FLYING THROUGH THE AIR.
THE ARCHER CRASHES TO THE GROUND...
THUMPH

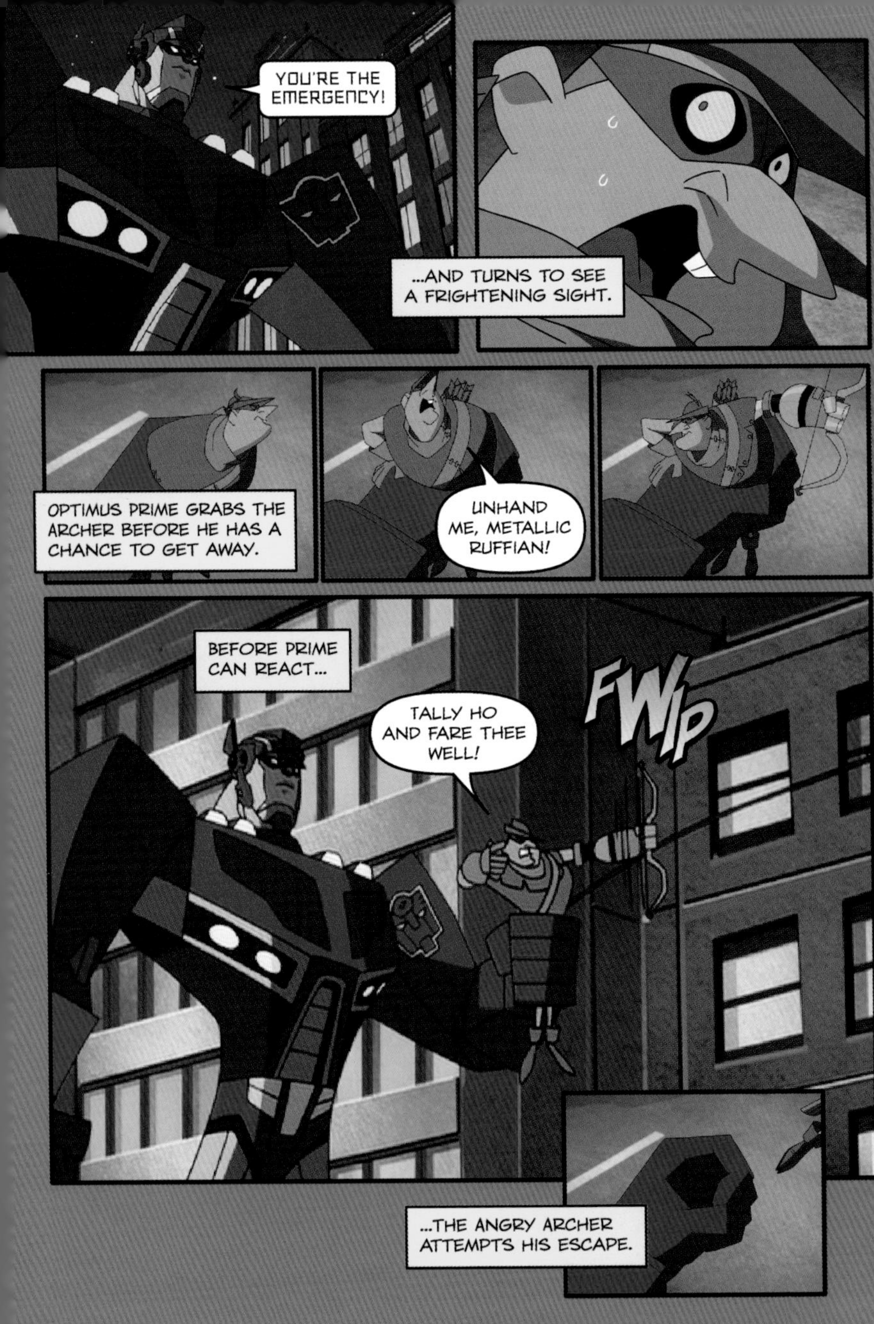

YOU'RE THE EMERGENCY!
...AND TURNS TO SEE A FRIGHTENING SIGHT.
OPTIMUS PRIME GRABS THE ARCHER BEFORE HE HAS A CHANCE TO GET AWAY.
UNHAND ME, METALLIC RUFFIAN!
BEFORE PRIME CAN REACT...
TALLY HO AND FARE THEE WELL!
FWIP
...THE ANGRY ARCHER ATTEMPTS HIS ESCAPE.

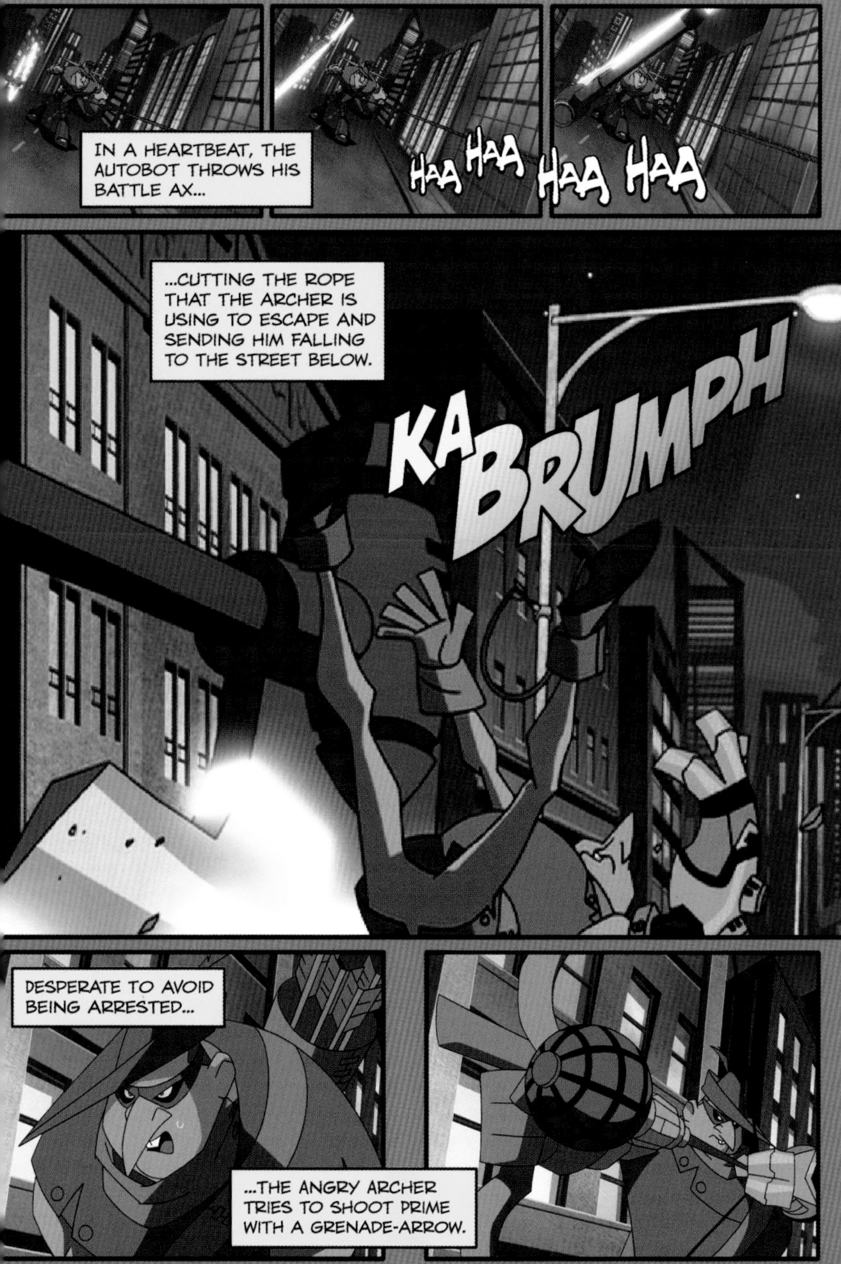
IN A HEARTBEAT, THE AUTOBOT THROWS HIS BATTLE AX...
HAA HAA HAA HAA
...CUTTING THE ROPE THAT THE ARCHER IS USING TO ESCAPE AND SENDING HIM FALLING TO THE STREET BELOW.
KA BRUMPH
DESPERATE TO AVOID BEING ARRESTED...
...THE ANGRY ARCHER TRIES TO SHOOT PRIME WITH A GRENADE-ARROW.

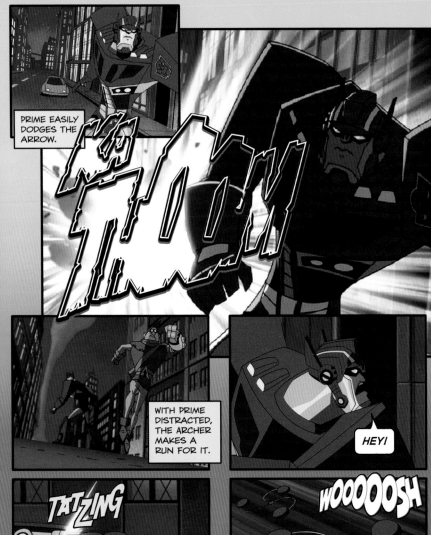

PRIME EASILY DODGES THE ARROW.

K TLOM

WITH PRIME DISTRACTED, THE ARCHER MAKES A RUN FOR IT.

HEY!

TAT ZING

WOOOOOSH

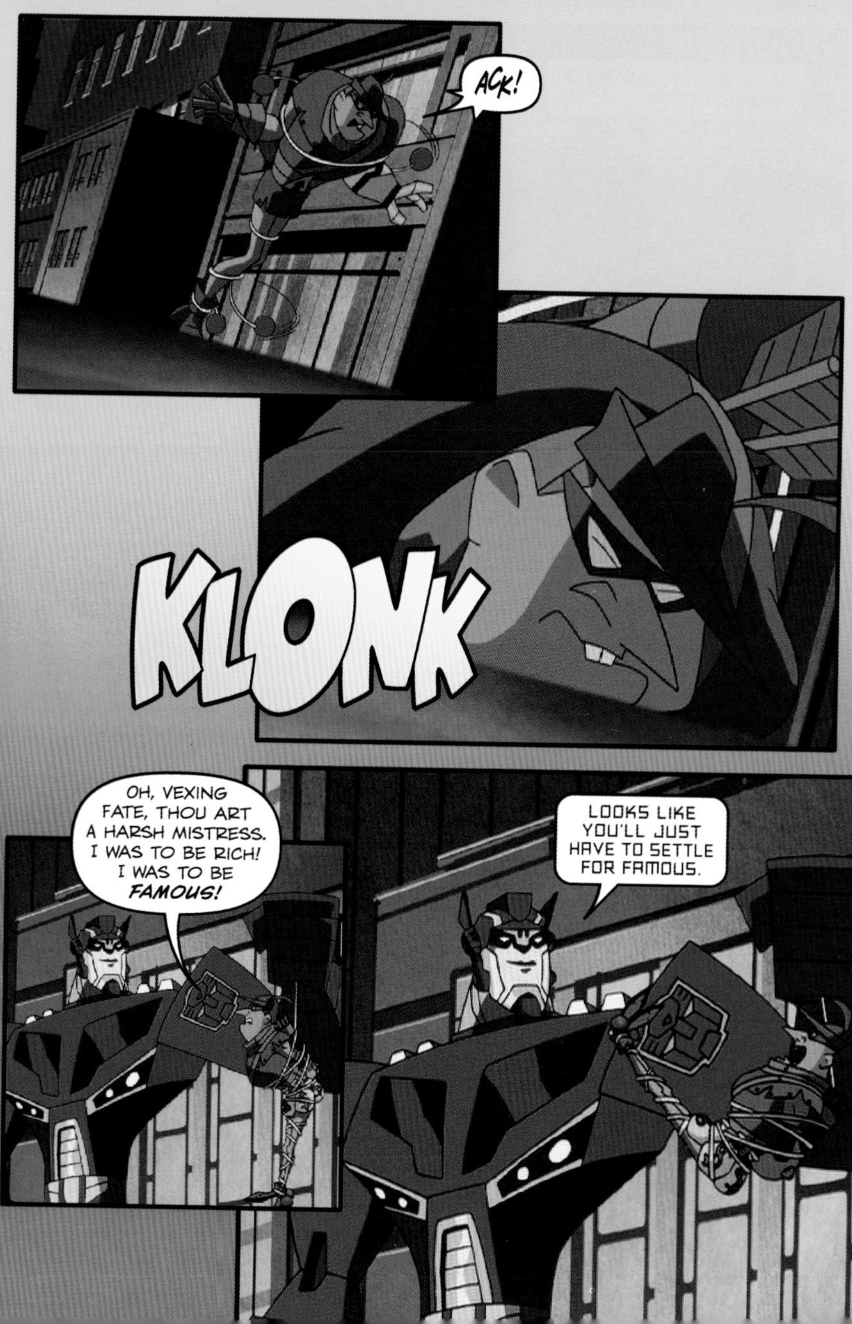
ACK!
KLONK
OH, VEXING FATE, THOU ART A HARSH MISTRESS. I WAS TO BE RICH! I WAS TO BE FAMOUS!
LOOKS LIKE YOU'LL JUST HAVE TO SETTLE FOR FAMOUS.

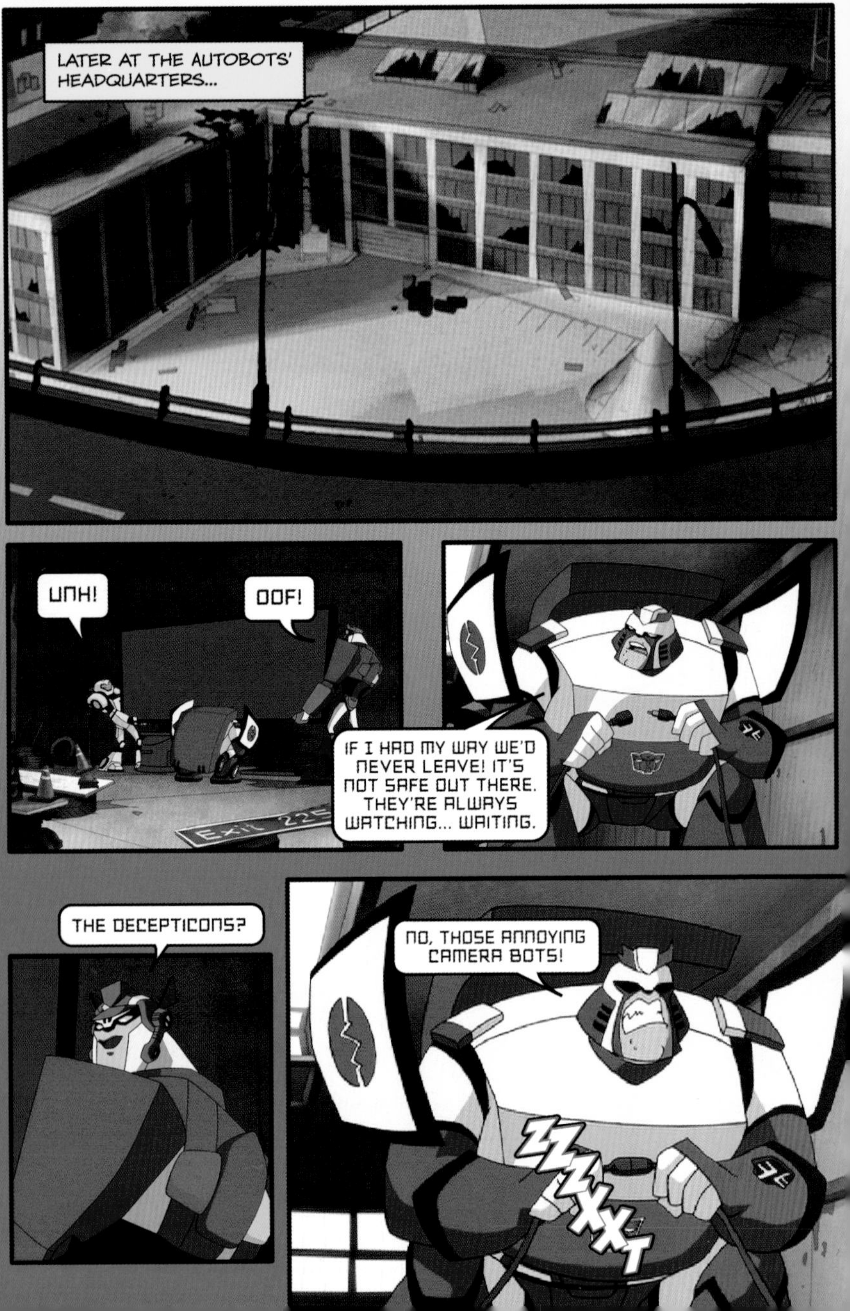
LATER AT THE AUTOBOTS' HEADQUARTERS...
UNH!
OOF!
IF I HAD MY WAY WE'D NEVER LEAVE! IT'S NOT SAFE OUT THERE. THEY'RE ALWAYS WATCHING... WAITING.
THE DECEPTICONS?
NO, THOSE ANNOYING CAMERA BOTS!
ZZZXXT

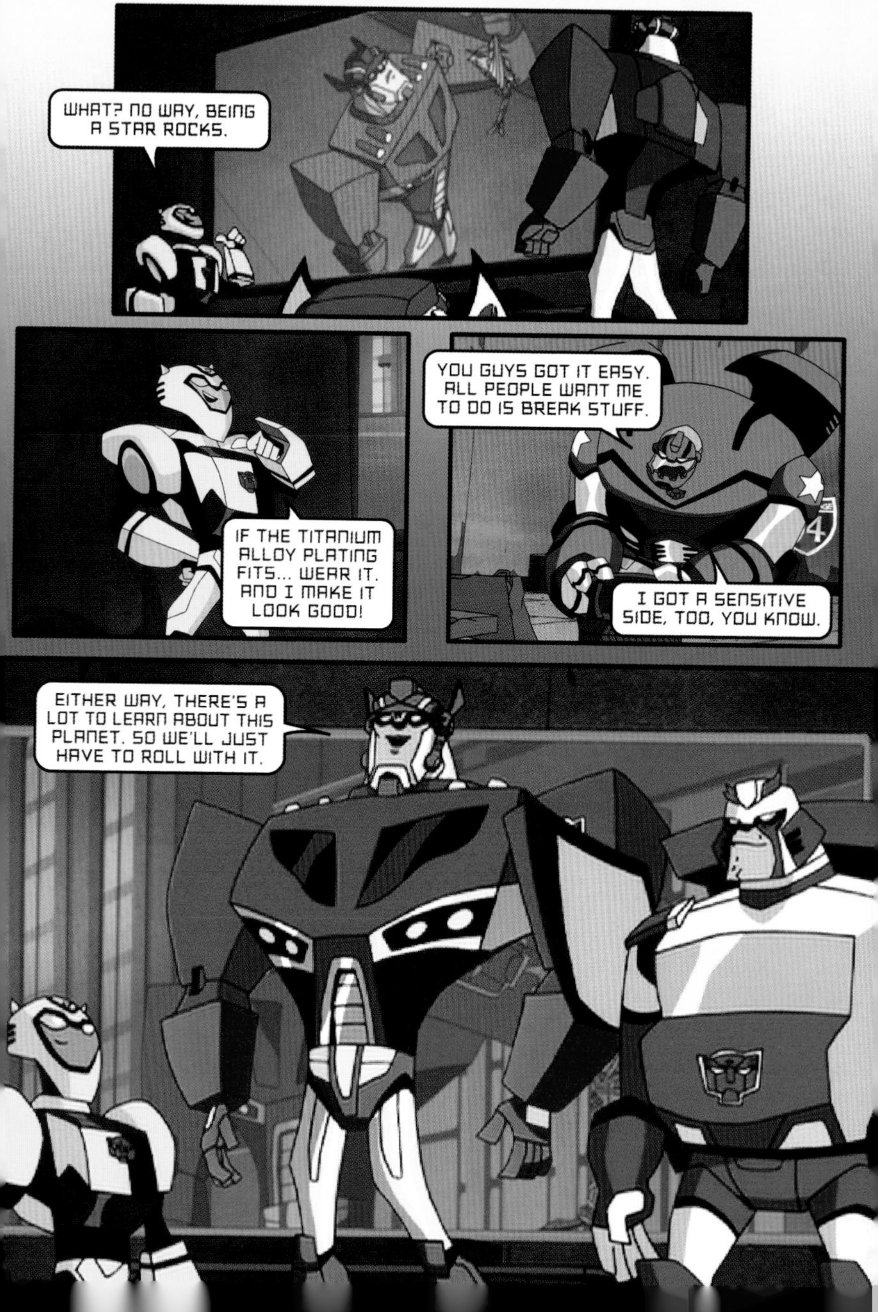
WHAT? NO WAY, BEING A STAR ROCKS.
IF THE TITANIUM ALLOY PLATING FITS... WEAR IT. AND I MAKE IT LOOK GOOD!
YOU GUYS GOT IT EASY. ALL PEOPLE WANT ME TO DO IS BREAK STUFF.
I GOT A SENSITIVE SIDE, TOO, YOU KNOW.
EITHER WAY, THERE'S A LOT TO LEARN ABOUT THIS PLANET. SO WE'LL JUST HAVE TO ROLL WITH IT.

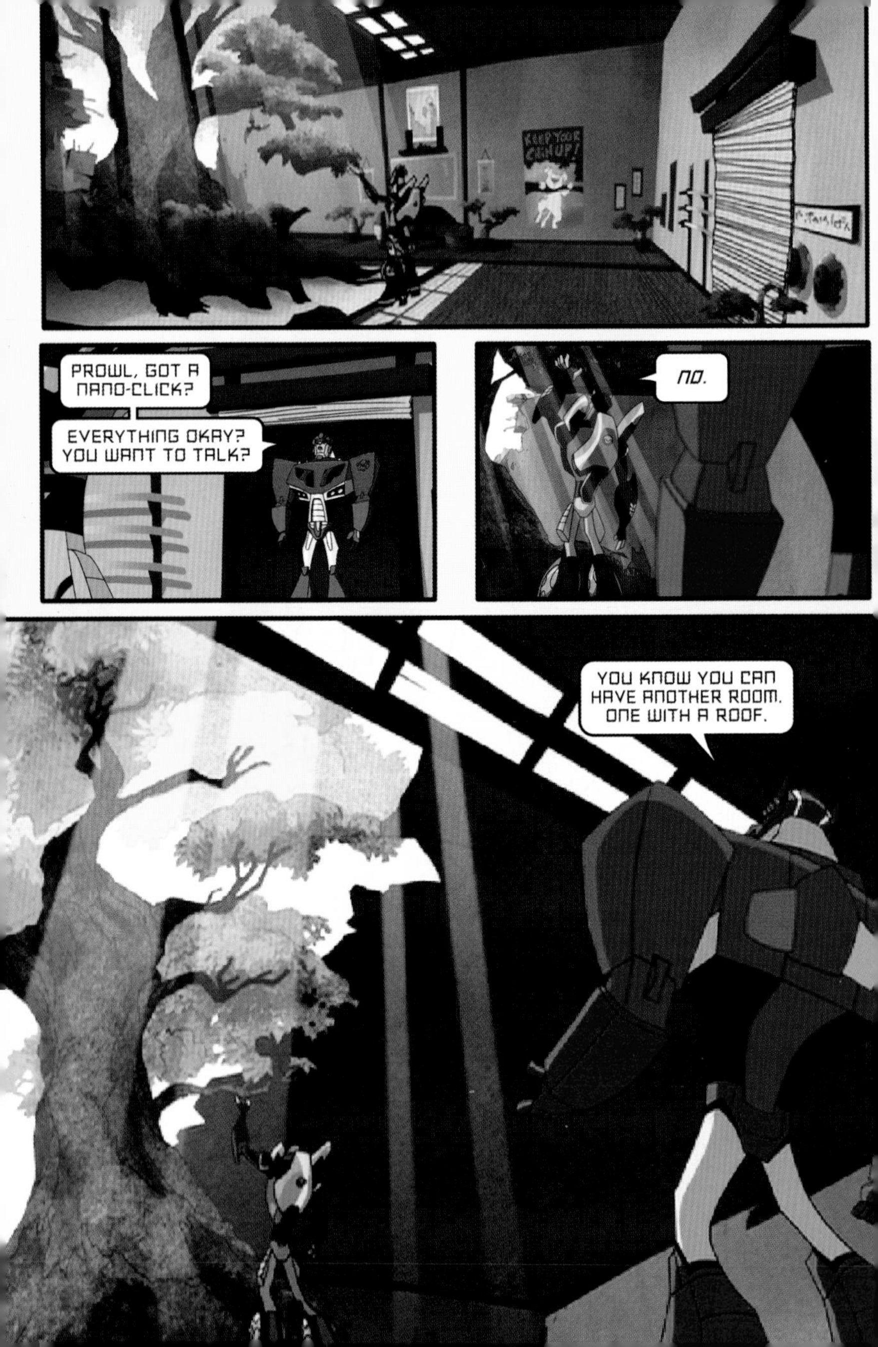
PROWL, GOT A NANO-CLICK?
EVERYTHING OKAY? YOU WANT TO TALK?
NO.
YOU KNOW YOU CAN HAVE ANOTHER ROOM. ONE WITH A ROOF.

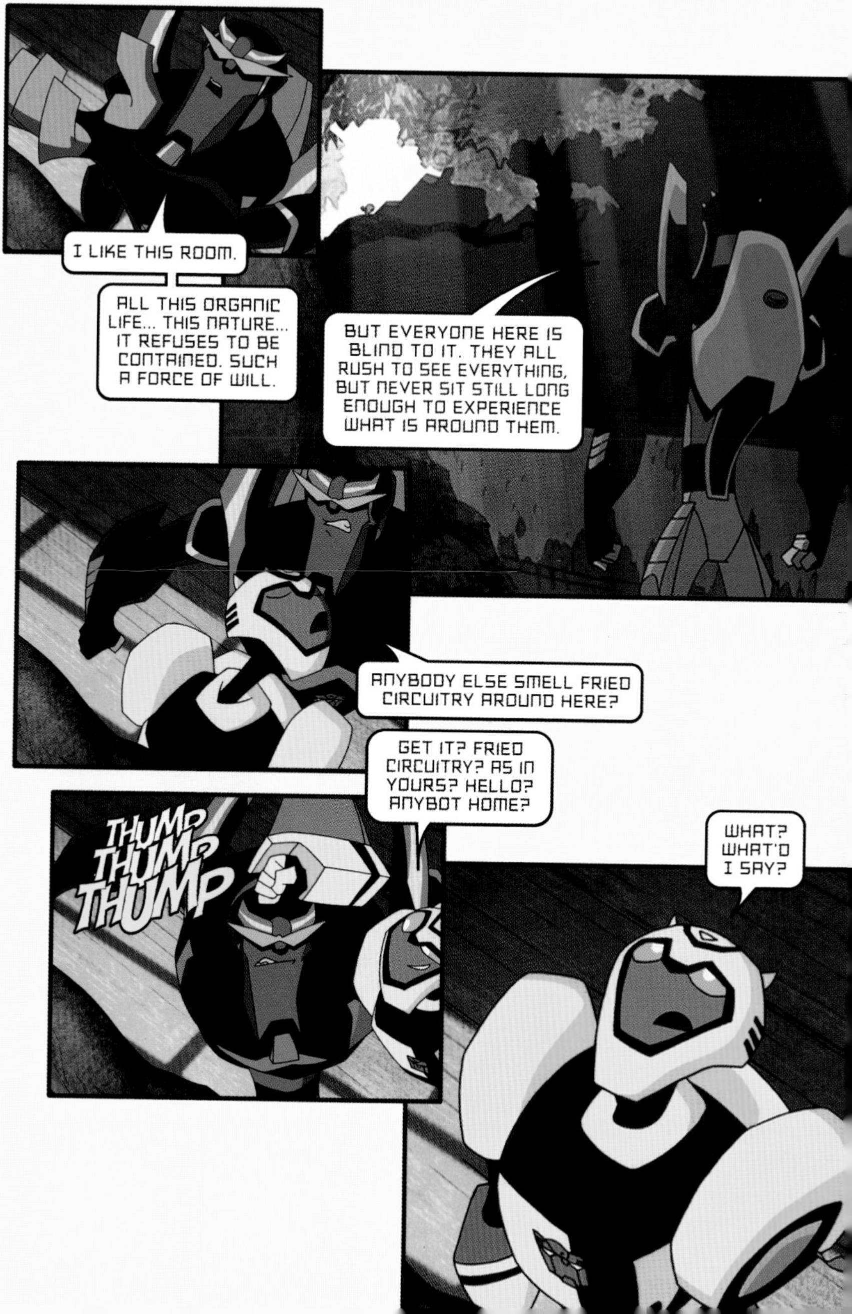

I LIKE THIS ROOM.
ALL THIS ORGANIC LIFE... THIS NATURE... IT REFUSES TO BE CONTAINED. SUCH A FORCE OF WILL.
BUT EVERYONE HERE IS BLIND TO IT. THEY ALL RUSH TO SEE EVERYTHING, BUT NEVER SIT STILL LONG ENOUGH TO EXPERIENCE WHAT IS AROUND THEM.
ANYBODY ELSE SMELL FRIED CIRCUITRY AROUND HERE?
GET IT? FRIED CIRCUITRY? AS IN YOURS? HELLO? ANYBOT HOME?
THUMP THUMP THUMP
WHAT? WHAT'D I SAY?

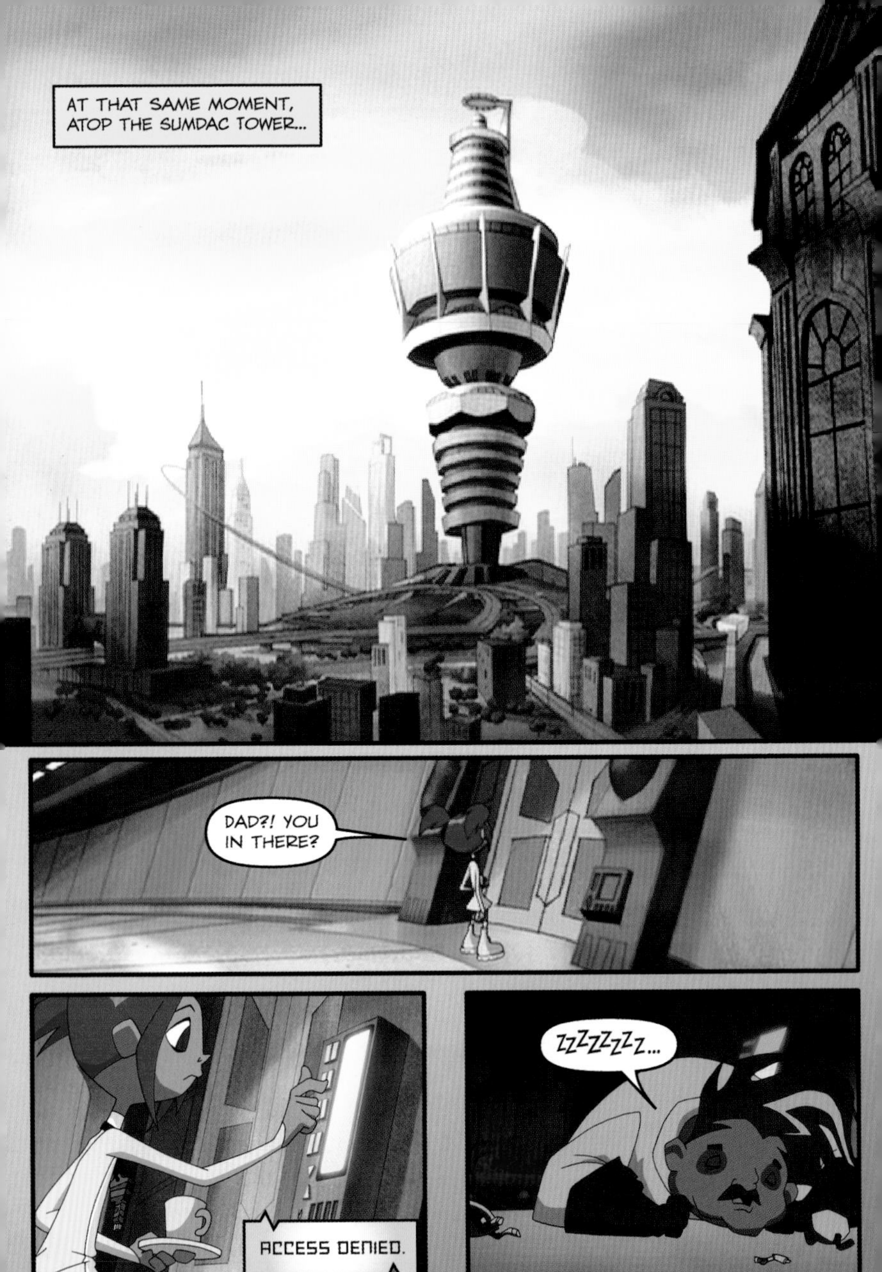
AT THAT SAME MOMENT, ATOP THE SUMDAC TOWER...
DAD?! YOU IN THERE?
ACCESS DENIED.
ZZZZZZZZ...

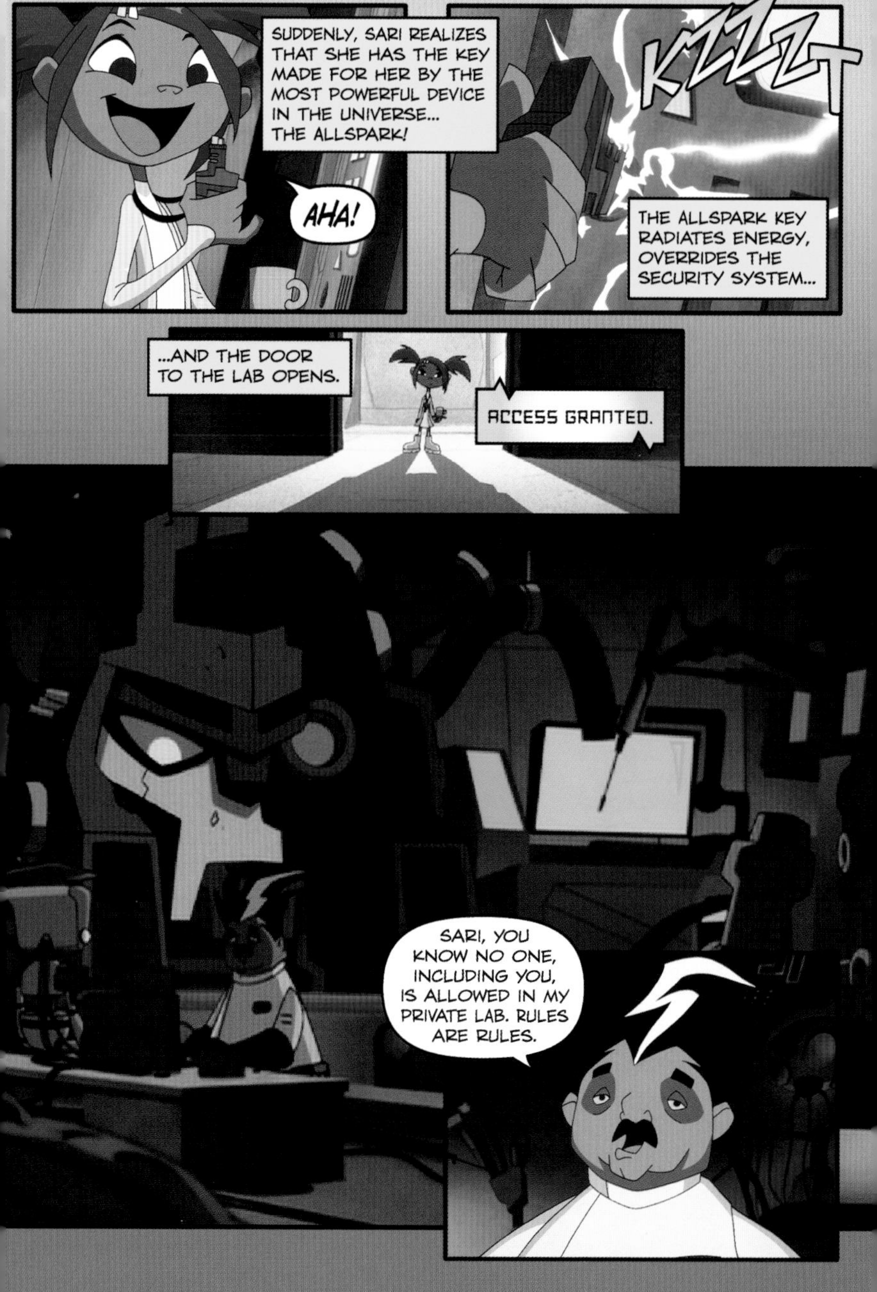
SUDDENLY, SARI REALIZES THAT SHE HAS THE KEY MADE FOR HER BY THE MOST POWERFUL DEVICE IN THE UNIVERSE... THE ALLSPARK!
AHA!
KZZZZT
THE ALLSPARK KEY RADIATES ENERGY, OVERRIDES THE SECURITY SYSTEM...
...AND THE DOOR TO THE LAB OPENS.
ACCESS GRANTED.
SARI, YOU KNOW NO ONE, INCLUDING YOU, IS ALLOWED IN MY PRIVATE LAB. RULES ARE RULES.

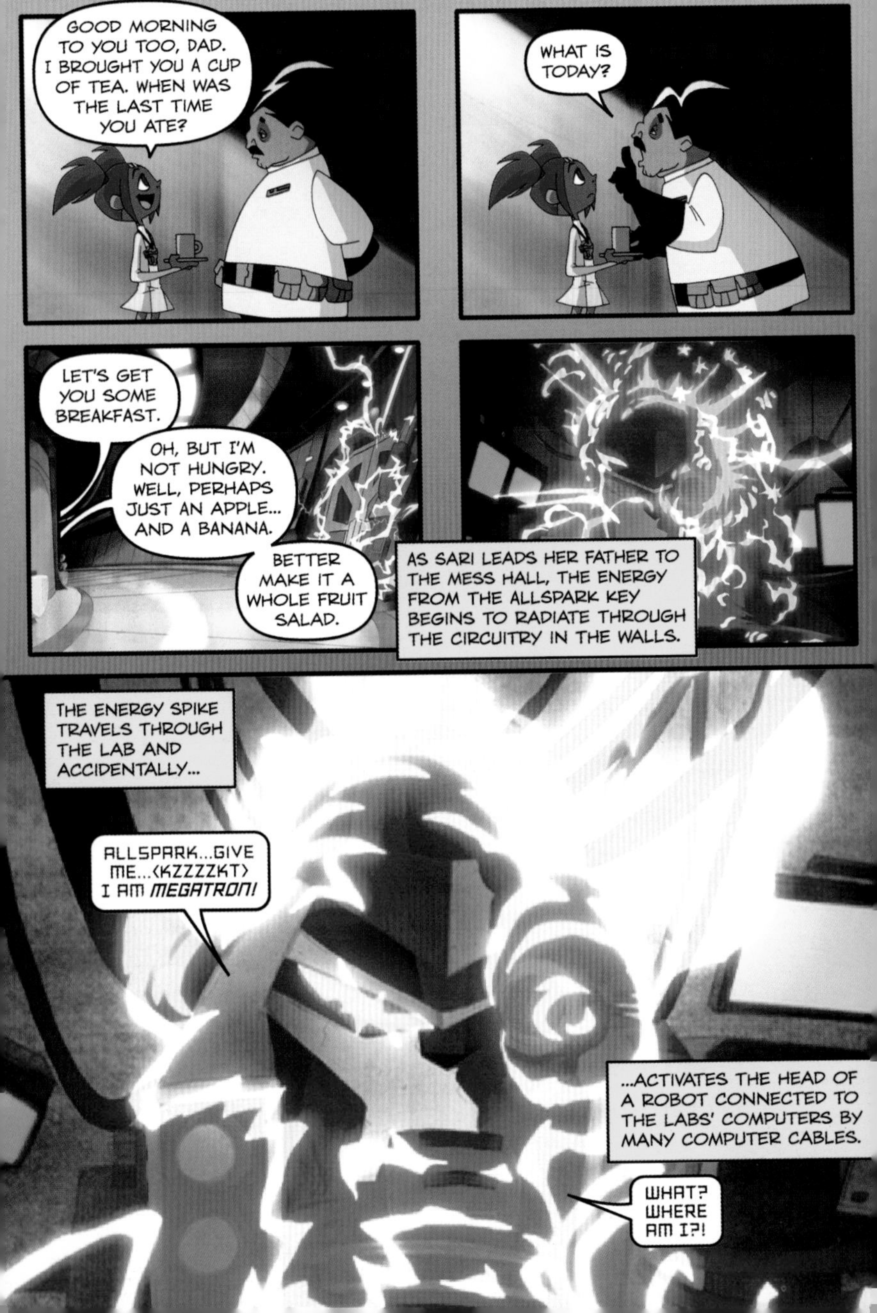
GOOD MORNING TO YOU TOO, DAD. I BROUGHT YOU A CUP OF TEA. WHEN WAS THE LAST TIME YOU ATE?
WHAT IS TODAY?
LET'S GET YOU SOME BREAKFAST.
OH, BUT I'M NOT HUNGRY. WELL, PERHAPS JUST AN APPLE... AND A BANANA.
BETTER MAKE IT A WHOLE FRUIT SALAD.
AS SARI LEADS HER FATHER TO THE MESS HALL, THE ENERGY FROM THE ALLSPARK KEY BEGINS TO RADIATE THROUGH THE CIRCUITRY IN THE WALLS.
THE ENERGY SPIKE TRAVELS THROUGH THE LAB AND ACCIDENTALLY...
ALLSPARK...GIVE ME...<KZZZZKT> I AM *MEGATRON!*
...ACTIVATES THE HEAD OF A ROBOT CONNECTED TO THE LABS' COMPUTERS BY MANY COMPUTER CABLES.
WHAT? WHERE AM I?!

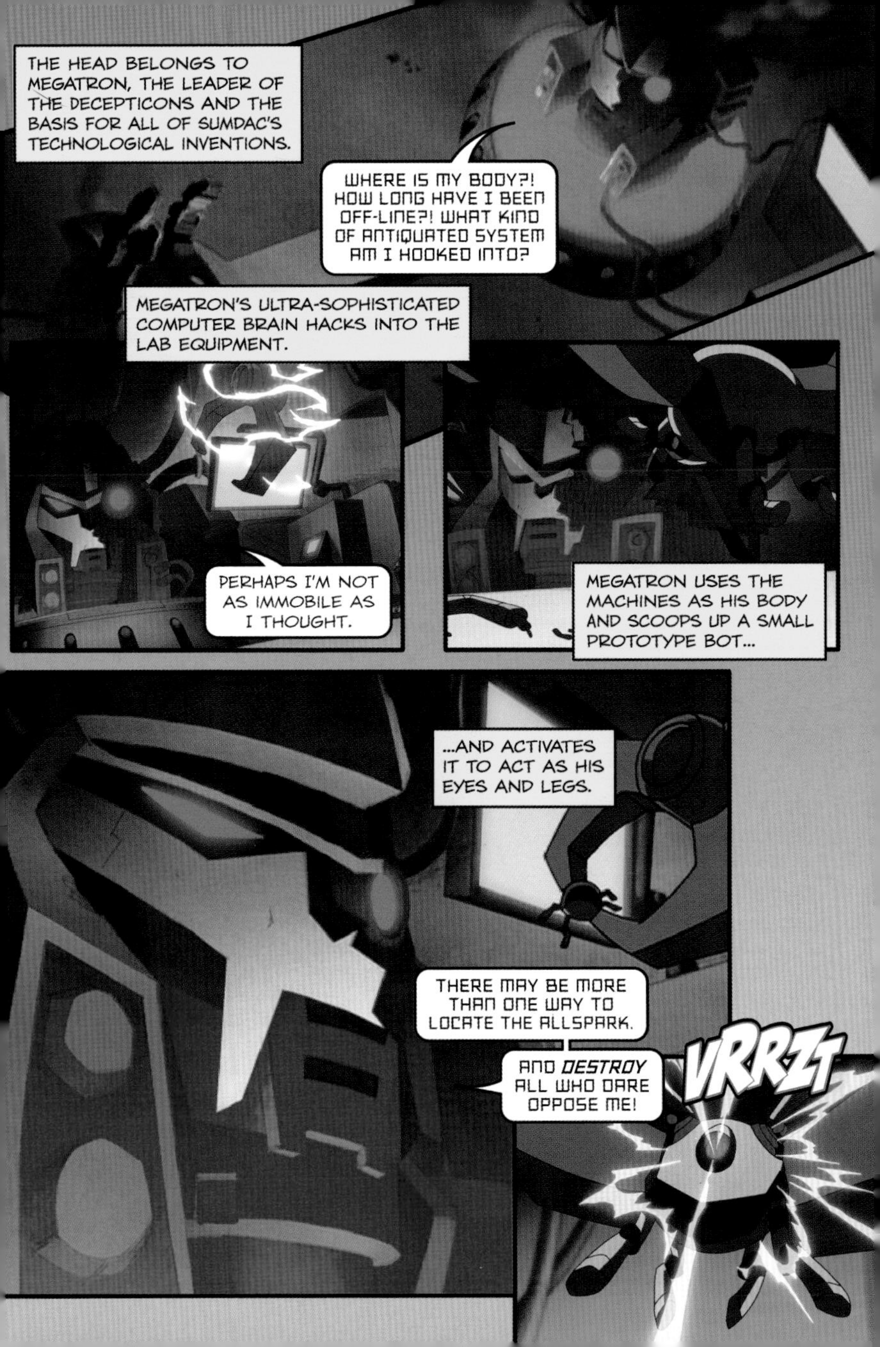
THE HEAD BELONGS TO MEGATRON, THE LEADER OF THE DECEPTICONS AND THE BASIS FOR ALL OF SUMDAC'S TECHNOLOGICAL INVENTIONS.
WHERE IS MY BODY?! HOW LONG HAVE I BEEN OFF-LINE?! WHAT KIND OF ANTIQUATED SYSTEM AM I HOOKED INTO?
MEGATRON'S ULTRA-SOPHISTICATED COMPUTER BRAIN HACKS INTO THE LAB EQUIPMENT.
PERHAPS I'M NOT AS IMMOBILE AS I THOUGHT.
MEGATRON USES THE MACHINES AS HIS BODY AND SCOOPS UP A SMALL PROTOTYPE BOT...
...AND ACTIVATES IT TO ACT AS HIS EYES AND LEGS.
THERE MAY BE MORE THAN ONE WAY TO LOCATE THE ALLSPARK.
AND *DESTROY* ALL WHO DARE OPPOSE ME!
VRRZT

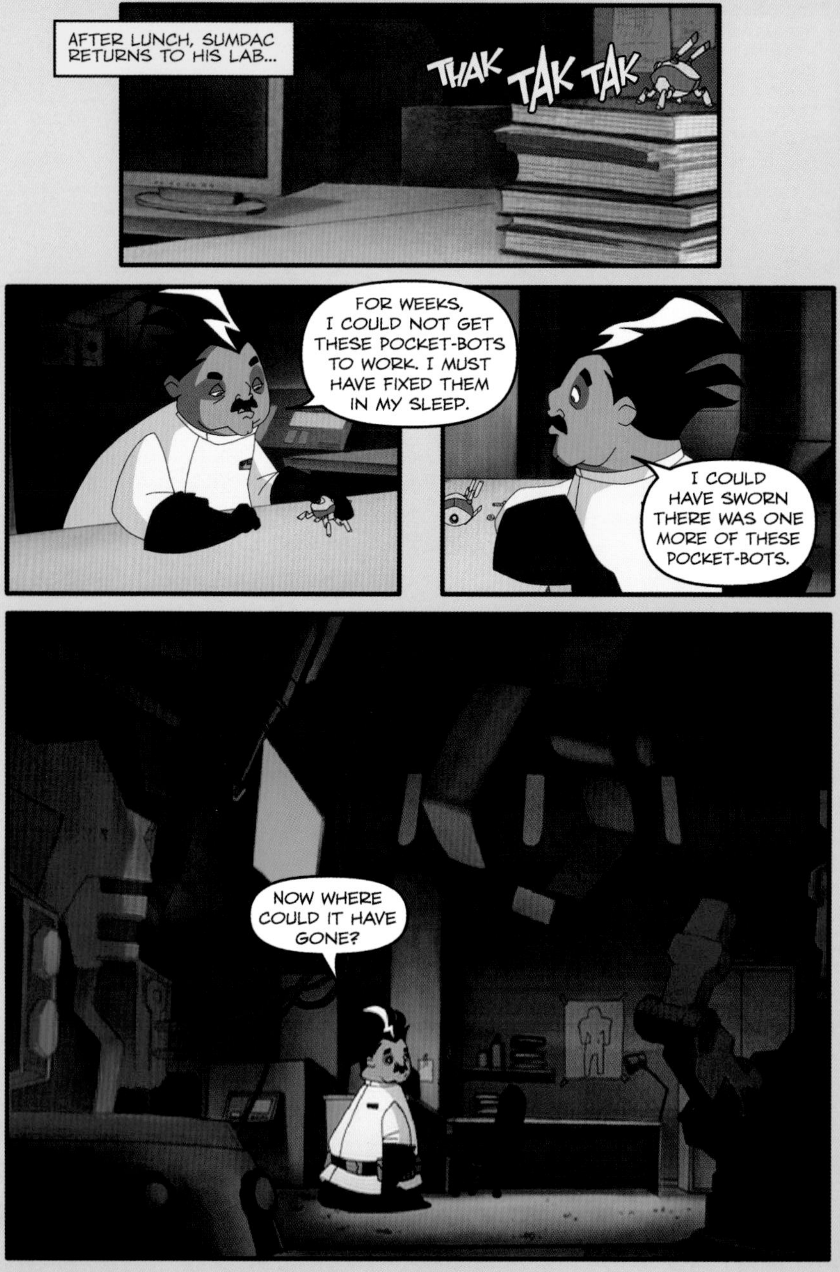

AFTER LUNCH, SUMDAC RETURNS TO HIS LAB...
THAK TAK TAK
FOR WEEKS, I COULD NOT GET THESE POCKET-BOTS TO WORK. I MUST HAVE FIXED THEM IN MY SLEEP.
I COULD HAVE SWORN THERE WAS ONE MORE OF THESE POCKET-BOTS.
NOW WHERE COULD IT HAVE GONE?

THAK TAK TAK

THAK TAK THAK

THAK TAK TAK

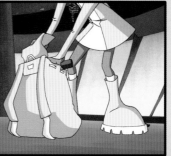

AUTOBOTS, HERE I COME!

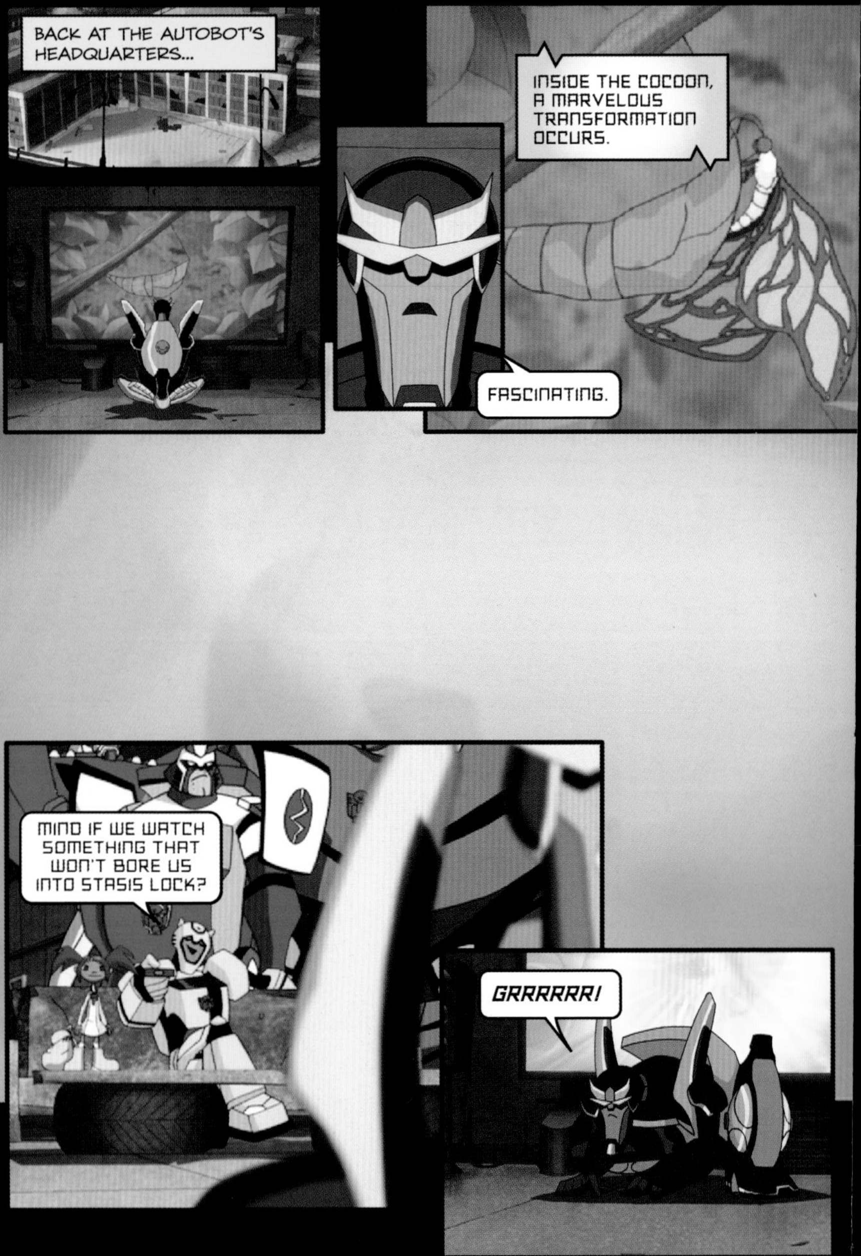
BACK AT THE AUTOBOT'S HEADQUARTERS...
INSIDE THE COCOON, A MARVELOUS TRANSFORMATION OCCURS.
FASCINATING.
MIND IF WE WATCH SOMETHING THAT WON'T BORE US INTO STASIS LOCK?
GRRRRRR!

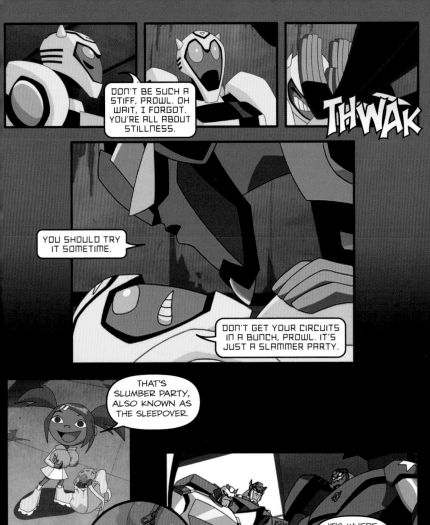

DON'T BE SUCH A STIFF, PROWL. OH WAIT, I FORGOT. YOU'RE ALL ABOUT STILLNESS.

THWAK

YOU SHOULD TRY IT SOMETIME.

DON'T GET YOUR CIRCUITS IN A BUNCH, PROWL. IT'S JUST A SLAMMER PARTY.

THAT'S SLUMBER PARTY, ALSO KNOWN AS THE SLEEPOVER.

IT'S WHERE A BUNCH OF FRIENDS GET TOGETHER AND HANG OUT.

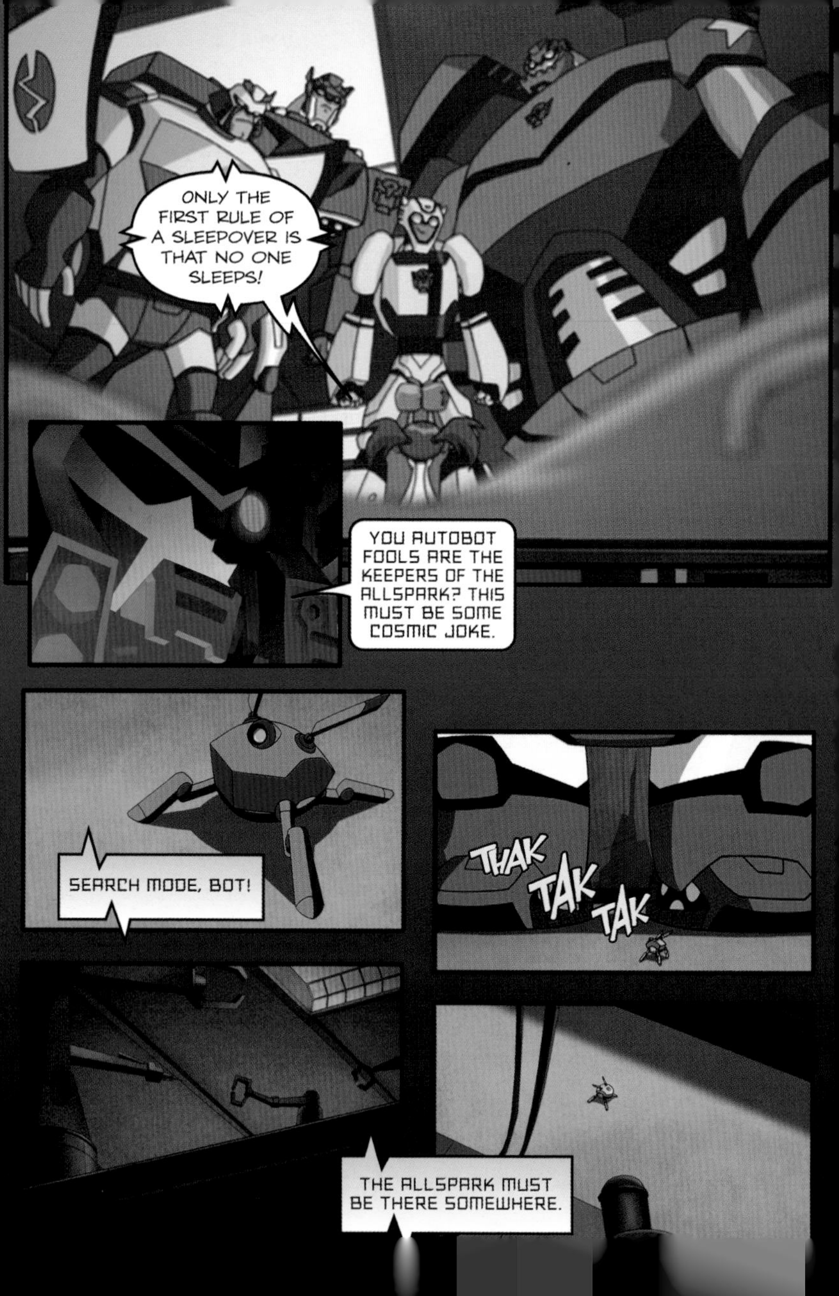
ONLY THE FIRST RULE OF A SLEEPOVER IS THAT NO ONE SLEEPS!
YOU AUTOBOT FOOLS ARE THE KEEPERS OF THE ALLSPARK? THIS MUST BE SOME COSMIC JOKE.
SEARCH MODE, BOT!
THAK
TAK
TAK
THE ALLSPARK MUST BE THERE SOMEWHERE.

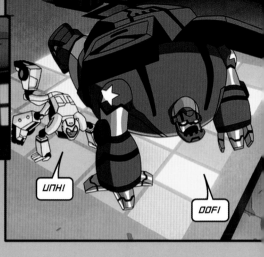

OKAY, LEFT HAND ON PURPLE.

UNH!

OOF!

SO THIS IS SOME KIND OF TRAINING EXERCISE TO BOOST DEXTERITY?

IT'S A GAME. FOR FUN.

RIGHT FOOT ON GREEN.

HEY PROWL! YOU'RE ALL INTO THAT BALANCE AND AGILITY GARBAGE. WANT IN ON THIS ACTION?

HEY! YOU WON!

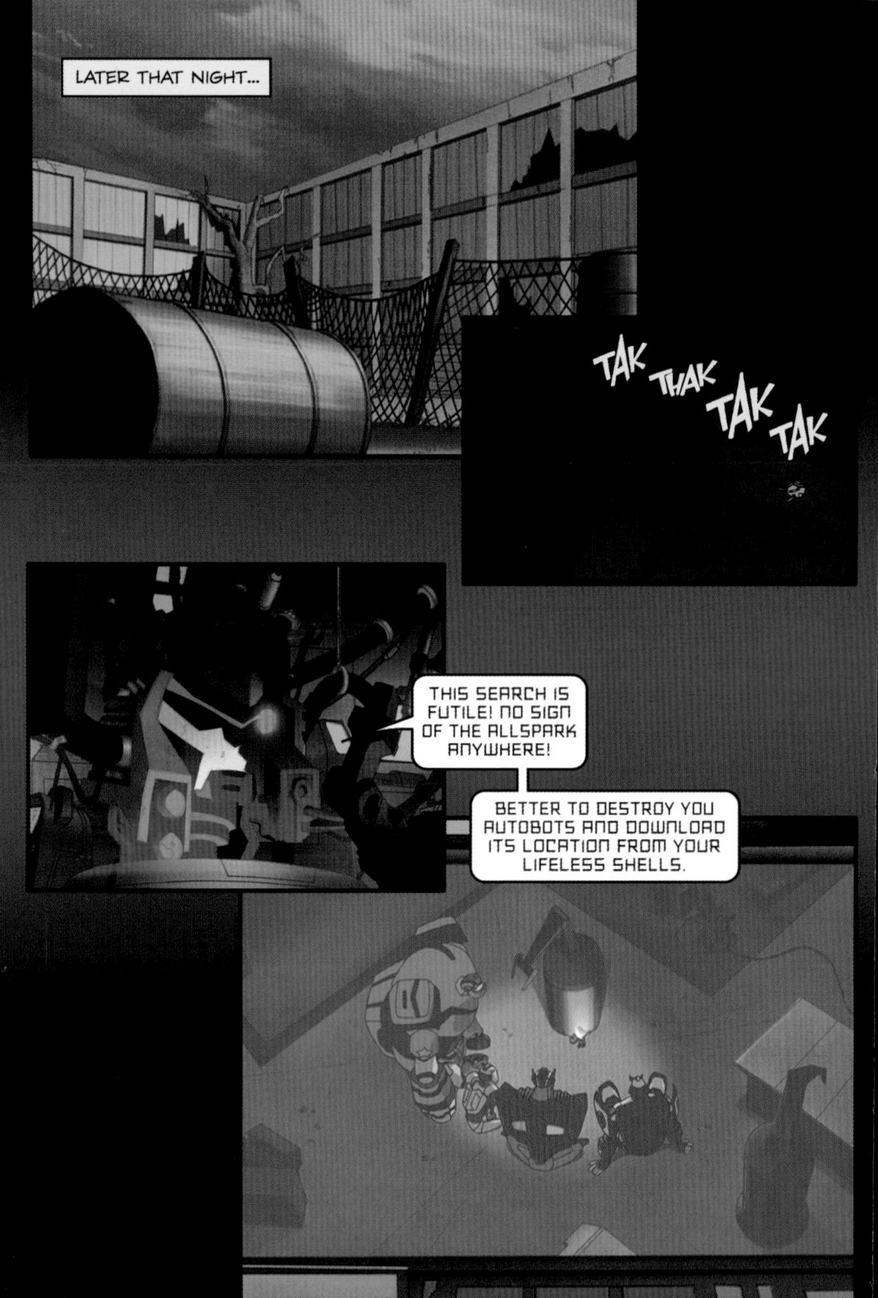
LATER THAT NIGHT...
TAK THAK TAK TAK
THIS SEARCH IS FUTILE! NO SIGN OF THE ALLSPARK ANYWHERE!
BETTER TO DESTROY YOU AUTOBOTS AND DOWNLOAD ITS LOCATION FROM YOUR LIFELESS SHELLS.

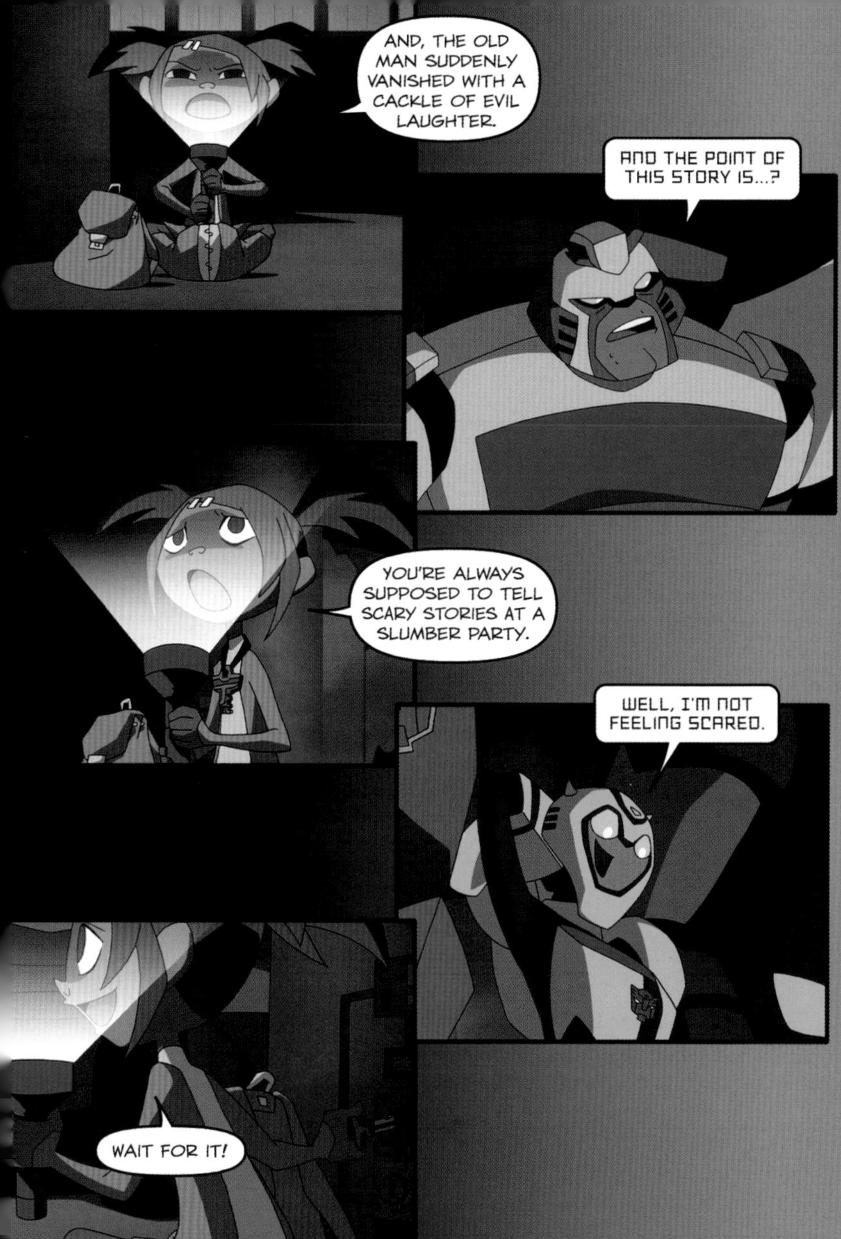

AND, THE OLD MAN SUDDENLY VANISHED WITH A CACKLE OF EVIL LAUGHTER.
AND THE POINT OF THIS STORY IS...?
YOU'RE ALWAYS SUPPOSED TO TELL SCARY STORIES AT A SLUMBER PARTY.
WELL, I'M NOT FEELING SCARED.
WAIT FOR IT!

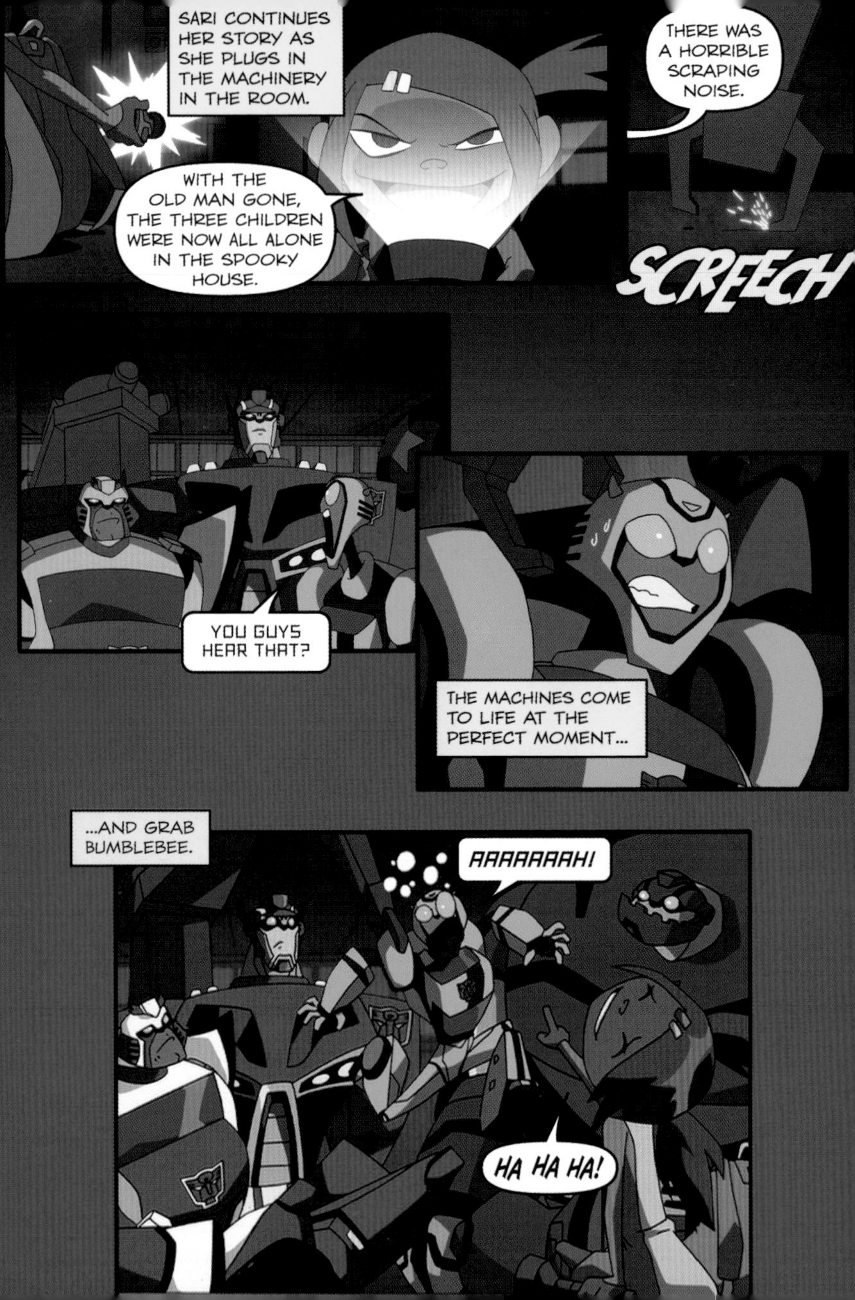
SARI CONTINUES HER STORY AS SHE PLUGS IN THE MACHINERY IN THE ROOM.
WITH THE OLD MAN GONE, THE THREE CHILDREN WERE NOW ALL ALONE IN THE SPOOKY HOUSE.
THERE WAS A HORRIBLE SCRAPING NOISE.
SCREECH
YOU GUYS HEAR THAT?
THE MACHINES COME TO LIFE AT THE PERFECT MOMENT...
...AND GRAB BUMBLEBEE.
AAAAAAAH!
HA HA HA!

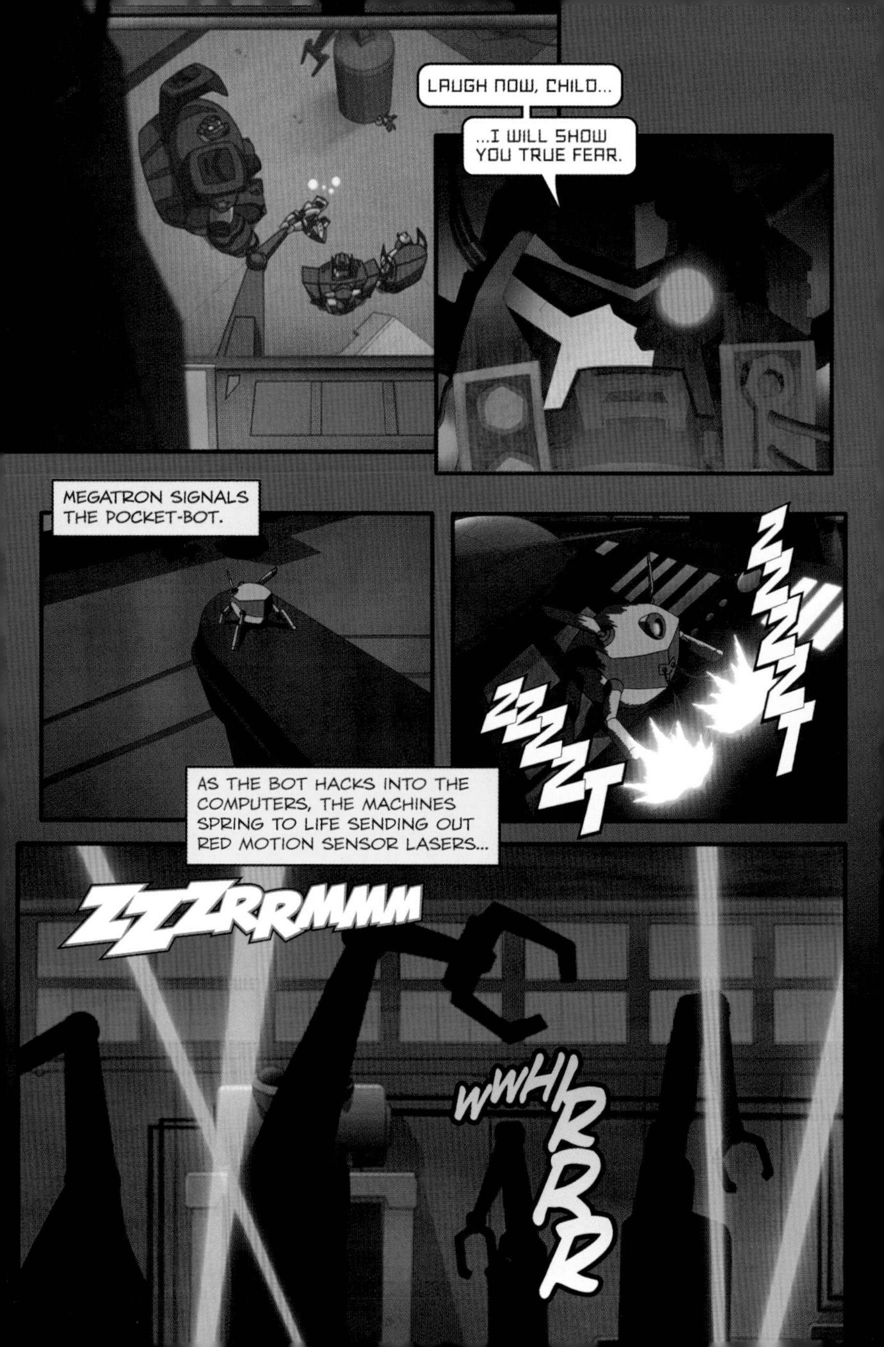
LAUGH NOW, CHILD...
...I WILL SHOW YOU TRUE FEAR.
MEGATRON SIGNALS THE POCKET-BOT.
ZZZZT
ZZZZZZT
AS THE BOT HACKS INTO THE COMPUTERS, THE MACHINES SPRING TO LIFE SENDING OUT RED MOTION SENSOR LASERS...
ZZZRRMMMM
WWHIRRR

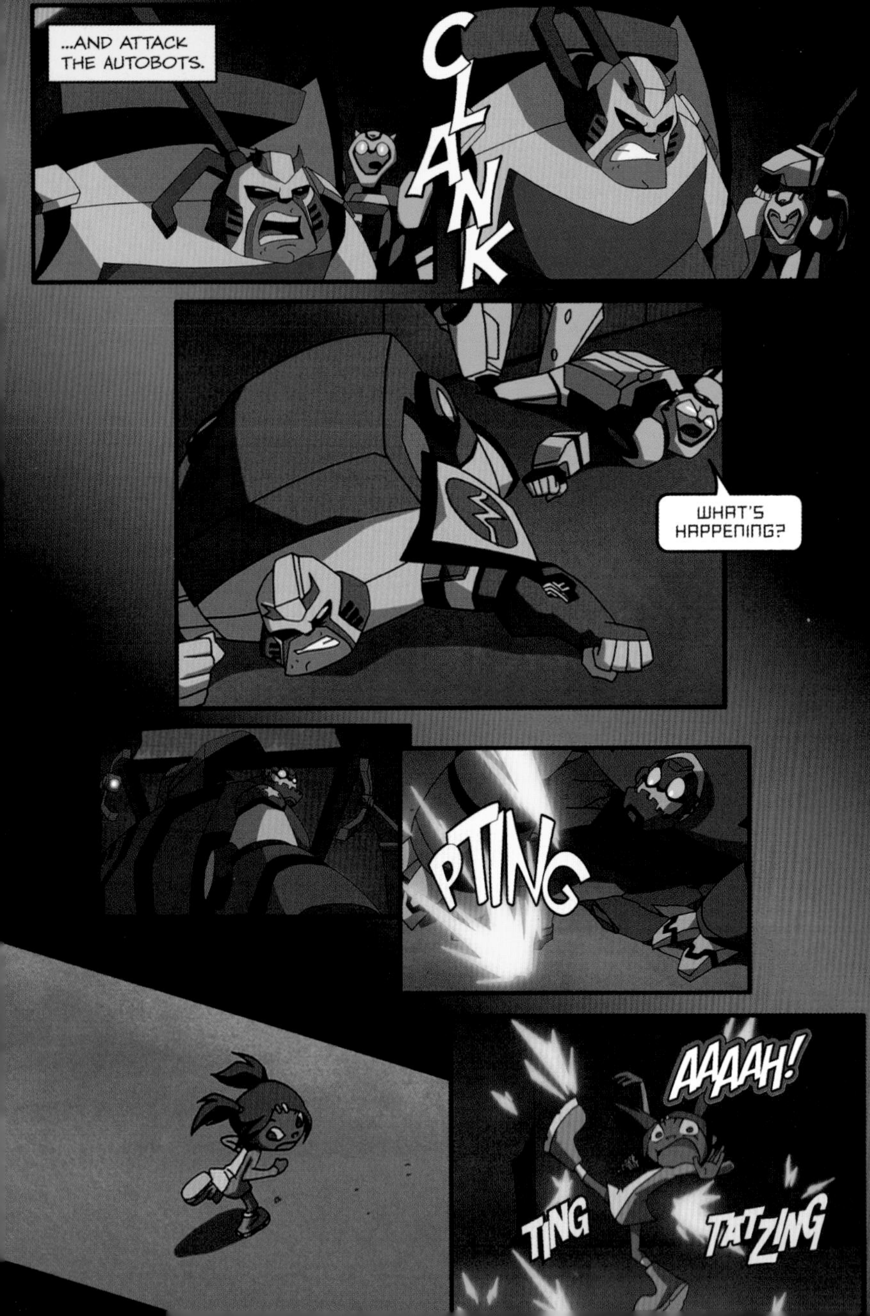
...AND ATTACK THE AUTOBOTS.
CLANK
WHAT'S HAPPENING?
PTING
AAAAH!
TING
TATZING

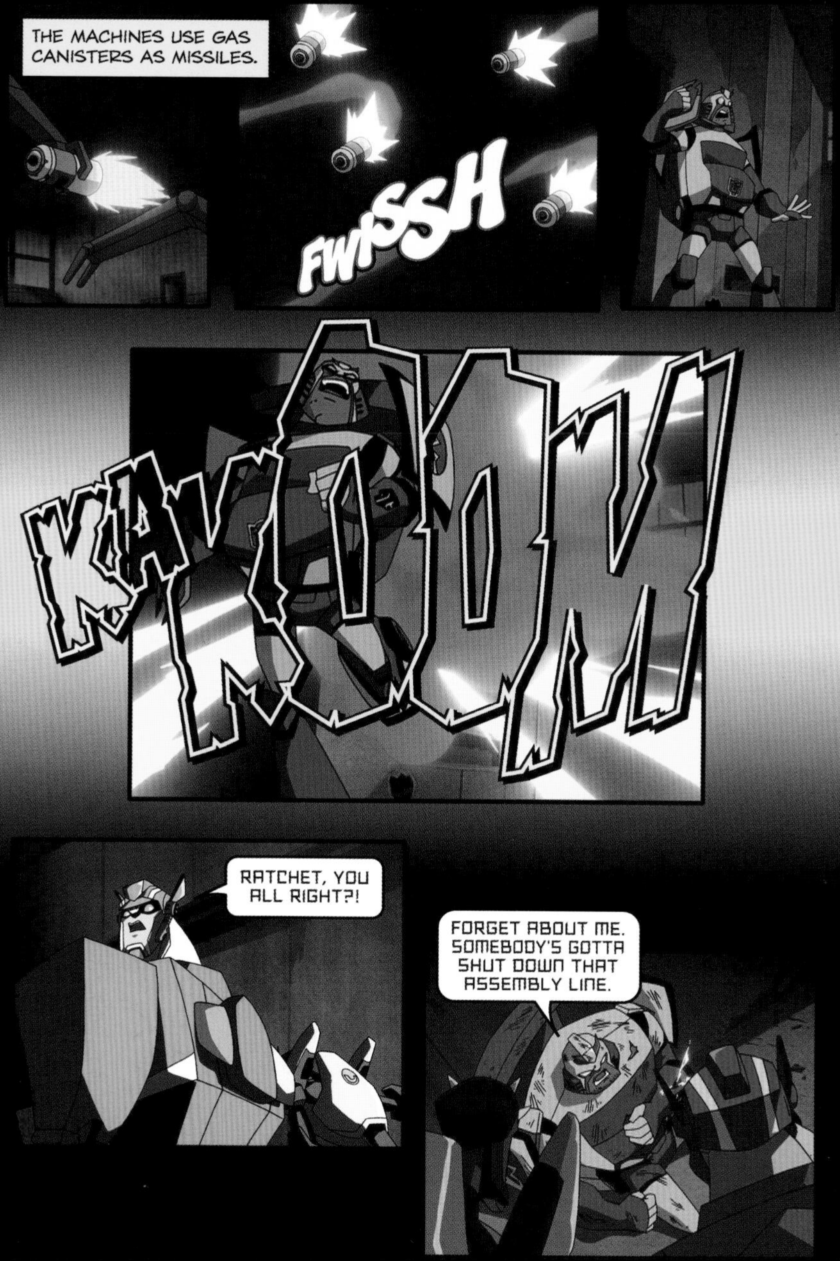
THE MACHINES USE GAS CANISTERS AS MISSILES.
FWISSH
KA-BOOM
RATCHET, YOU ALL RIGHT?!
FORGET ABOUT ME. SOMEBODY'S GOTTA SHUT DOWN THAT ASSEMBLY LINE.

EACH OF THE AUTOBOTS TRY TO TURN-OFF THE MACHINE...

THIS LOOKS LIKE A JOB FOR WHEELS ON HEELS!

HEY!

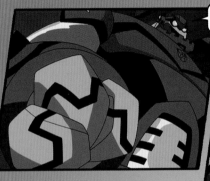

WHO NEEDS SENSITIVE? SMASHING STUFF IS FUN!

URK! THAT CAN'T BE GOOD.

HANG ON, BULKHEAD!

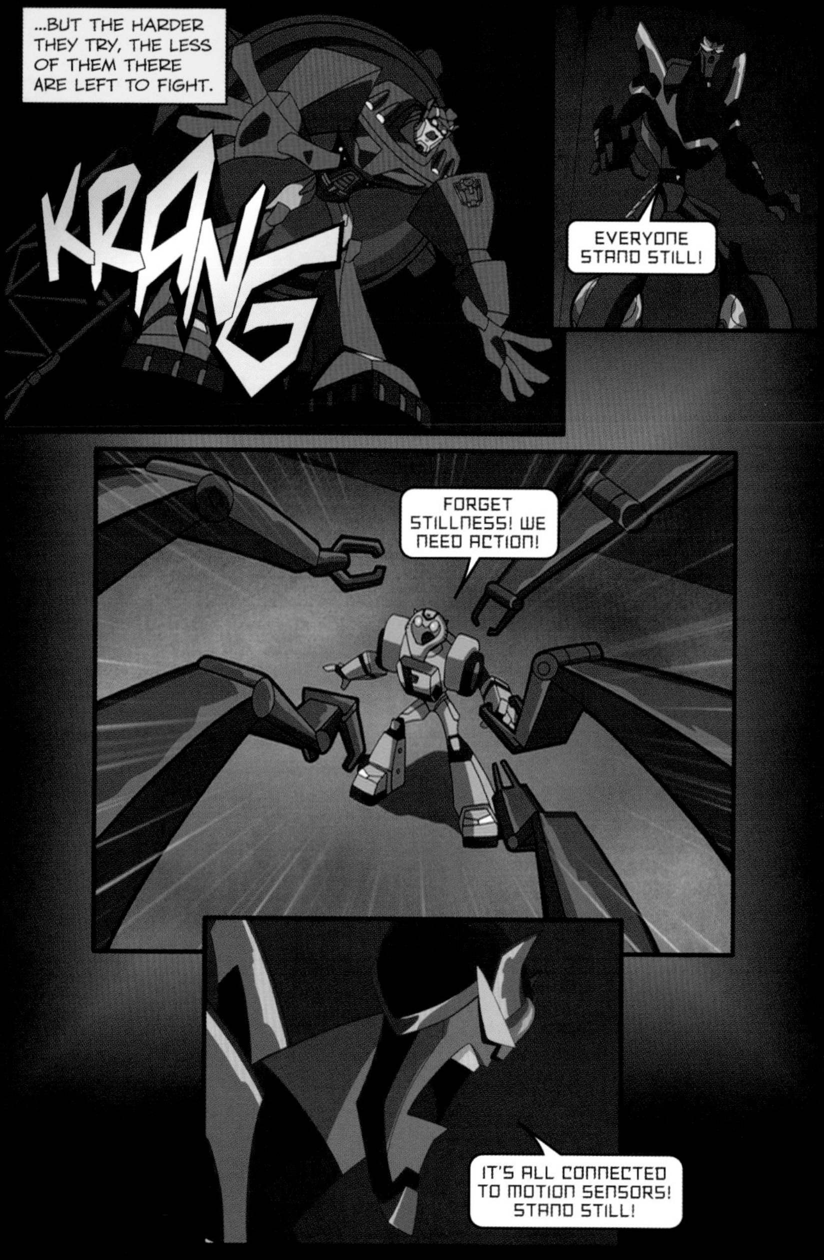
...BUT THE HARDER THEY TRY, THE LESS OF THEM THERE ARE LEFT TO FIGHT.
KRANG
EVERYONE STAND STILL!
FORGET STILLNESS! WE NEED ACTION!
IT'S ALL CONNECTED TO MOTION SENSORS! STAND STILL!

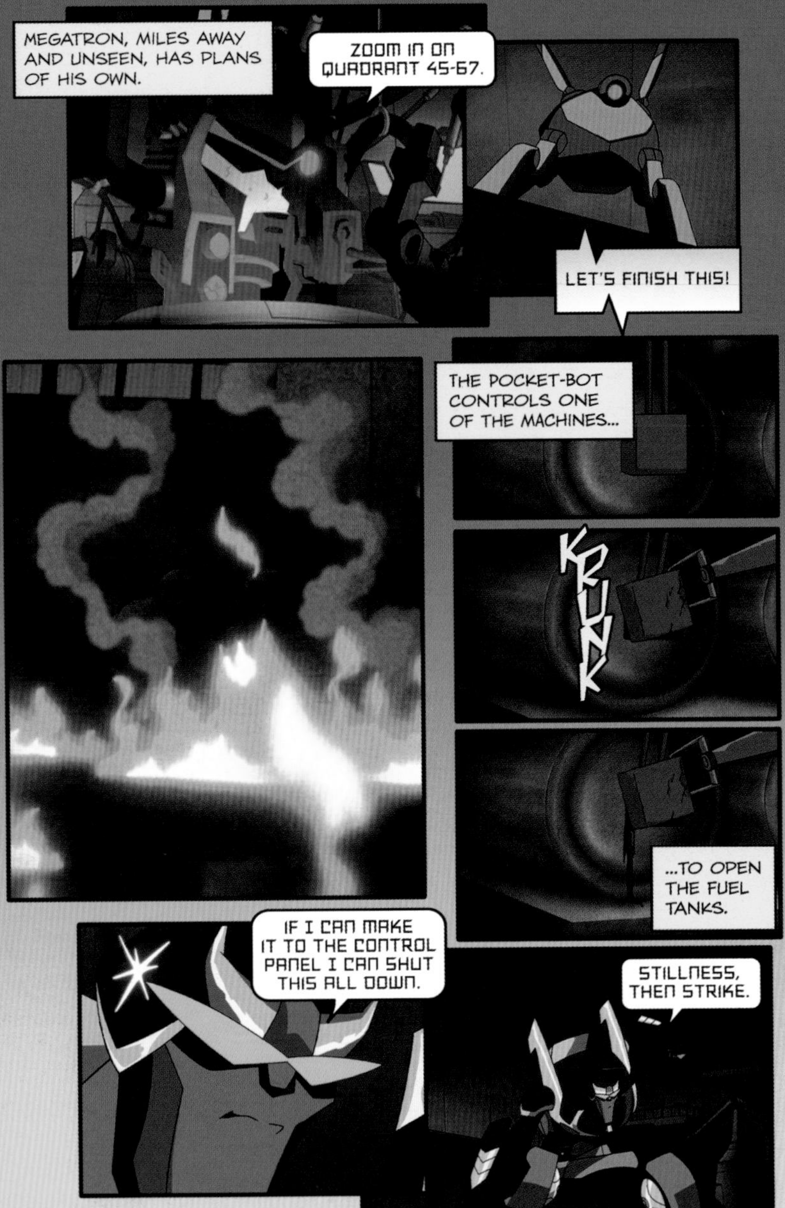
MEGATRON, MILES AWAY AND UNSEEN, HAS PLANS OF HIS OWN.
ZOOM IN ON QUADRANT 45-67.
LET'S FINISH THIS!
THE POCKET-BOT CONTROLS ONE OF THE MACHINES...
KRUNK
...TO OPEN THE FUEL TANKS.
IF I CAN MAKE IT TO THE CONTROL PANEL I CAN SHUT THIS ALL DOWN.
STILLNESS, THEN STRIKE.

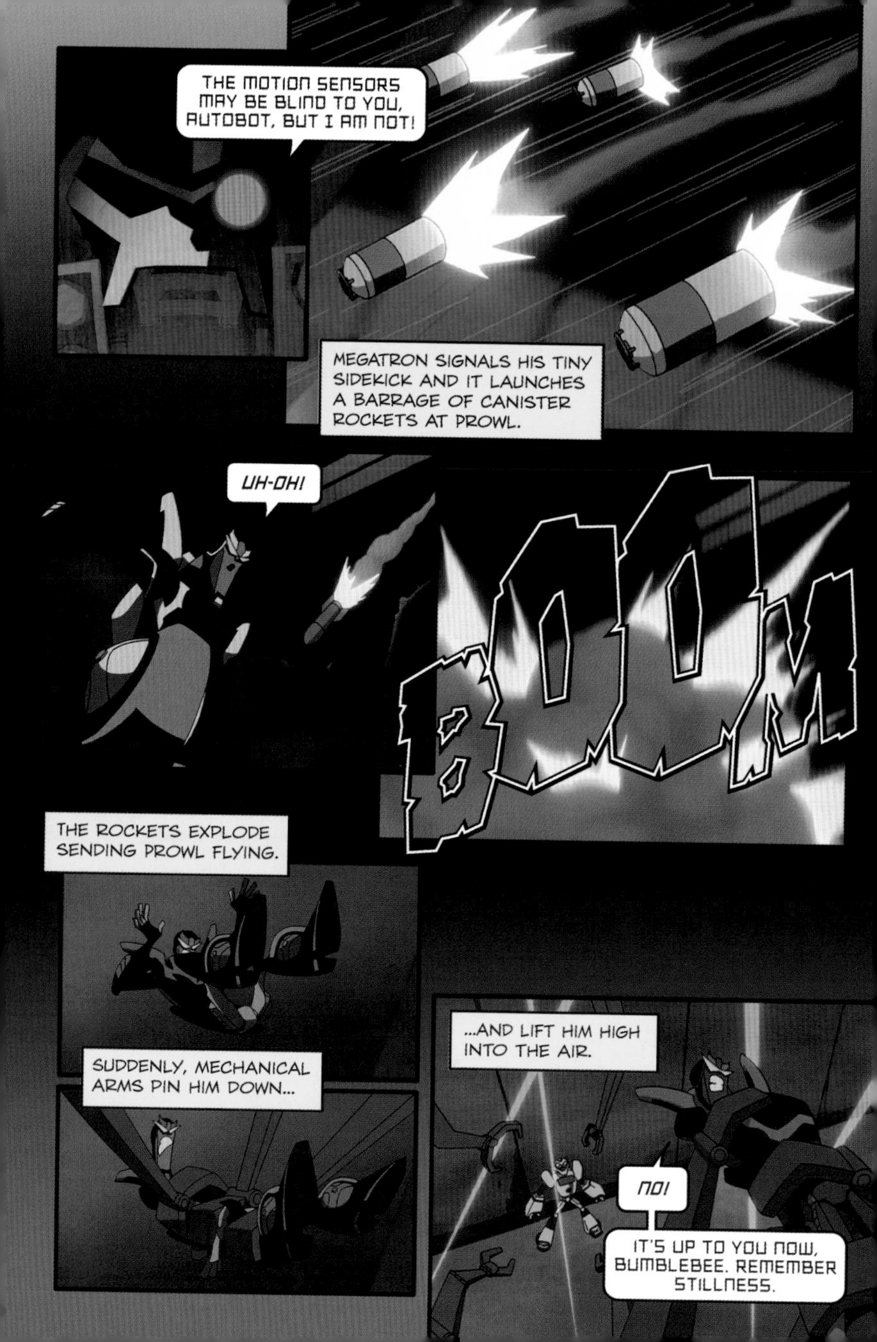
THE MOTION SENSORS MAY BE BLIND TO YOU, AUTOBOT, BUT I AM NOT!
MEGATRON SIGNALS HIS TINY SIDEKICK AND IT LAUNCHES A BARRAGE OF CANISTER ROCKETS AT PROWL.
UH-OH!
BOOM
THE ROCKETS EXPLODE SENDING PROWL FLYING.
SUDDENLY, MECHANICAL ARMS PIN HIM DOWN...
...AND LIFT HIM HIGH INTO THE AIR.
NO!
IT'S UP TO YOU NOW, BUMBLEBEE. REMEMBER STILLNESS.

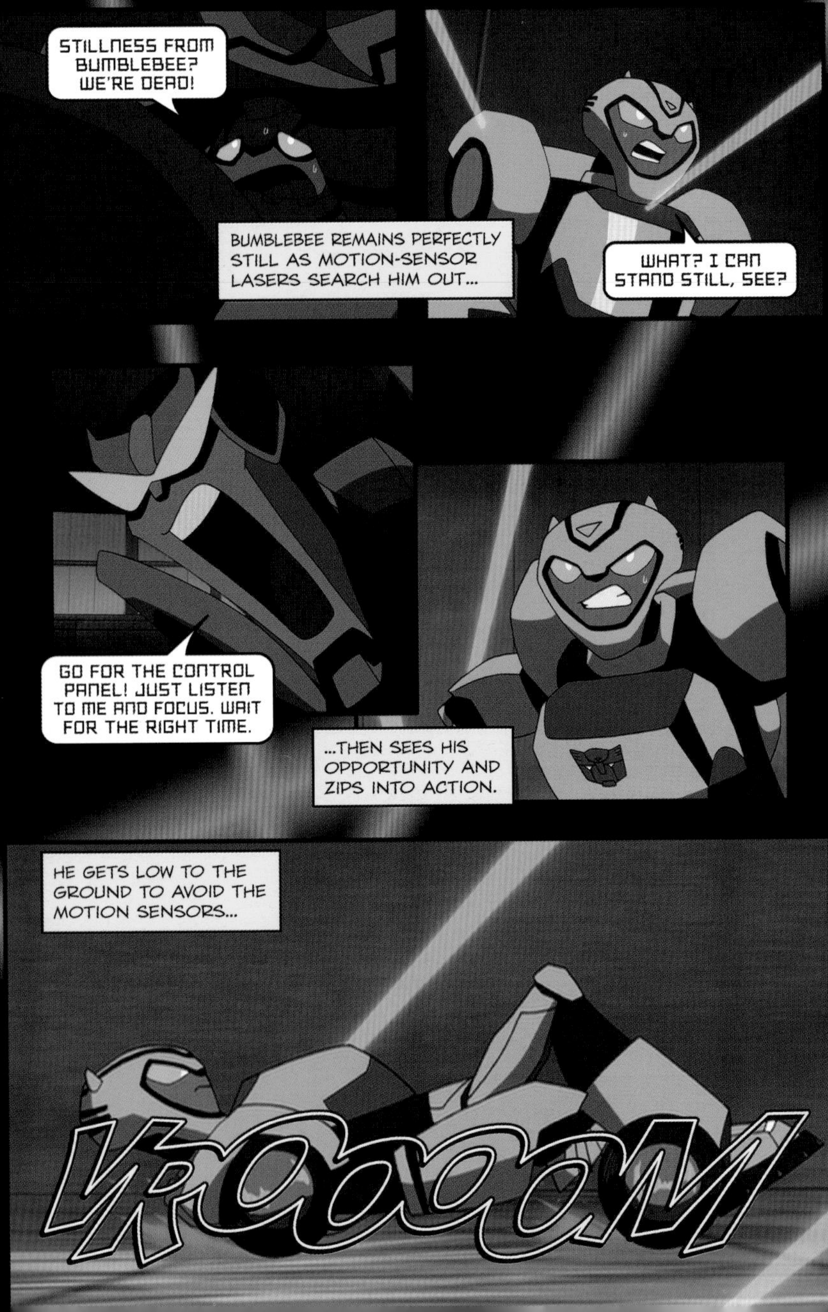
STILLNESS FROM BUMBLEBEE? WE'RE DEAD!
BUMBLEBEE REMAINS PERFECTLY STILL AS MOTION-SENSOR LASERS SEARCH HIM OUT...
WHAT? I CAN STAND STILL, SEE?
GO FOR THE CONTROL PANEL! JUST LISTEN TO ME AND FOCUS. WAIT FOR THE RIGHT TIME.
...THEN SEES HIS OPPORTUNITY AND ZIPS INTO ACTION.
HE GETS LOW TO THE GROUND TO AVOID THE MOTION SENSORS...
VROOOOM

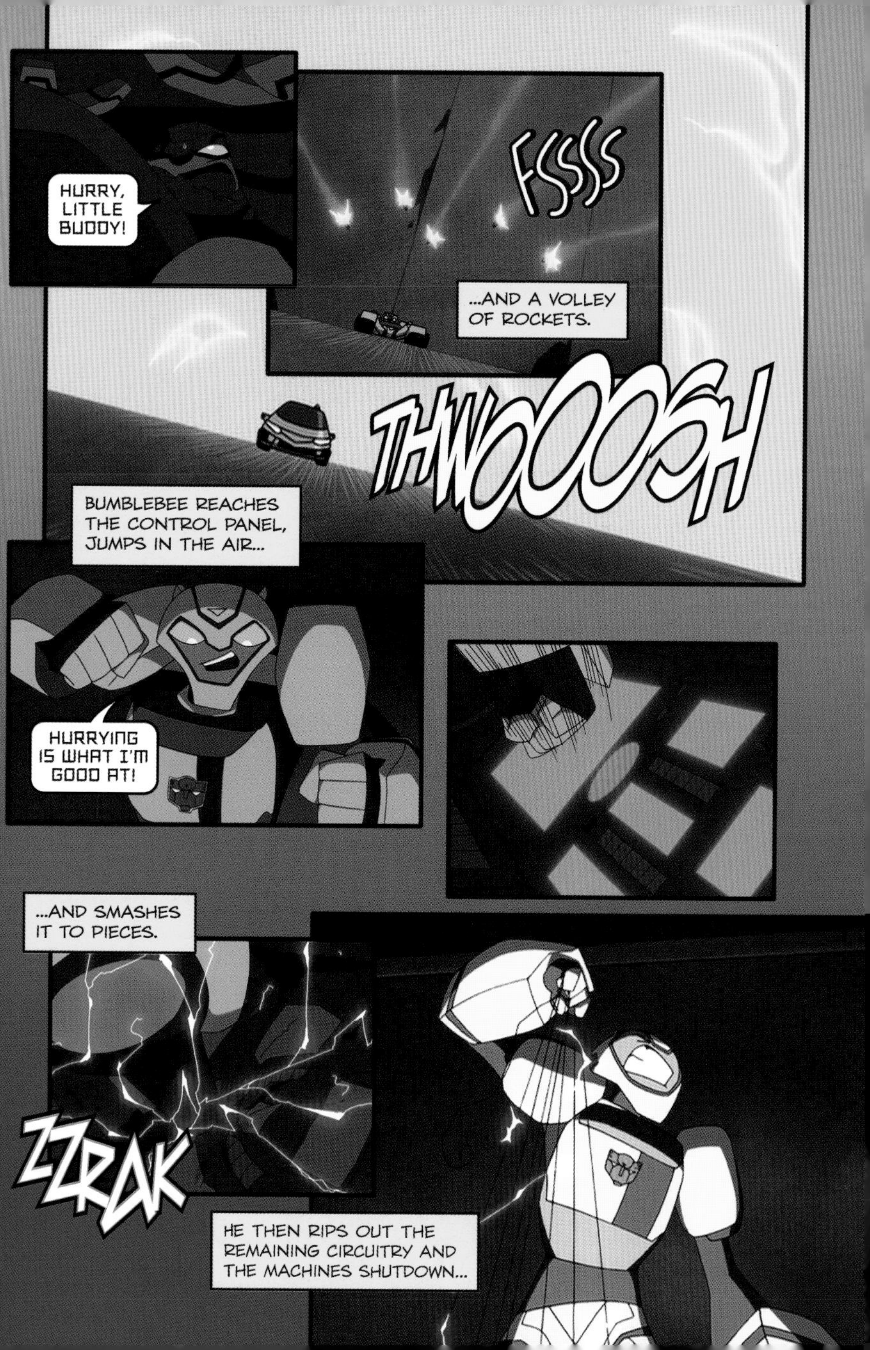
HURRY, LITTLE BUDDY!
FSSSS
...AND A VOLLEY OF ROCKETS.
THWOOOSH
BUMBLEBEE REACHES THE CONTROL PANEL, JUMPS IN THE AIR...
HURRYING IS WHAT I'M GOOD AT!
...AND SMASHES IT TO PIECES.
ZZRAK
HE THEN RIPS OUT THE REMAINING CIRCUITRY AND THE MACHINES SHUTDOWN...

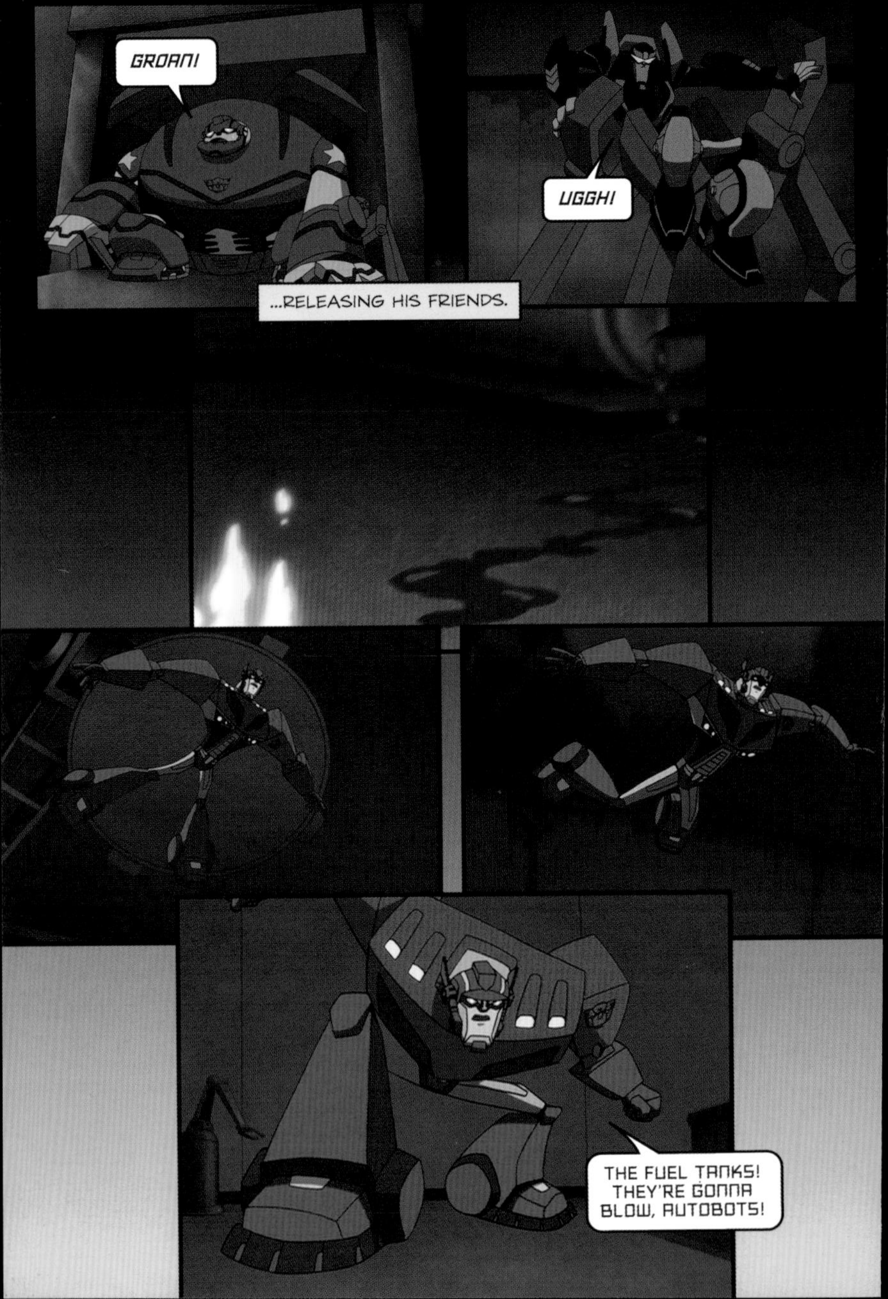
GROAN!
UGGH!
...RELEASING HIS FRIENDS.
THE FUEL TANKS! THEY'RE GONNA BLOW, AUTOBOTS!

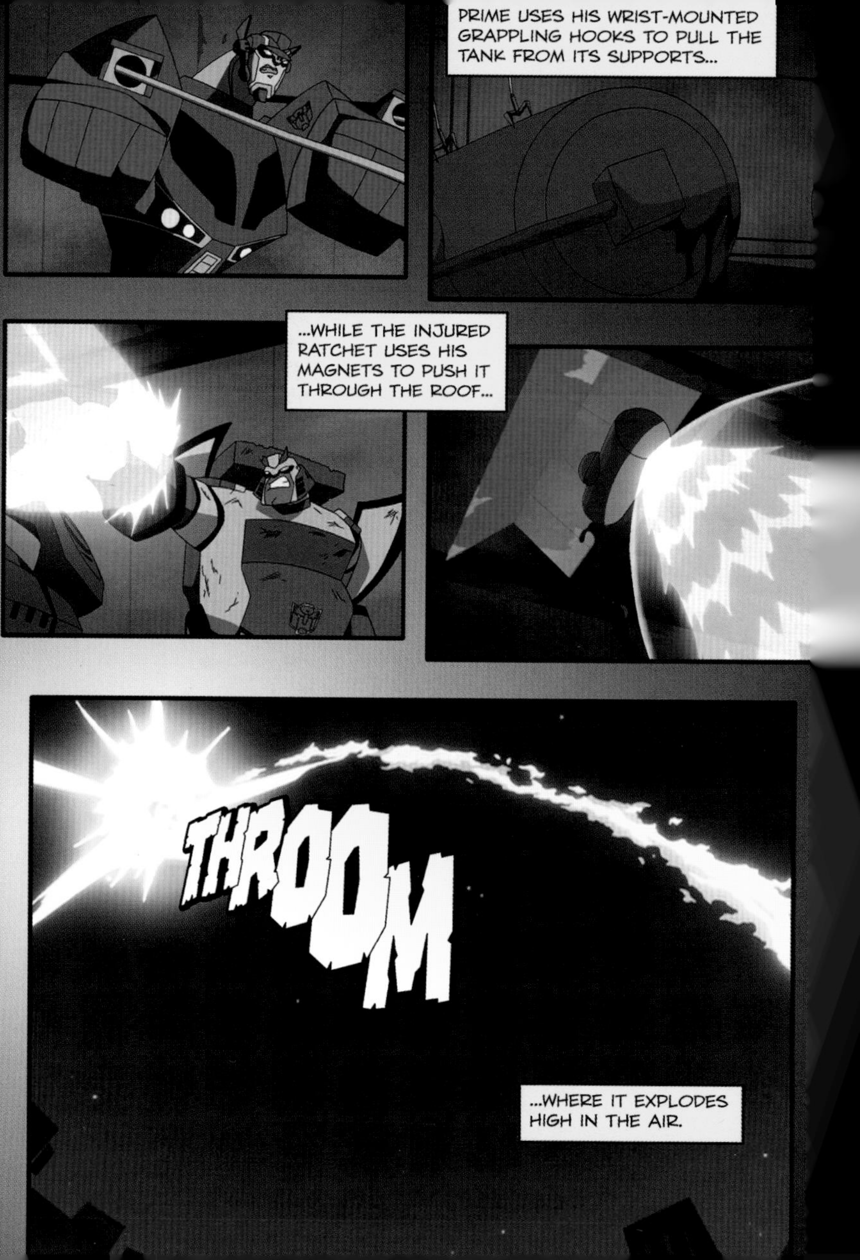
PRIME USES HIS WRIST-MOUNTED GRAPPLING HOOKS TO PULL THE TANK FROM ITS SUPPORTS...
...WHILE THE INJURED RATCHET USES HIS MAGNETS TO PUSH IT THROUGH THE ROOF...
THROOM
...WHERE IT EXPLODES HIGH IN THE AIR.

SOON...

SO IF MY KEY DIDN'T DO THIS, THEN WHAT DID?

PRIME PLUCKS UP THE TINY BOT.

I THINK THIS MIGHT BE THE CULPRIT.

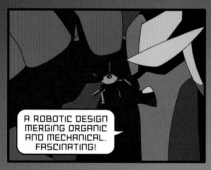

A ROBOTIC DESIGN MERGING ORGANIC AND MECHANICAL. FASCINATING!

IT FREES ITSELF FROM PRIME'S GRASP AND TRIES TO ESCAPE.

CATCH IT! WE NEED TO EXAMINE IT!

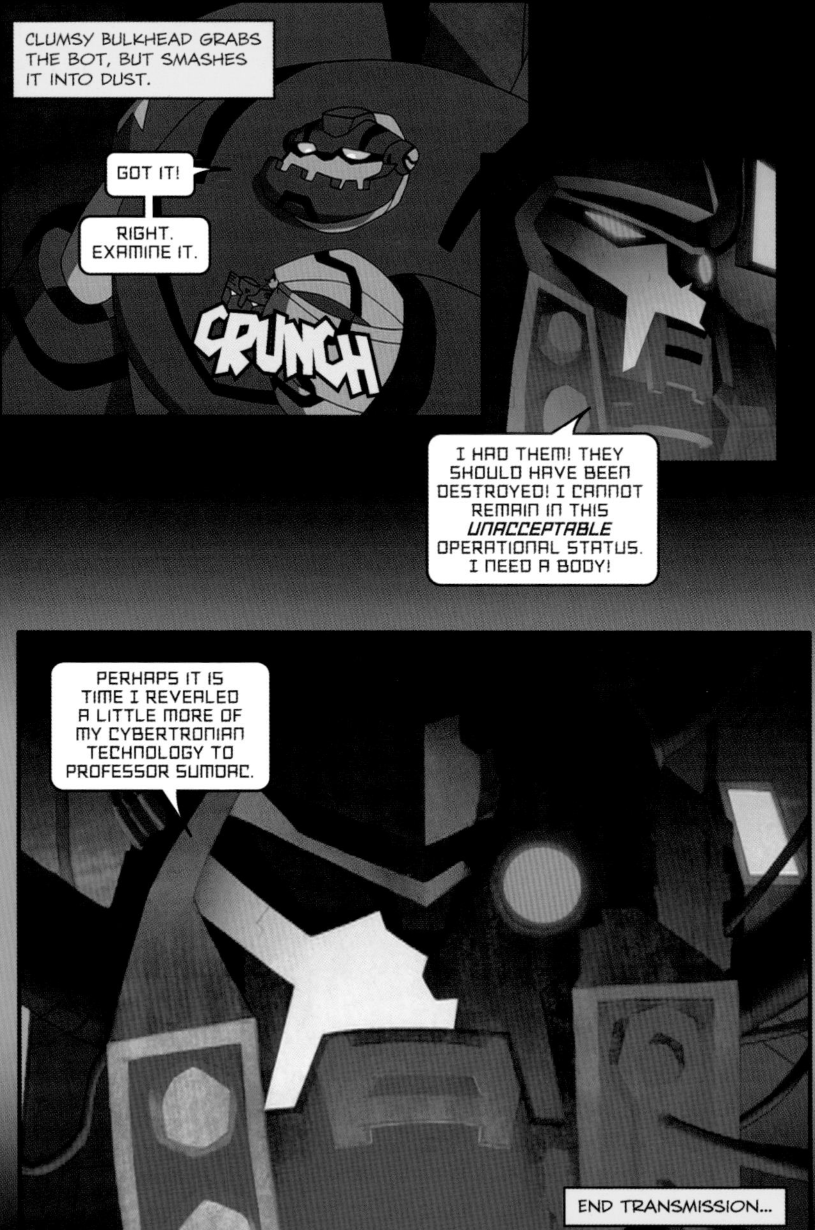
CLUMSY BULKHEAD GRABS THE BOT, BUT SMASHES IT INTO DUST.
GOT IT!
RIGHT. EXAMINE IT.
CRUNCH
I HAD THEM! THEY SHOULD HAVE BEEN DESTROYED! I CANNOT REMAIN IN THIS *UNACCEPTABLE* OPERATIONAL STATUS. I NEED A BODY!
PERHAPS IT IS TIME I REVEALED A LITTLE MORE OF MY CYBERTRONIAN TECHNOLOGY TO PROFESSOR SUMDAC.
END TRANSMISSION...

THE TRANSFORMERS IN TOTAL MELTDOWN

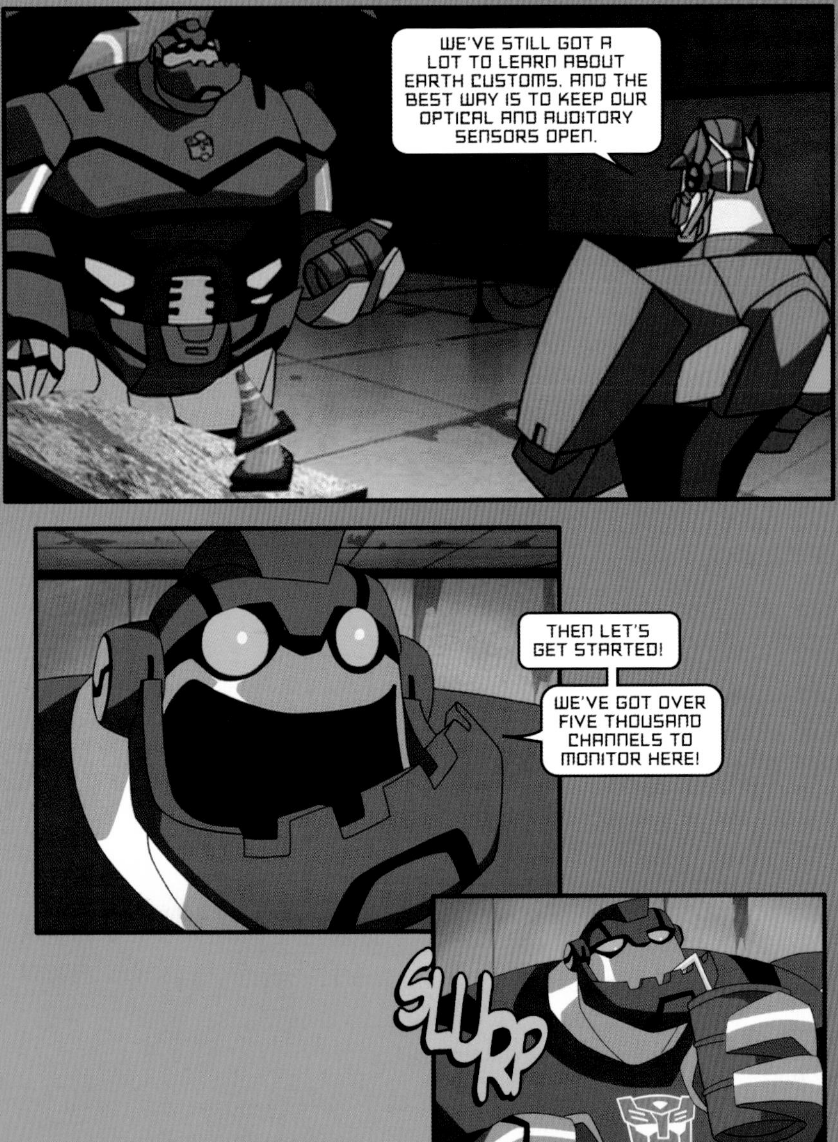

WE'VE STILL GOT A LOT TO LEARN ABOUT EARTH CUSTOMS. AND THE BEST WAY IS TO KEEP OUR OPTICAL AND AUDITORY SENSORS OPEN.
THEN LET'S GET STARTED!
WE'VE GOT OVER FIVE THOUSAND CHANNELS TO MONITOR HERE!
SLURP

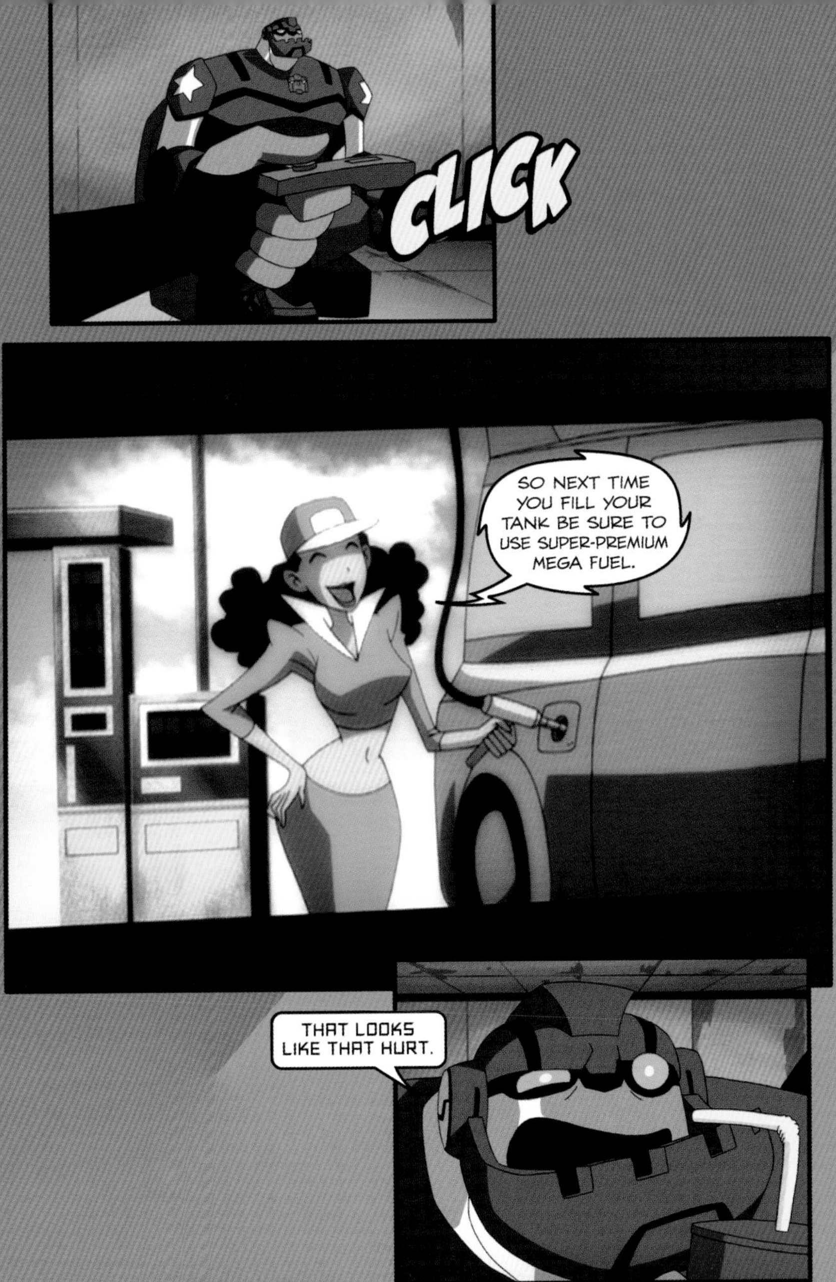
CLICK
SO NEXT TIME YOU FILL YOUR TANK BE SURE TO USE SUPER-PREMIUM MEGA FUEL.
THAT LOOKS LIKE THAT HURT.

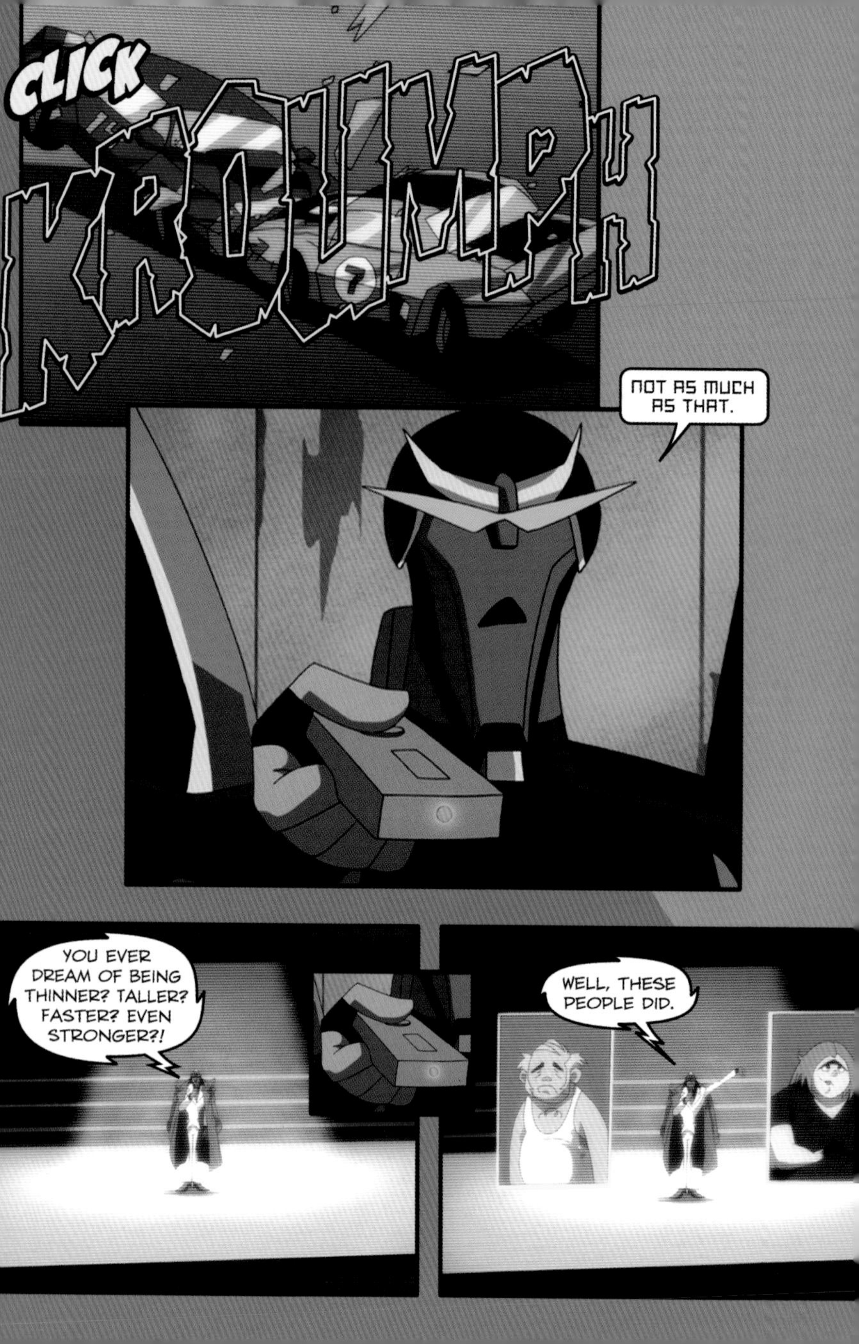
CLICK
KROOMPH
NOT AS MUCH AS THAT.
YOU EVER DREAM OF BEING THINNER? TALLER? FASTER? EVEN STRONGER?!
WELL, THESE PEOPLE DID.

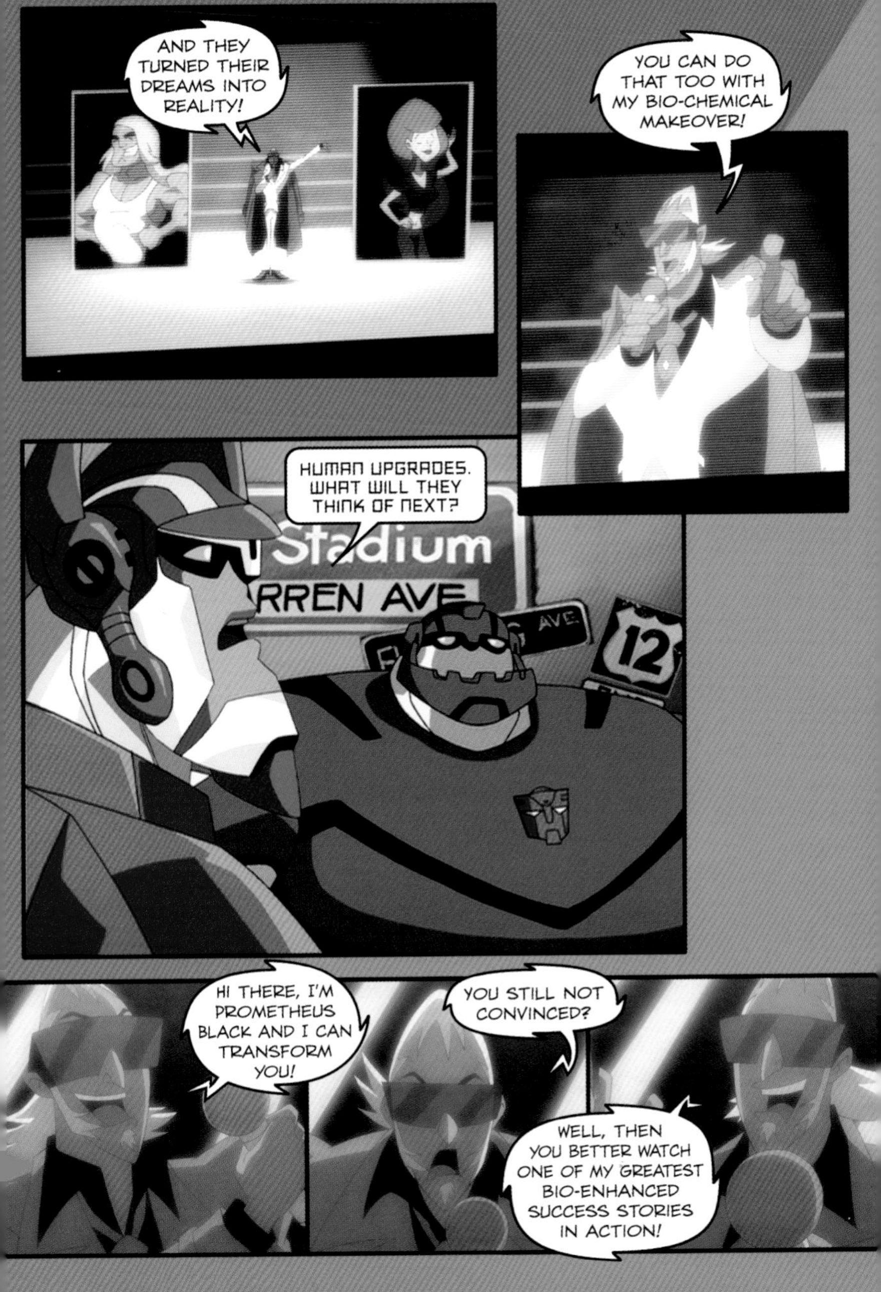
AND THEY TURNED THEIR DREAMS INTO REALITY!
YOU CAN DO THAT TOO WITH MY BIO-CHEMICAL MAKEOVER!
HUMAN UPGRADES. WHAT WILL THEY THINK OF NEXT?
Stadium
RREN AVE
AVE
12
HI THERE, I'M PROMETHEUS BLACK AND I CAN TRANSFORM YOU!
YOU STILL NOT CONVINCED?
WELL, THEN YOU BETTER WATCH ONE OF MY GREATEST BIO-ENHANCED SUCCESS STORIES IN ACTION!

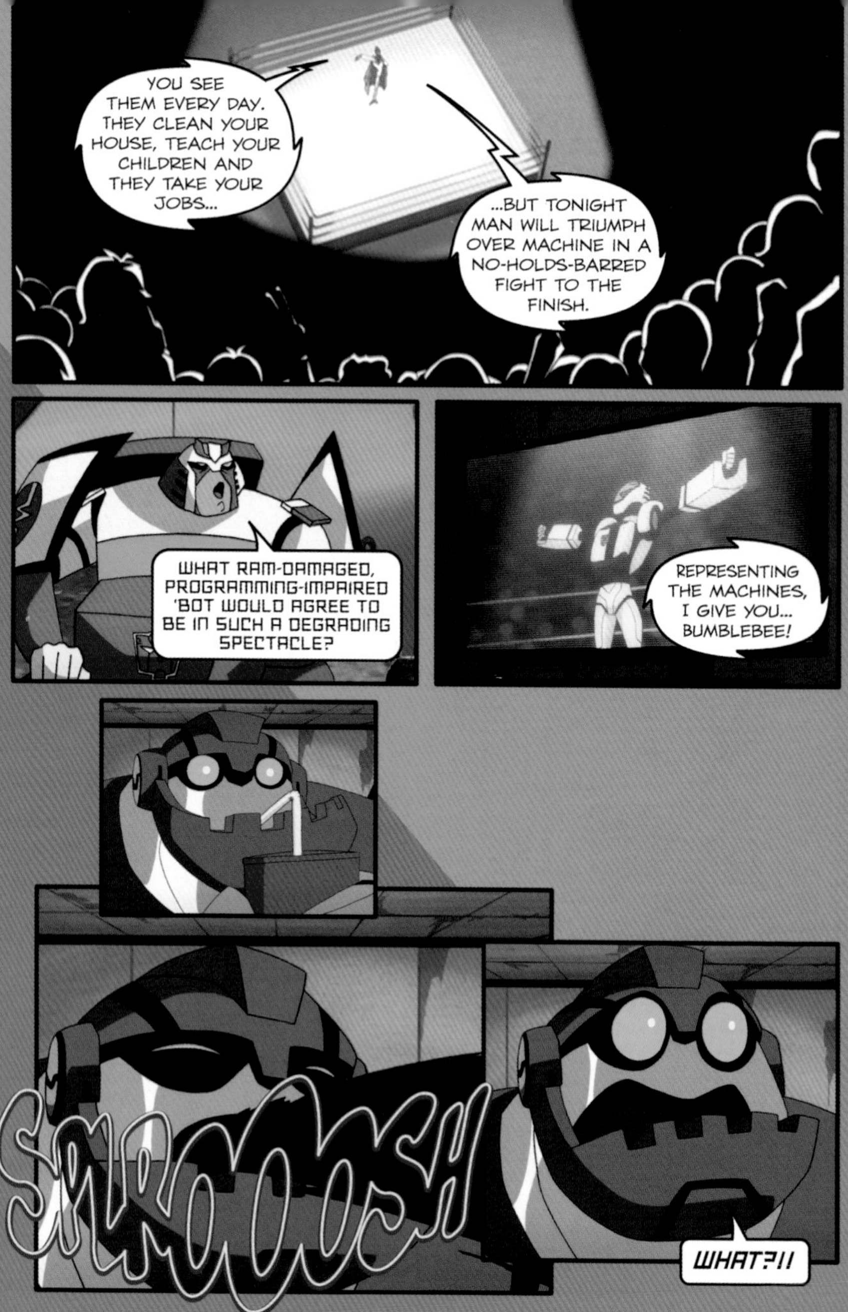

YOU SEE THEM EVERY DAY. THEY CLEAN YOUR HOUSE, TEACH YOUR CHILDREN AND THEY TAKE YOUR JOBS...
...BUT TONIGHT MAN WILL TRIUMPH OVER MACHINE IN A NO-HOLDS-BARRED FIGHT TO THE FINISH.
WHAT RAM-DAMAGED, PROGRAMMING-IMPAIRED 'BOT WOULD AGREE TO BE IN SUCH A DEGRADING SPECTACLE?
REPRESENTING THE MACHINES, I GIVE YOU... BUMBLEBEE!
SPROOOSH
WHAT?!!

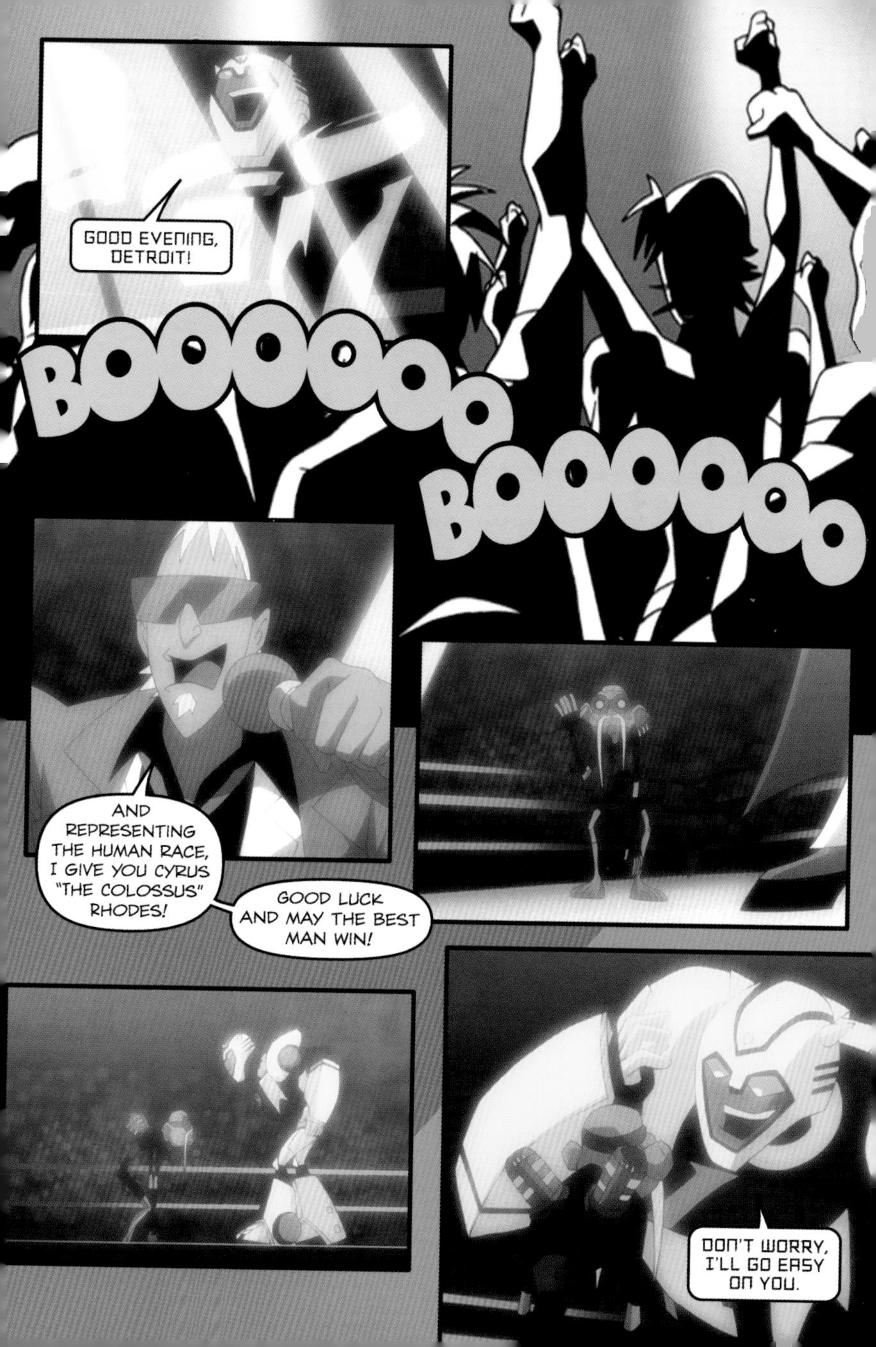
GOOD EVENING, DETROIT!
BOOOOOO
BOOOOOO
AND REPRESENTING THE HUMAN RACE, I GIVE YOU CYRUS "THE COLOSSUS" RHODES!
GOOD LUCK AND MAY THE BEST MAN WIN!
DON'T WORRY, I'LL GO EASY ON YOU.

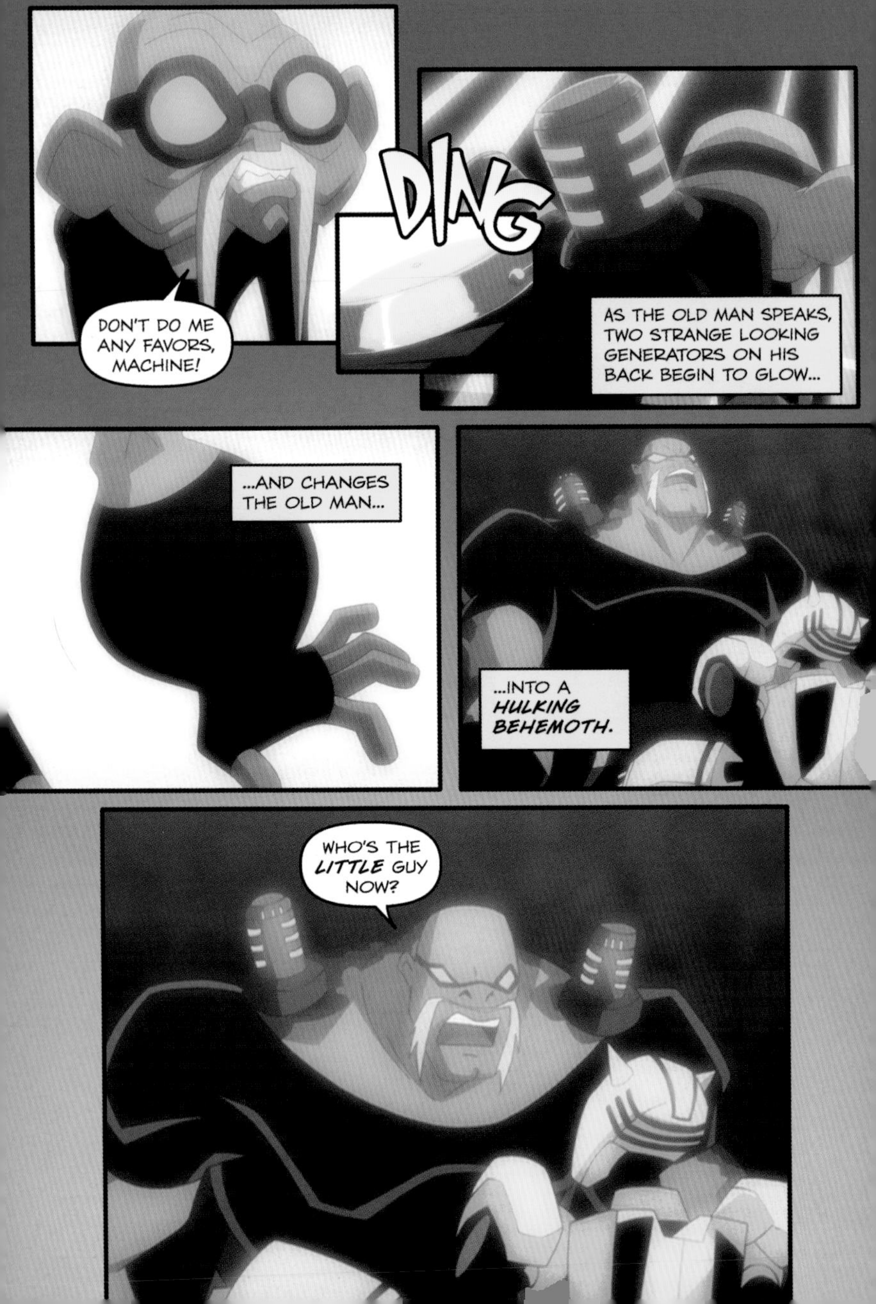
DON'T DO ME ANY FAVORS, MACHINE!
DING
AS THE OLD MAN SPEAKS, TWO STRANGE LOOKING GENERATORS ON HIS BACK BEGIN TO GLOW...
...AND CHANGES THE OLD MAN...
...INTO A *HULKING BEHEMOTH.*
WHO'S THE *LITTLE* GUY NOW?

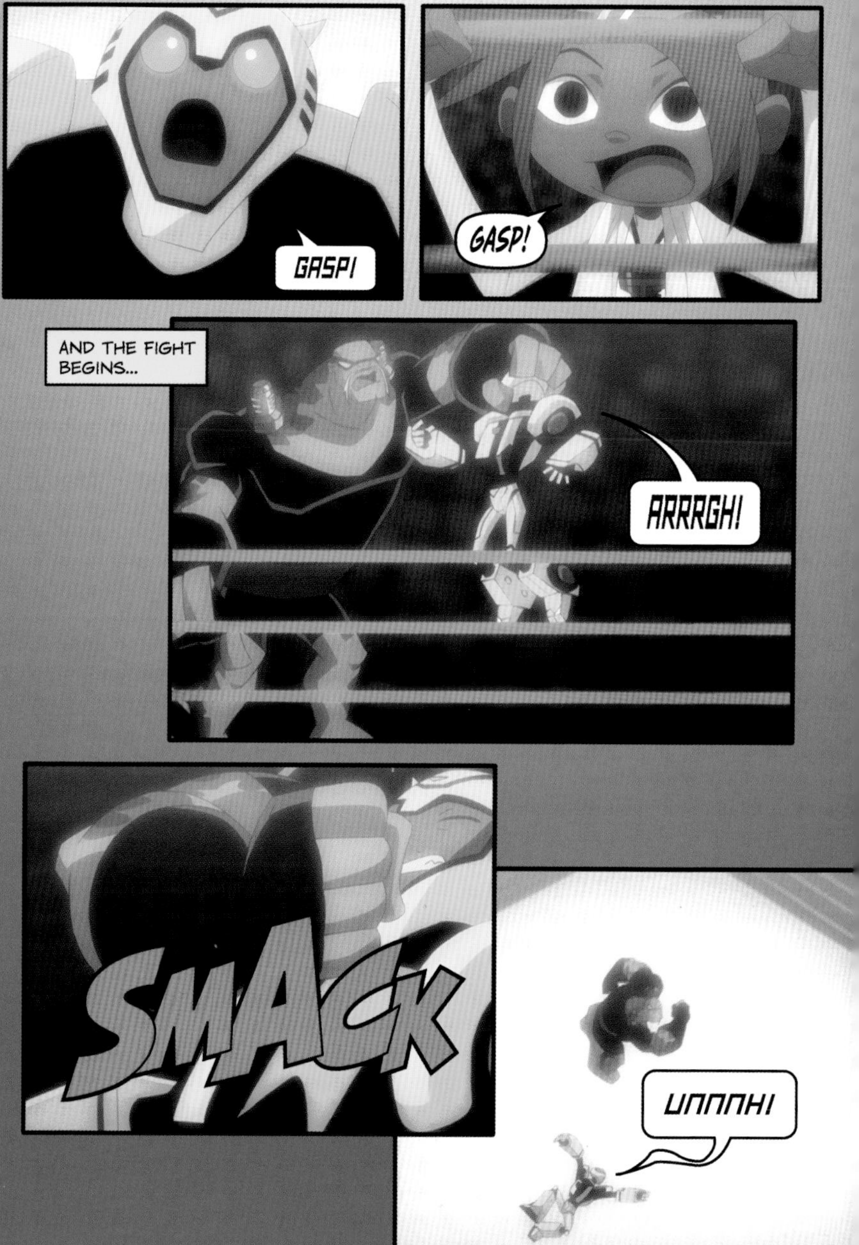
GASP!
GASP!
AND THE FIGHT BEGINS...
ARRRGH!
SMACK
UNNNH!

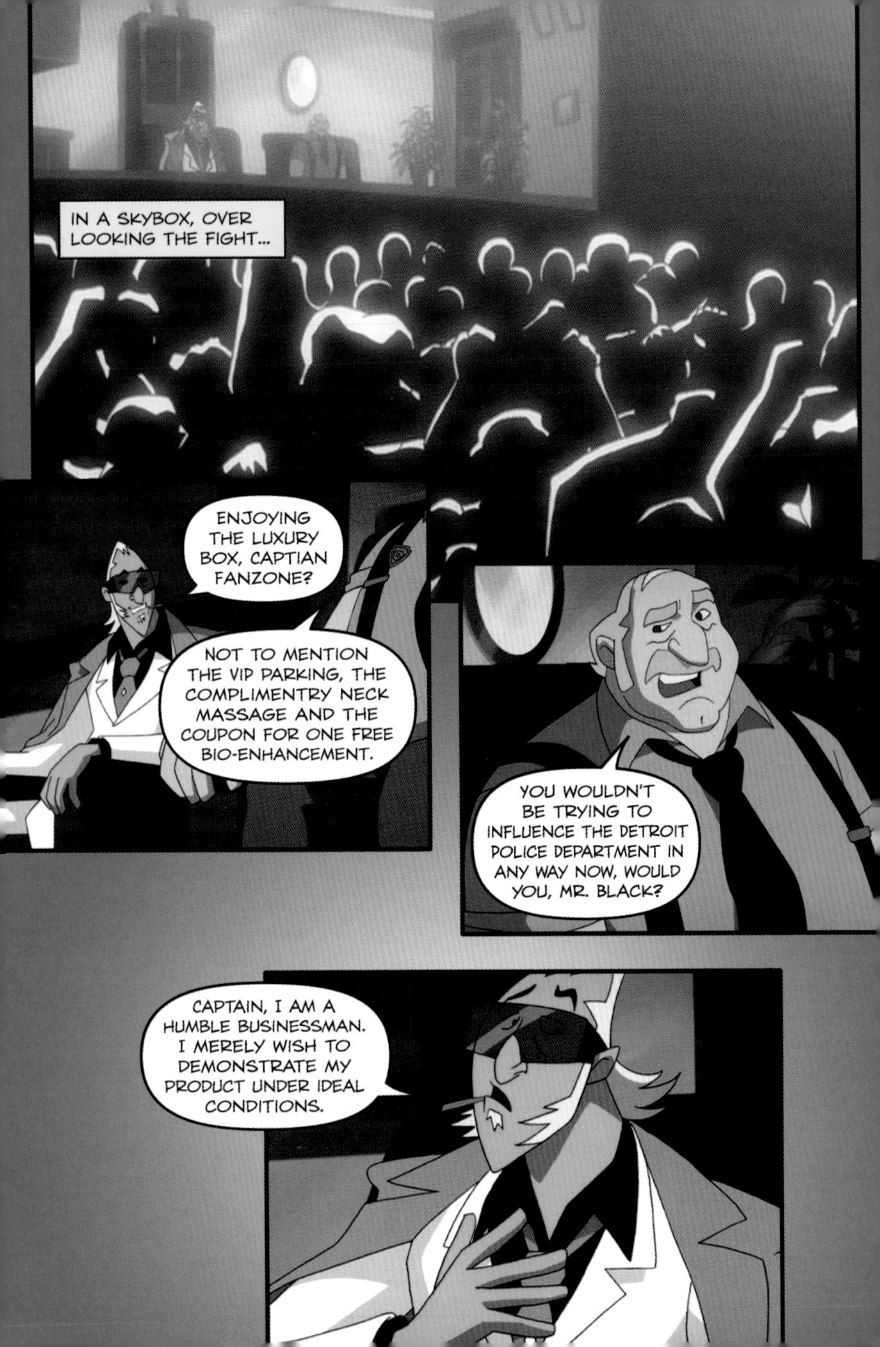
IN A SKYBOX, OVER LOOKING THE FIGHT...
ENJOYING THE LUXURY BOX, CAPTIAN FANZONE?
NOT TO MENTION THE VIP PARKING, THE COMPLIMENTRY NECK MASSAGE AND THE COUPON FOR ONE FREE BIO-ENHANCEMENT.
YOU WOULDN'T BE TRYING TO INFLUENCE THE DETROIT POLICE DEPARTMENT IN ANY WAY NOW, WOULD YOU, MR. BLACK?
CAPTAIN, I AM A HUMBLE BUSINESSMAN. I MERELY WISH TO DEMONSTRATE MY PRODUCT UNDER IDEAL CONDITIONS.

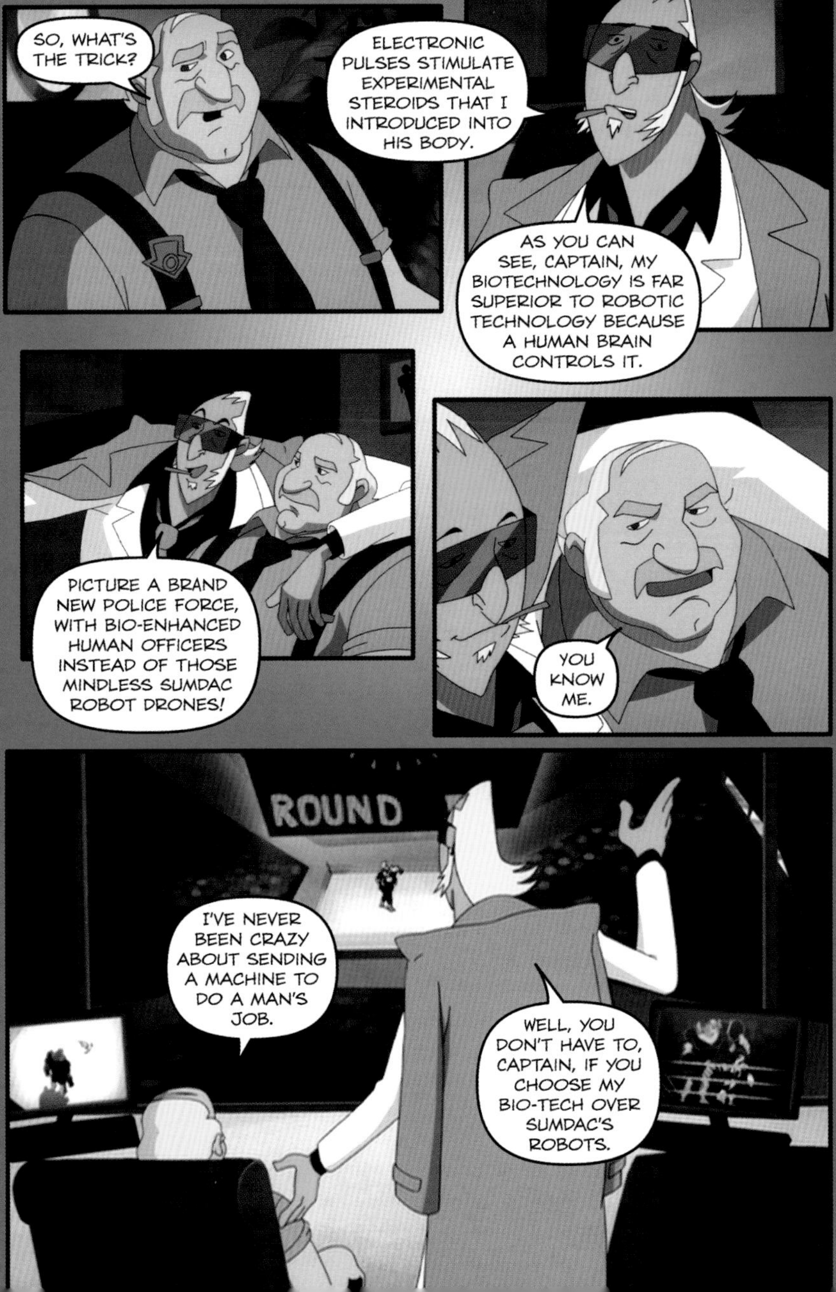
SO, WHAT'S THE TRICK?
ELECTRONIC PULSES STIMULATE EXPERIMENTAL STEROIDS THAT I INTRODUCED INTO HIS BODY.
AS YOU CAN SEE, CAPTAIN, MY BIOTECHNOLOGY IS FAR SUPERIOR TO ROBOTIC TECHNOLOGY BECAUSE A HUMAN BRAIN CONTROLS IT.
PICTURE A BRAND NEW POLICE FORCE, WITH BIO-ENHANCED HUMAN OFFICERS INSTEAD OF THOSE MINDLESS SUMDAC ROBOT DRONES!
YOU KNOW ME.
ROUND
I'VE NEVER BEEN CRAZY ABOUT SENDING A MACHINE TO DO A MAN'S JOB.
WELL, YOU DON'T HAVE TO, CAPTAIN, IF YOU CHOOSE MY BIO-TECH OVER SUMDAC'S ROBOTS.

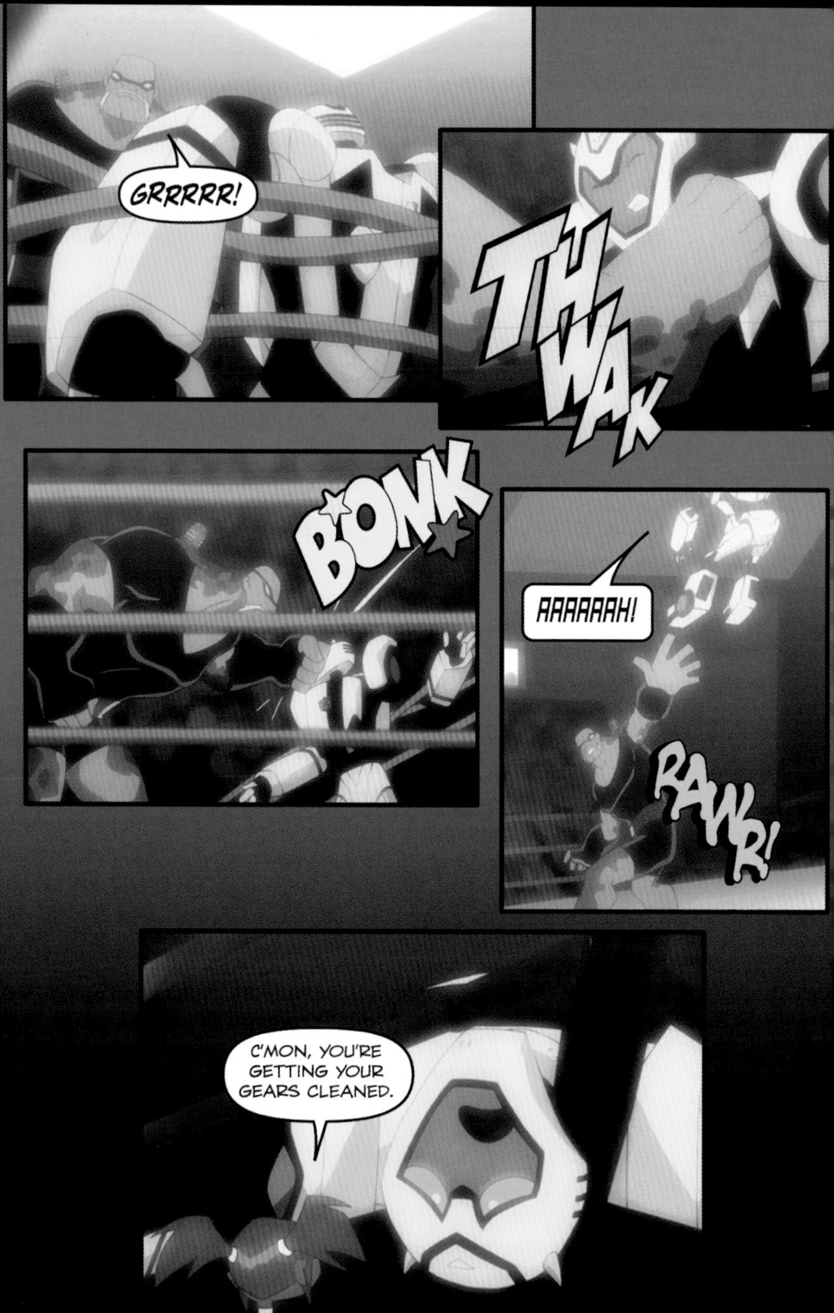
GRRRRR!
THWAK
BONK
AAAAAAH!
RAWR!
C'MON, YOU'RE GETTING YOUR GEARS CLEANED.

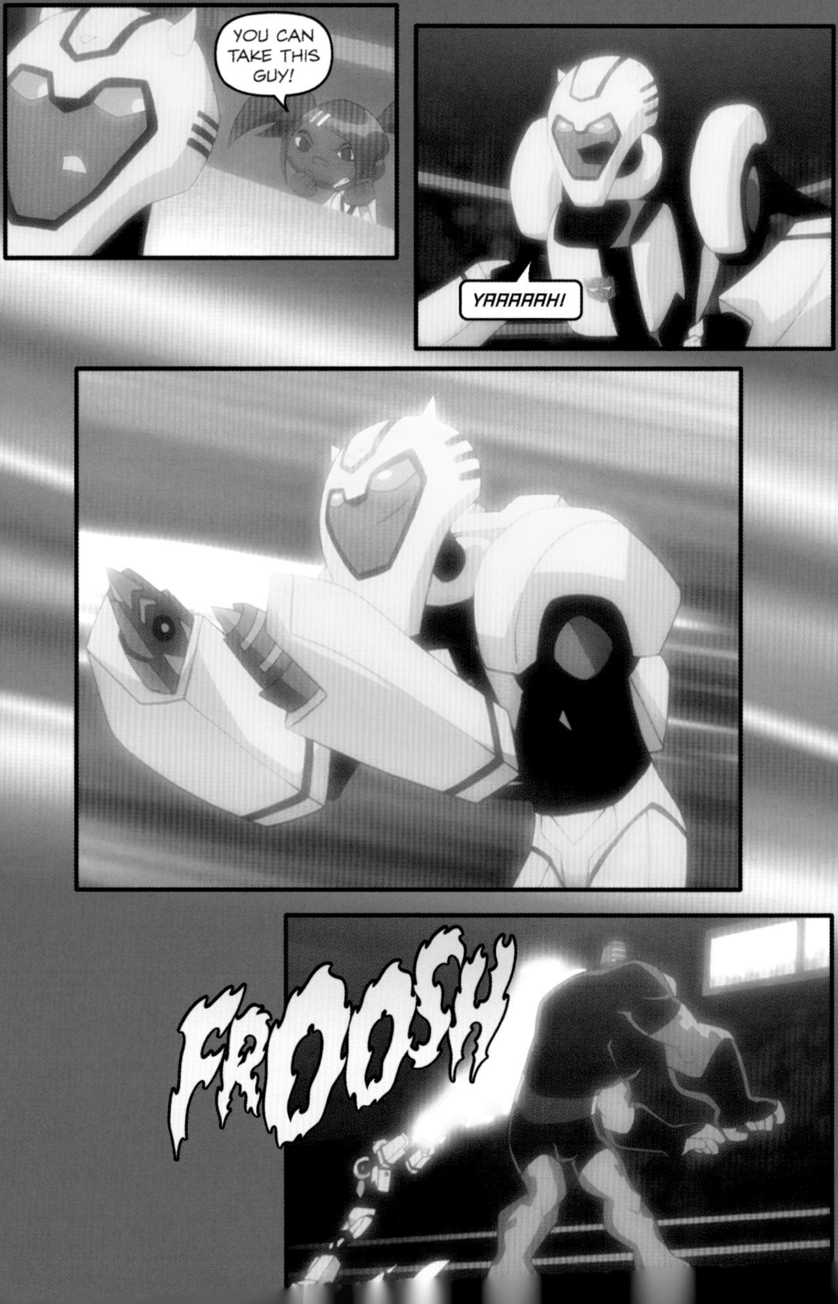
YOU CAN TAKE THIS GUY!
YAAAAAH!
FROOSH

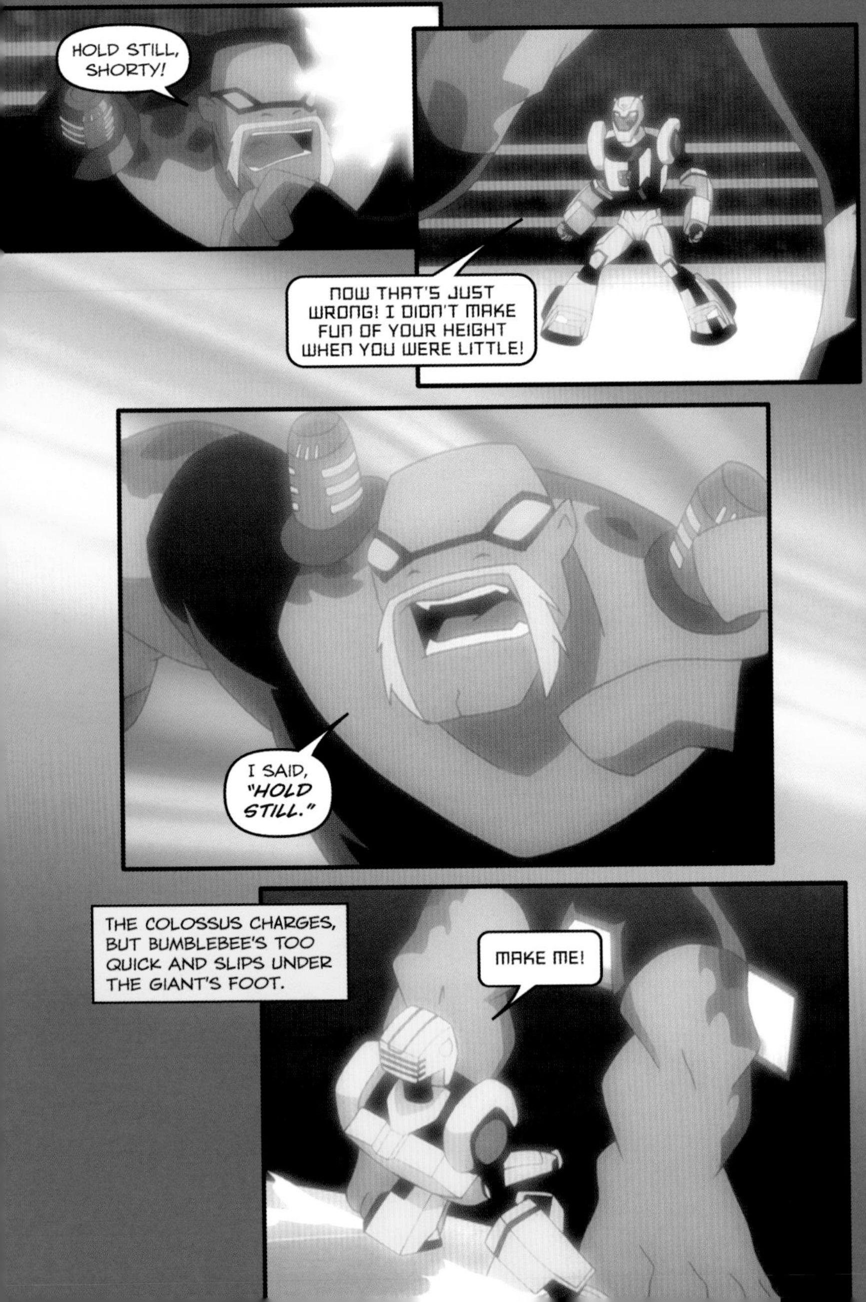
HOLD STILL, SHORTY!
NOW THAT'S JUST WRONG! I DIDN'T MAKE FUN OF YOUR HEIGHT WHEN YOU WERE LITTLE!
I SAID, "HOLD STILL."
THE COLOSSUS CHARGES, BUT BUMBLEBEE'S TOO QUICK AND SLIPS UNDER THE GIANT'S FOOT.
MAKE ME!

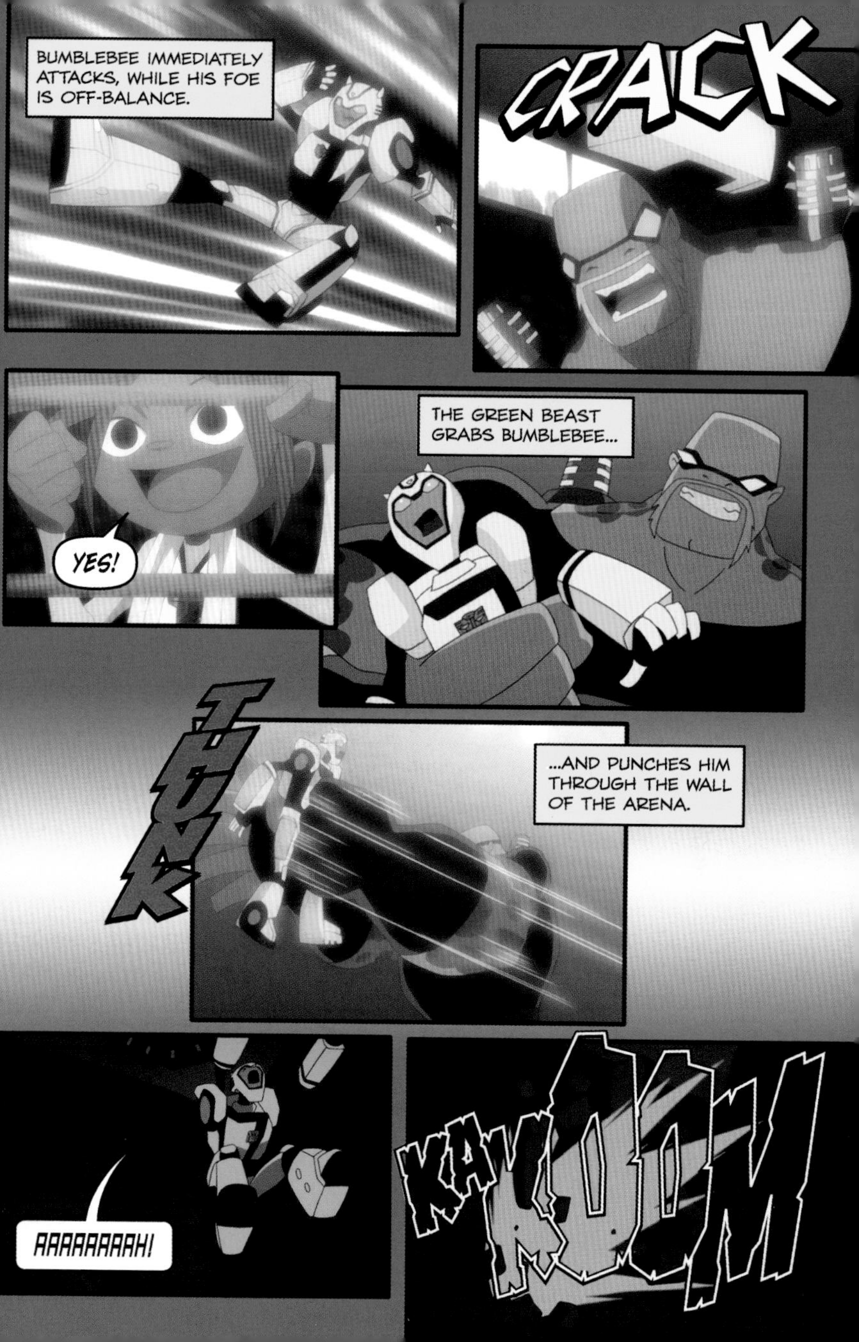
BUMBLEBEE IMMEDIATELY ATTACKS, WHILE HIS FOE IS OFF-BALANCE.
CRACK
YES!
THE GREEN BEAST GRABS BUMBLEBEE...
THUNK
...AND PUNCHES HIM THROUGH THE WALL OF THE ARENA.
AAAAAAAAH!
KA-BOOM

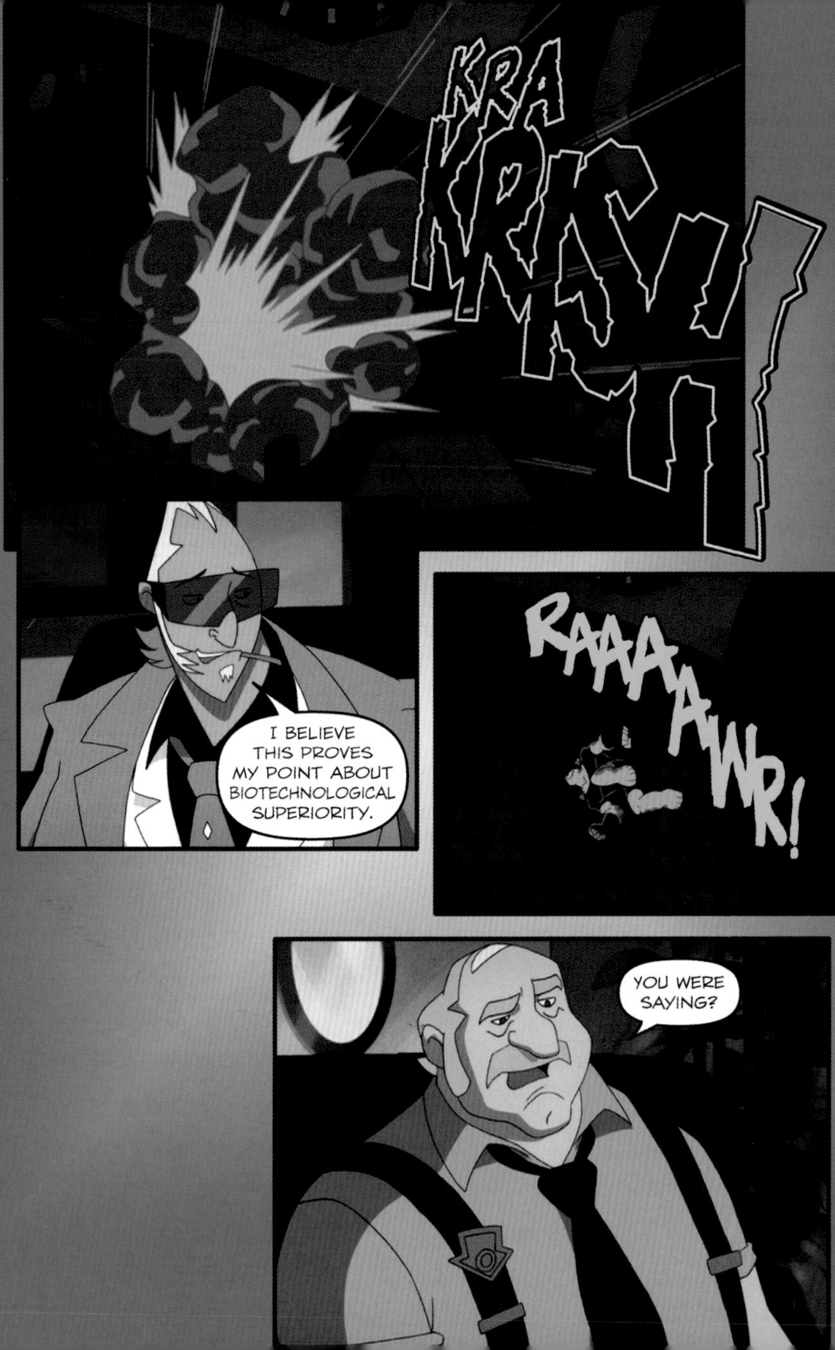
KRA KRASH!
I BELIEVE THIS PROVES MY POINT ABOUT BIOTECHNOLOGICAL SUPERIORITY.
RAAAAWR!
YOU WERE SAYING?

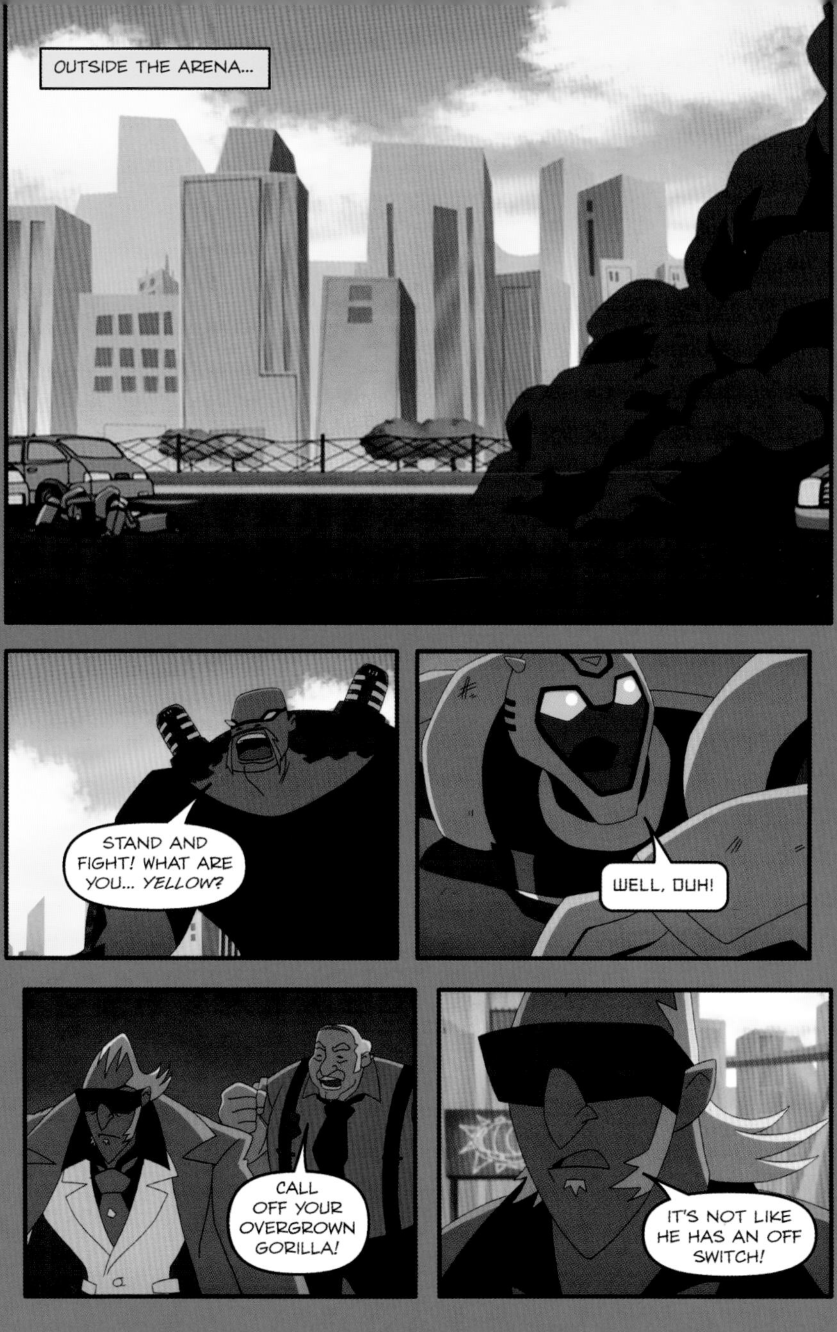
OUTSIDE THE ARENA...
STAND AND FIGHT! WHAT ARE YOU... YELLOW?
WELL, DUH!
CALL OFF YOUR OVERGROWN GORILLA!
IT'S NOT LIKE HE HAS AN OFF SWITCH!

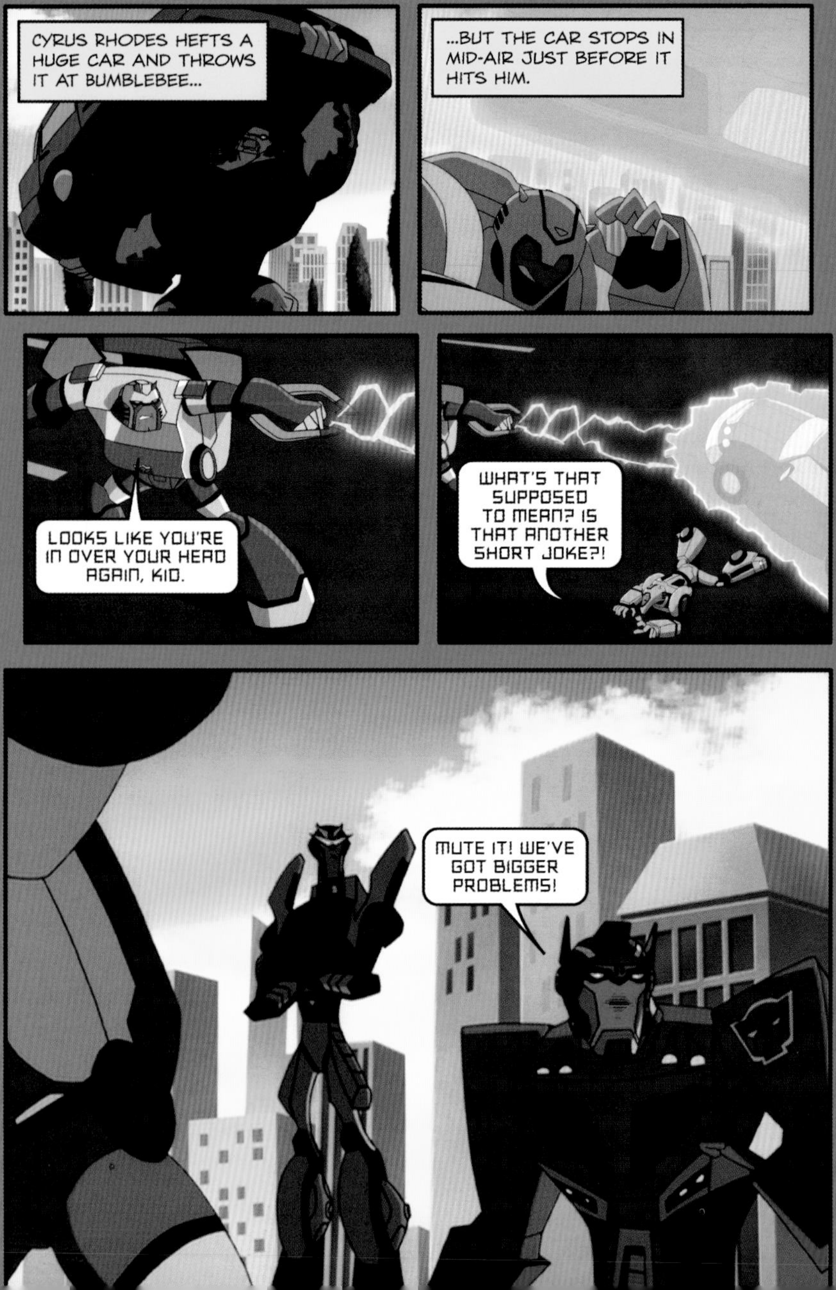
CYRUS RHODES HEFTS A HUGE CAR AND THROWS IT AT BUMBLEBEE...
...BUT THE CAR STOPS IN MID-AIR JUST BEFORE IT HITS HIM.
LOOKS LIKE YOU'RE IN OVER YOUR HEAD AGAIN, KID.
WHAT'S THAT SUPPOSED TO MEAN? IS THAT ANOTHER SHORT JOKE?!
MUTE IT! WE'VE GOT BIGGER PROBLEMS!

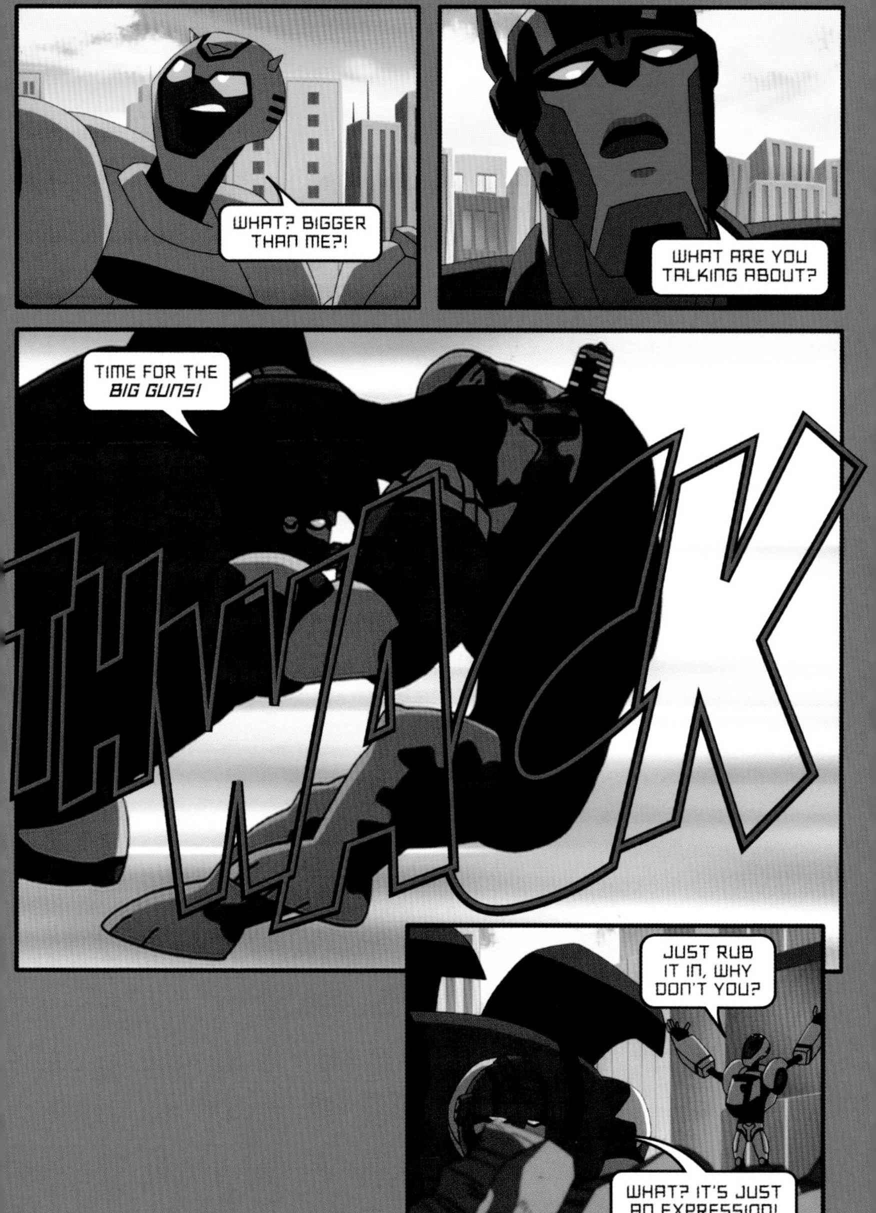
WHAT? BIGGER THAN ME?!
WHAT ARE YOU TALKING ABOUT?
TIME FOR THE *BIG GUNS!*
THWACK
JUST RUB IT IN, WHY DON'T YOU?
WHAT? IT'S JUST AN EXPRESSION!

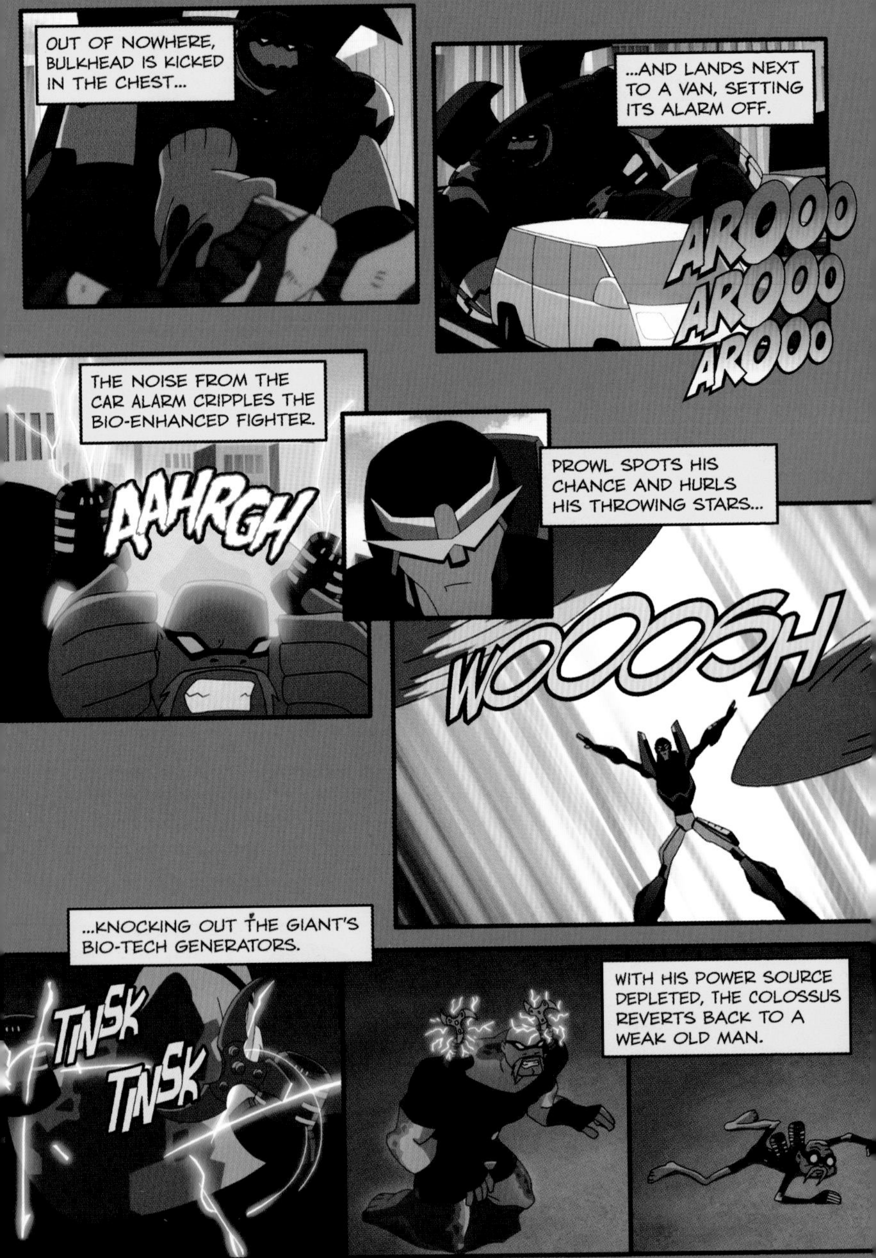
OUT OF NOWHERE, BULKHEAD IS KICKED IN THE CHEST...
...AND LANDS NEXT TO A VAN, SETTING ITS ALARM OFF.
AROOO AROOO AROOO
THE NOISE FROM THE CAR ALARM CRIPPLES THE BIO-ENHANCED FIGHTER.
AAHRGH
PROWL SPOTS HIS CHANCE AND HURLS HIS THROWING STARS...
WOOOSH
...KNOCKING OUT THE GIANT'S BIO-TECH GENERATORS.
TINSK TINSK
WITH HIS POWER SOURCE DEPLETED, THE COLOSSUS REVERTS BACK TO A WEAK OLD MAN.

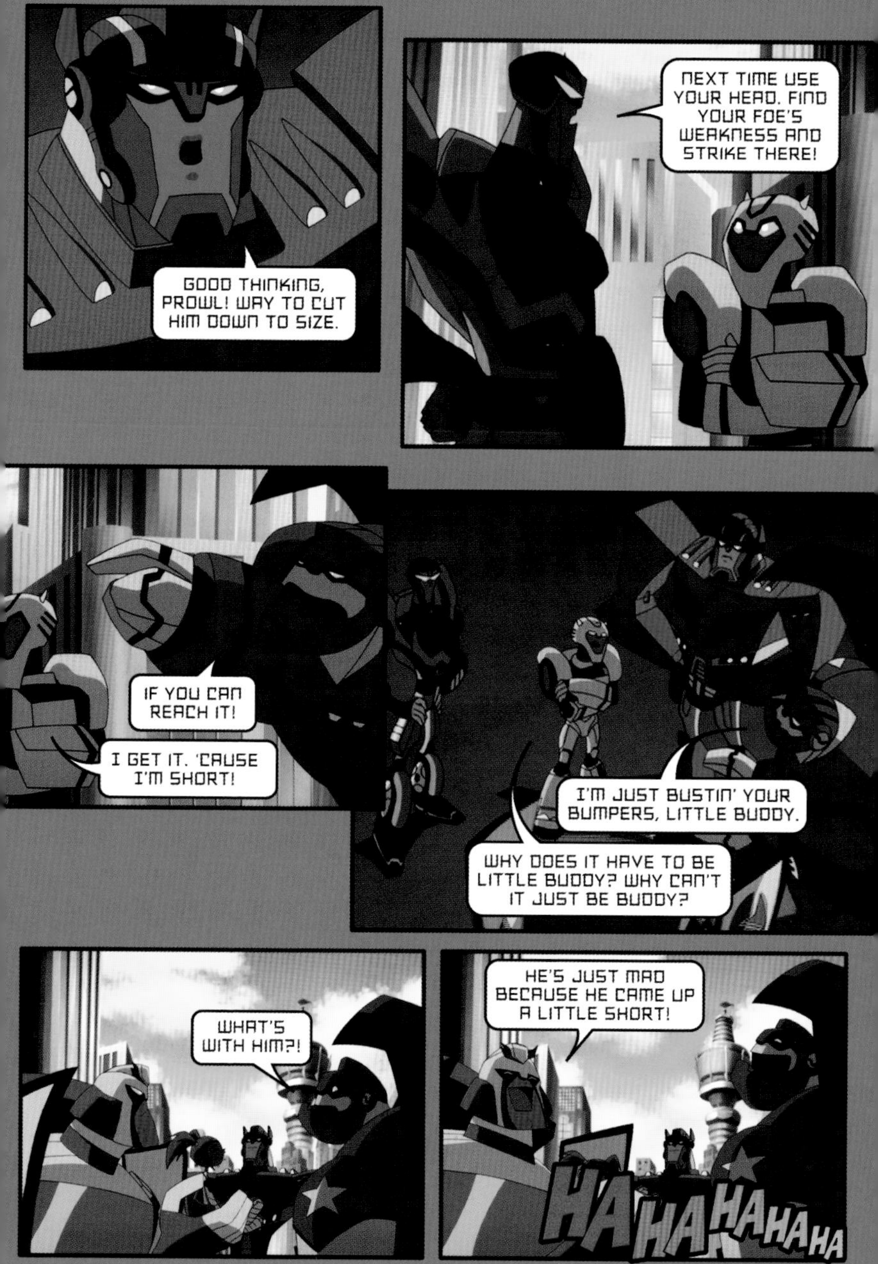
GOOD THINKING, PROWL! WAY TO CUT HIM DOWN TO SIZE.
NEXT TIME USE YOUR HEAD. FIND YOUR FOE'S WEAKNESS AND STRIKE THERE!
IF YOU CAN REACH IT!
I GET IT. 'CAUSE I'M SHORT!
I'M JUST BUSTIN' YOUR BUMPERS, LITTLE BUDDY.
WHY DOES IT HAVE TO BE LITTLE BUDDY? WHY CAN'T IT JUST BE BUDDY?
WHAT'S WITH HIM?!
HE'S JUST MAD BECAUSE HE CAME UP A LITTLE SHORT!
HA HA HA HA HA HA

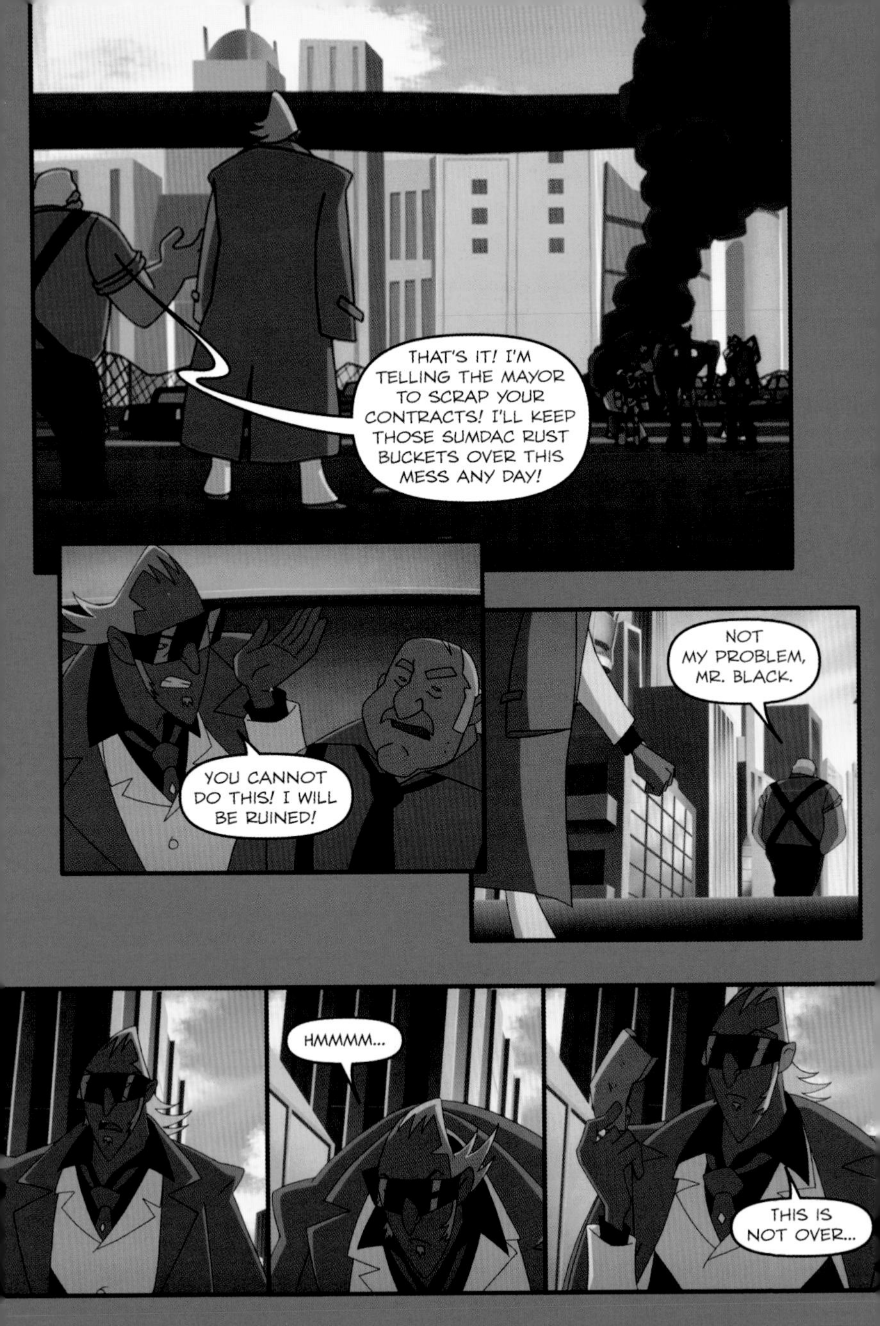
THAT'S IT! I'M TELLING THE MAYOR TO SCRAP YOUR CONTRACTS! I'LL KEEP THOSE SUMDAC RUST BUCKETS OVER THIS MESS ANY DAY!
YOU CANNOT DO THIS! I WILL BE RUINED!
NOT MY PROBLEM, MR. BLACK.
HMMMM...
THIS IS NOT OVER...

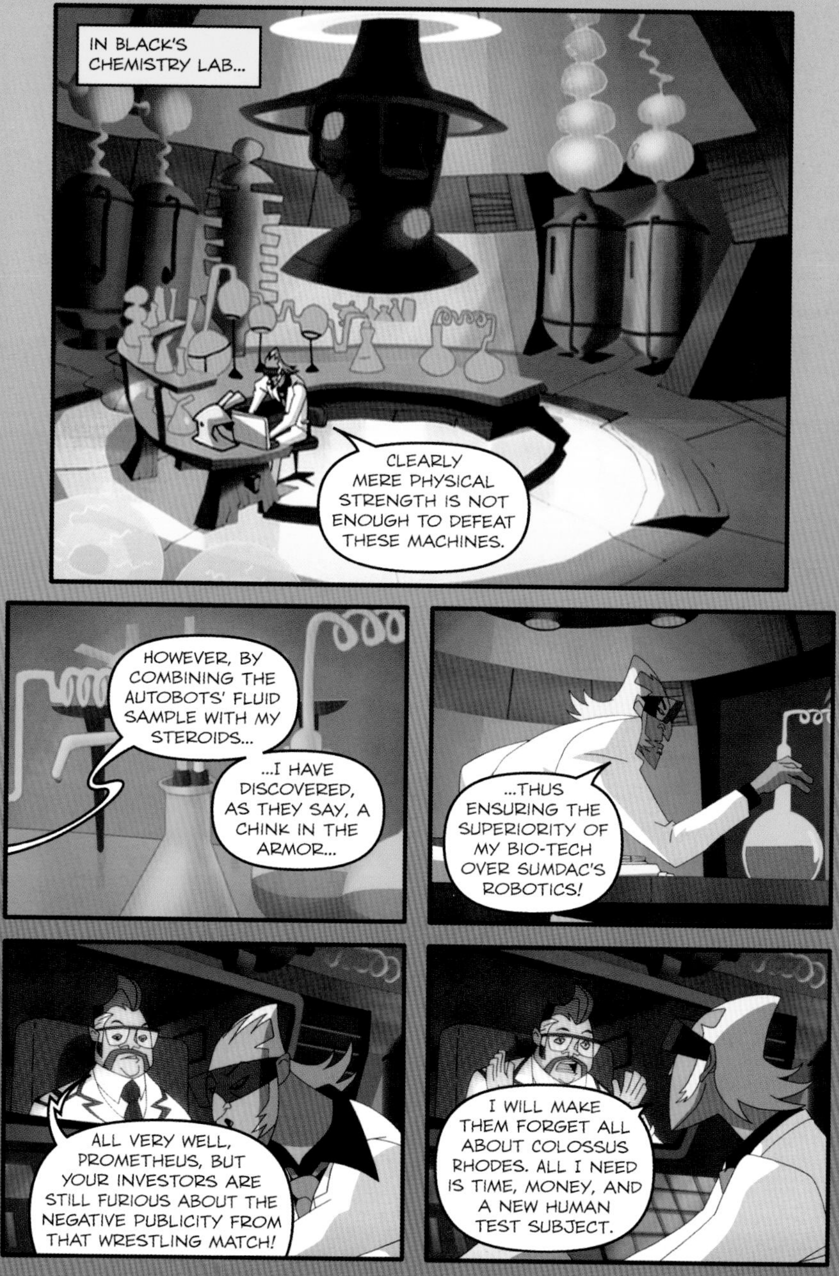
IN BLACK'S CHEMISTRY LAB...
CLEARLY MERE PHYSICAL STRENGTH IS NOT ENOUGH TO DEFEAT THESE MACHINES.
HOWEVER, BY COMBINING THE AUTOBOTS' FLUID SAMPLE WITH MY STEROIDS...
...I HAVE DISCOVERED, AS THEY SAY, A CHINK IN THE ARMOR...
...THUS ENSURING THE SUPERIORITY OF MY BIO-TECH OVER SUMDAC'S ROBOTICS!
ALL VERY WELL, PROMETHEUS, BUT YOUR INVESTORS ARE STILL FURIOUS ABOUT THE NEGATIVE PUBLICITY FROM THAT WRESTLING MATCH!
I WILL MAKE THEM FORGET ALL ABOUT COLOSSUS RHODES. ALL I NEED IS TIME, MONEY, AND A NEW HUMAN TEST SUBJECT.

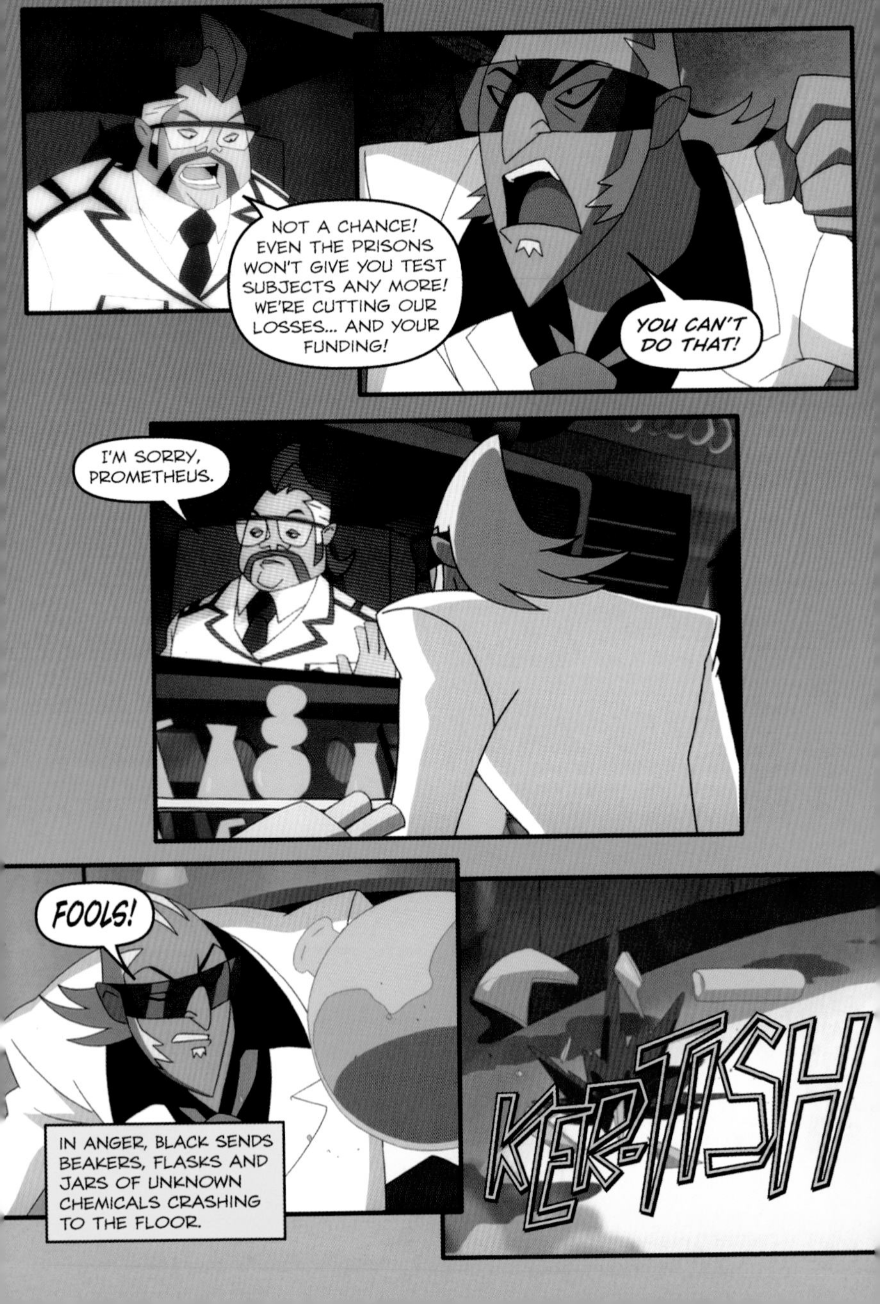
NOT A CHANCE! EVEN THE PRISONS WON'T GIVE YOU TEST SUBJECTS ANY MORE! WE'RE CUTTING OUR LOSSES... AND YOUR FUNDING!
YOU CAN'T DO THAT!
I'M SORRY, PROMETHEUS.
FOOLS!
IN ANGER, BLACK SENDS BEAKERS, FLASKS AND JARS OF UNKNOWN CHEMICALS CRASHING TO THE FLOOR.
KER-TISH

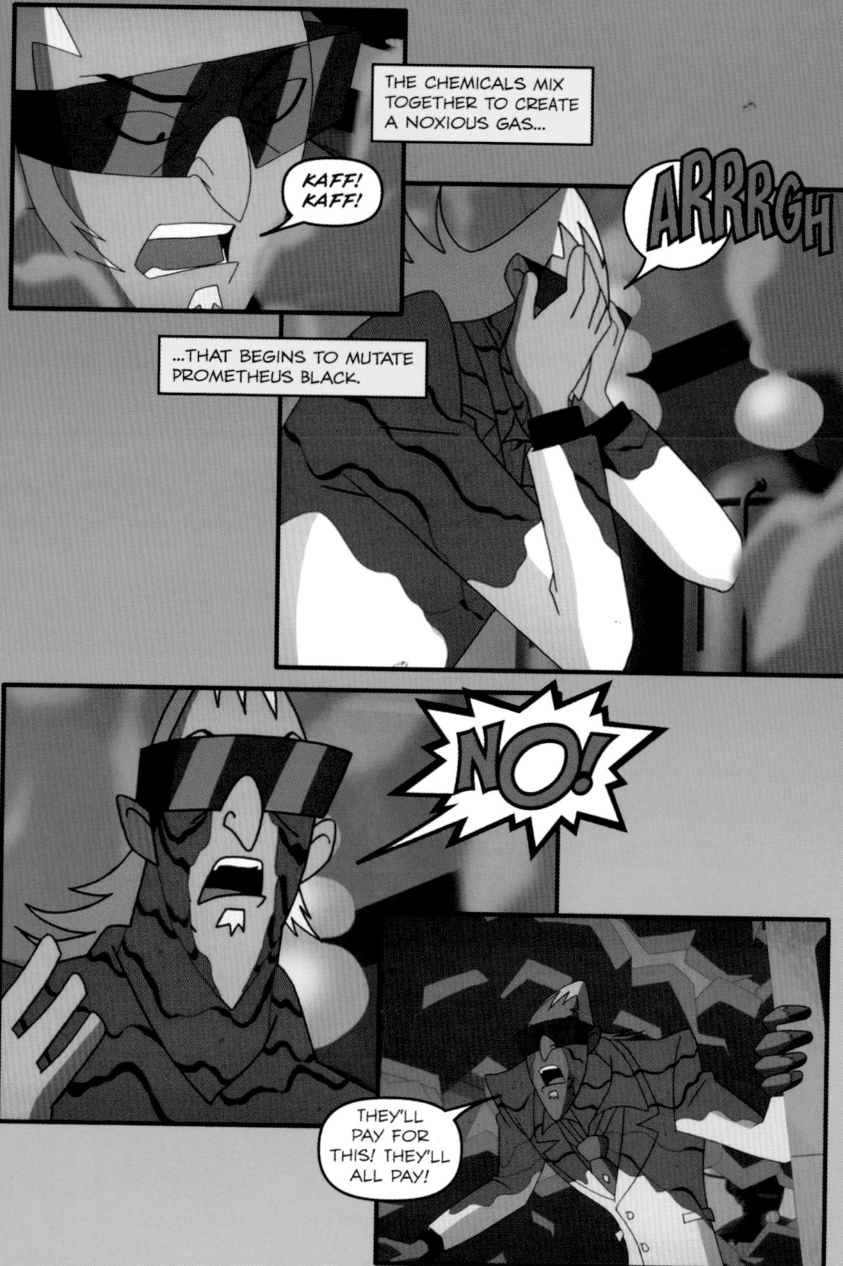
THE CHEMICALS MIX TOGETHER TO CREATE A NOXIOUS GAS...
KAFF! KAFF!
ARRRGH
...THAT BEGINS TO MUTATE PROMETHEUS BLACK.
NO!
THEY'LL PAY FOR THIS! THEY'LL ALL PAY!

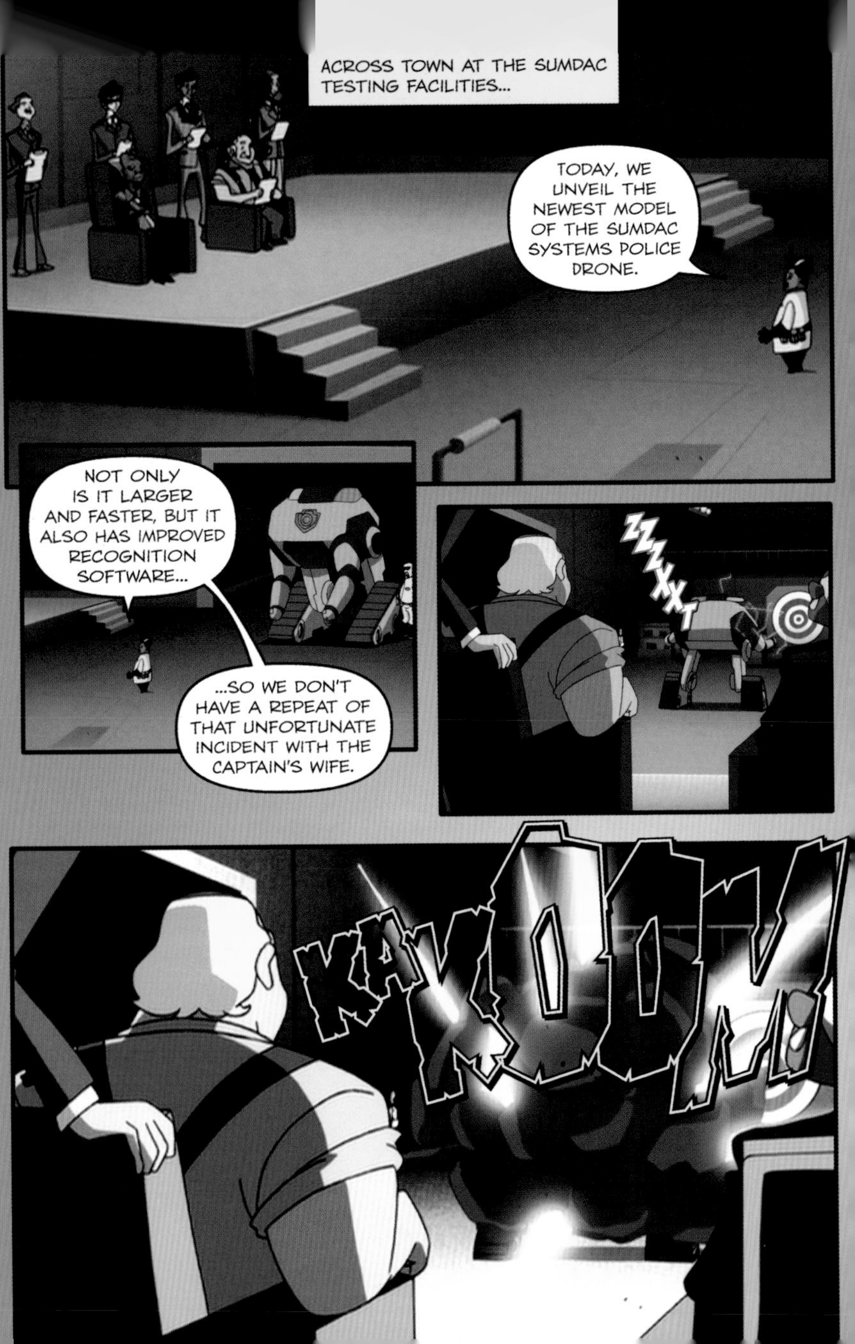
ACROSS TOWN AT THE SUMDAC TESTING FACILITIES...
TODAY, WE UNVEIL THE NEWEST MODEL OF THE SUMDAC SYSTEMS POLICE DRONE.
NOT ONLY IS IT LARGER AND FASTER, BUT IT ALSO HAS IMPROVED RECOGNITION SOFTWARE...
...SO WE DON'T HAVE A REPEAT OF THAT UNFORTUNATE INCIDENT WITH THE CAPTAIN'S WIFE.
ZZZXXT
KAKOOM

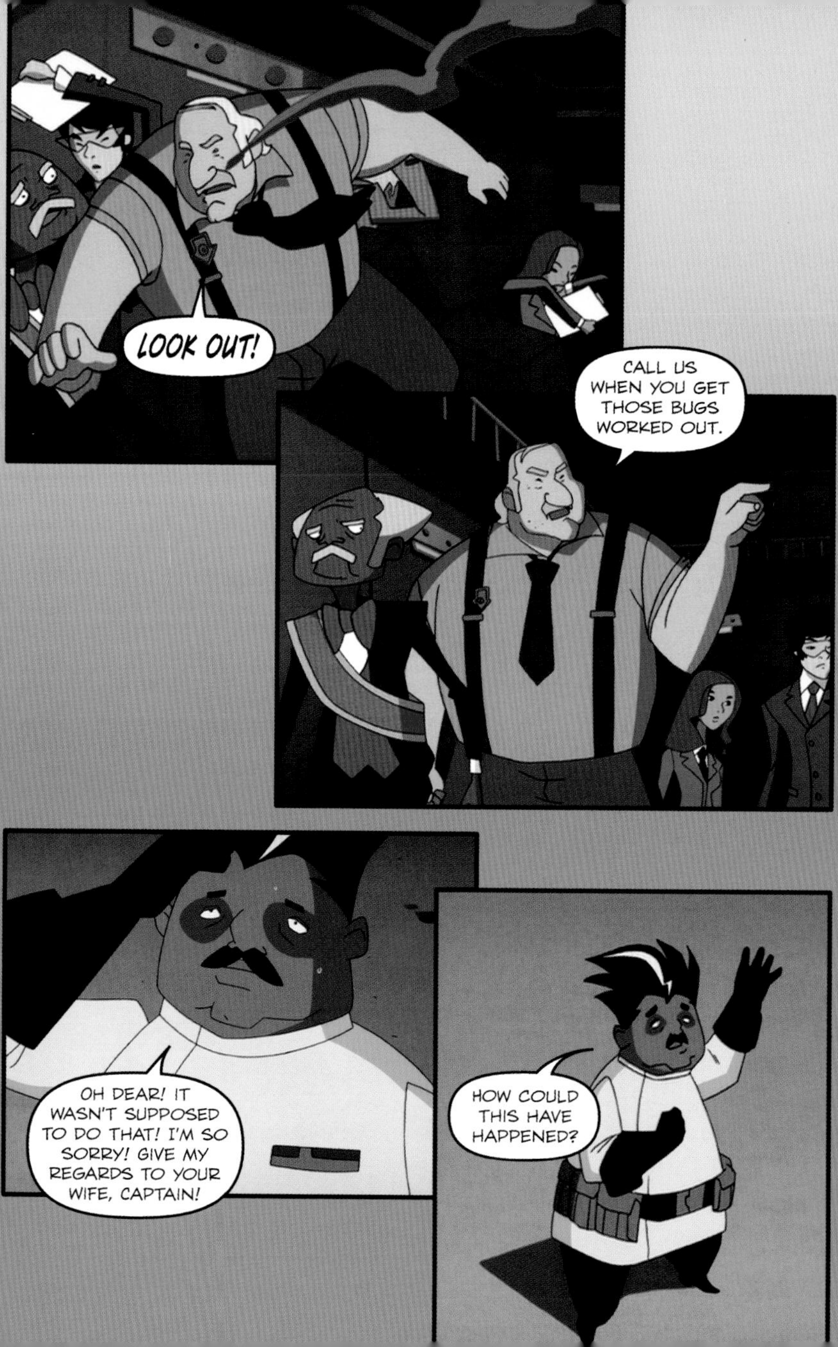
LOOK OUT!
CALL US WHEN YOU GET THOSE BUGS WORKED OUT.
OH DEAR! IT WASN'T SUPPOSED TO DO THAT! I'M SO SORRY! GIVE MY REGARDS TO YOUR WIFE, CAPTAIN!
HOW COULD THIS HAVE HAPPENED?

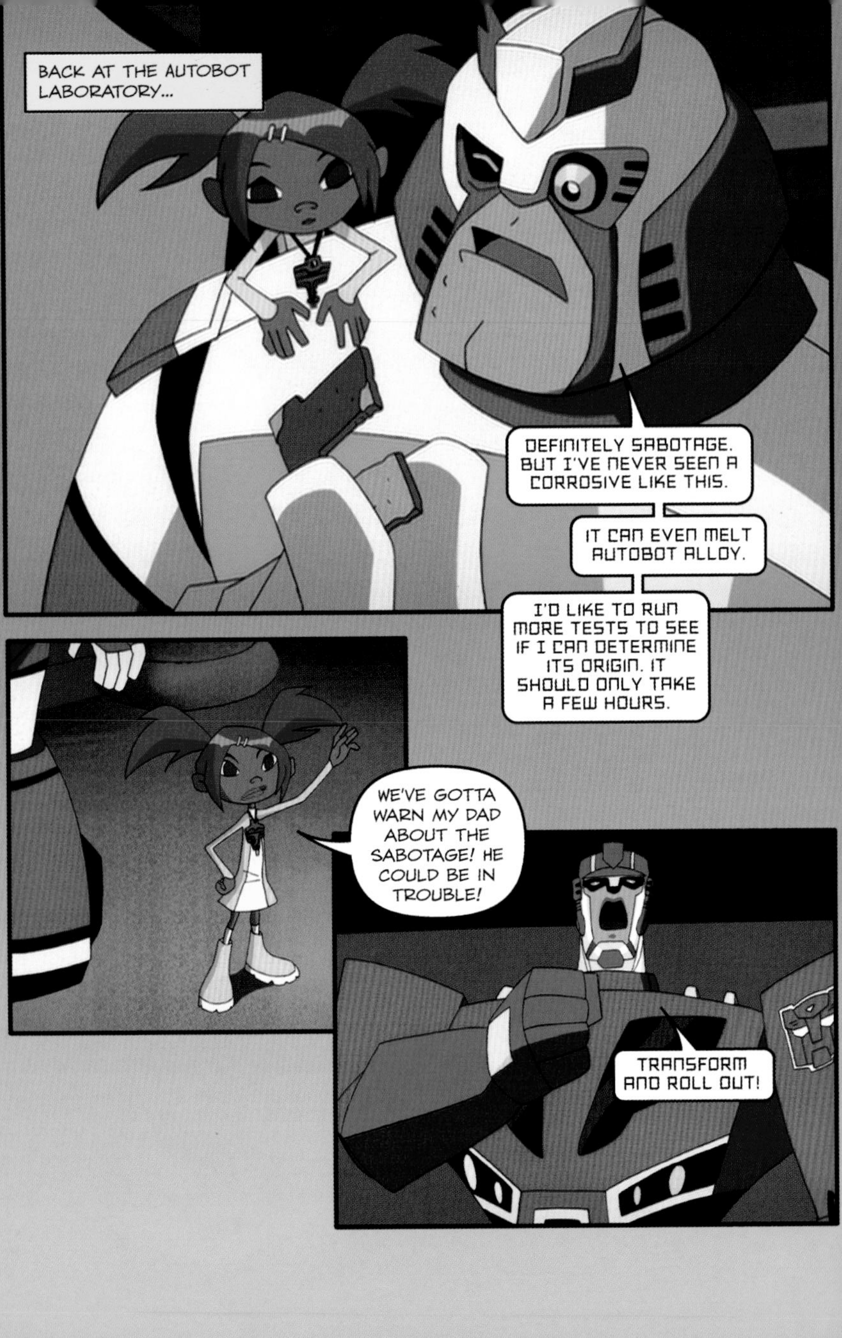
BACK AT THE AUTOBOT LABORATORY...
DEFINITELY SABOTAGE. BUT I'VE NEVER SEEN A CORROSIVE LIKE THIS.
IT CAN EVEN MELT AUTOBOT ALLOY.
I'D LIKE TO RUN MORE TESTS TO SEE IF I CAN DETERMINE ITS ORIGIN. IT SHOULD ONLY TAKE A FEW HOURS.
WE'VE GOTTA WARN MY DAD ABOUT THE SABOTAGE! HE COULD BE IN TROUBLE!
TRANSFORM AND ROLL OUT!

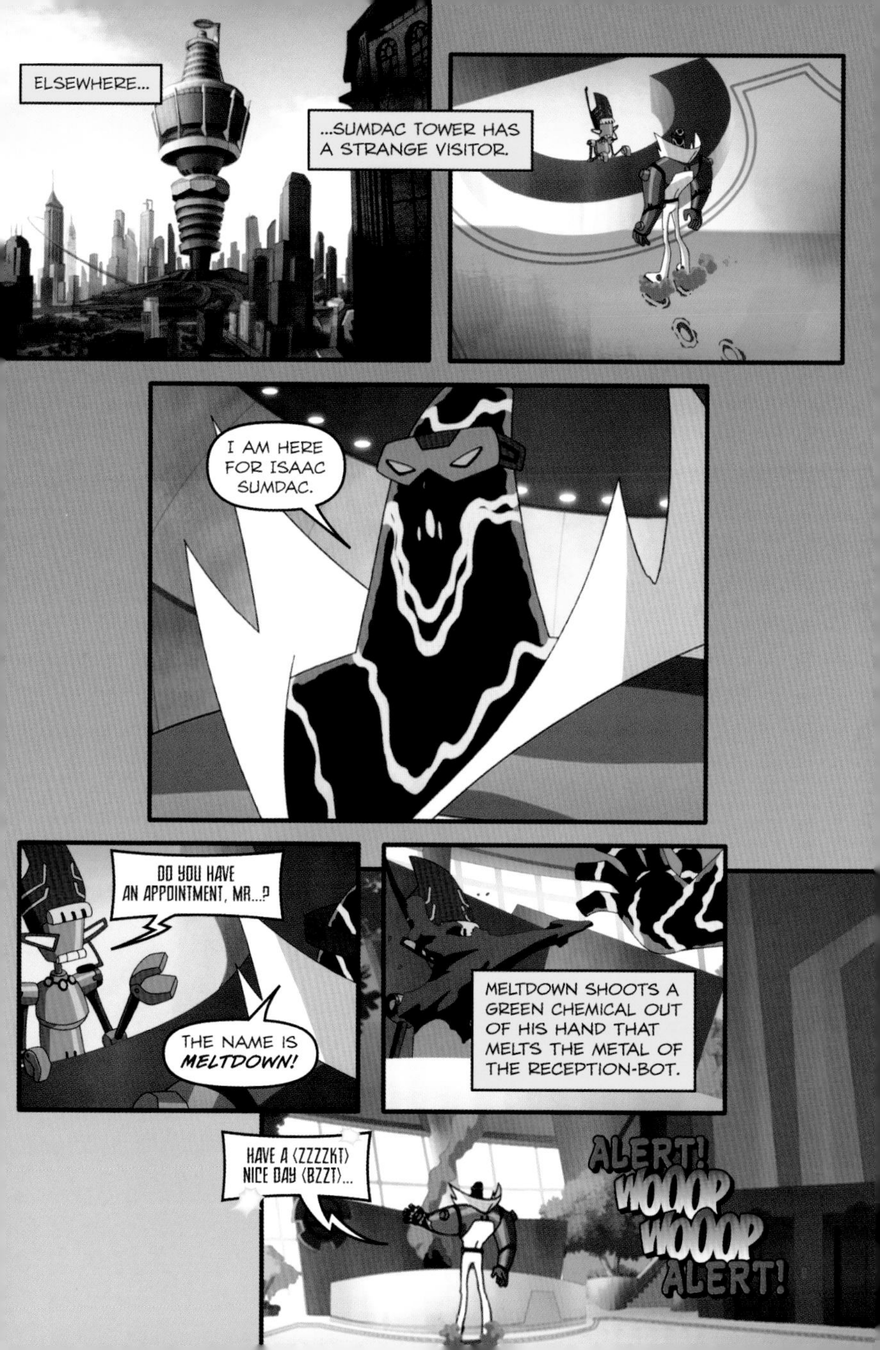
ELSEWHERE...
...SUMDAC TOWER HAS A STRANGE VISITOR.
I AM HERE FOR ISAAC SUMDAC.
DO YOU HAVE AN APPOINTMENT, MR...?
THE NAME IS MELTDOWN!
MELTDOWN SHOOTS A GREEN CHEMICAL OUT OF HIS HAND THAT MELTS THE METAL OF THE RECEPTION-BOT.
HAVE A (ZZZZKT) NICE DAY (BZZT)...
ALERT! WOOOP WOOOP ALERT!

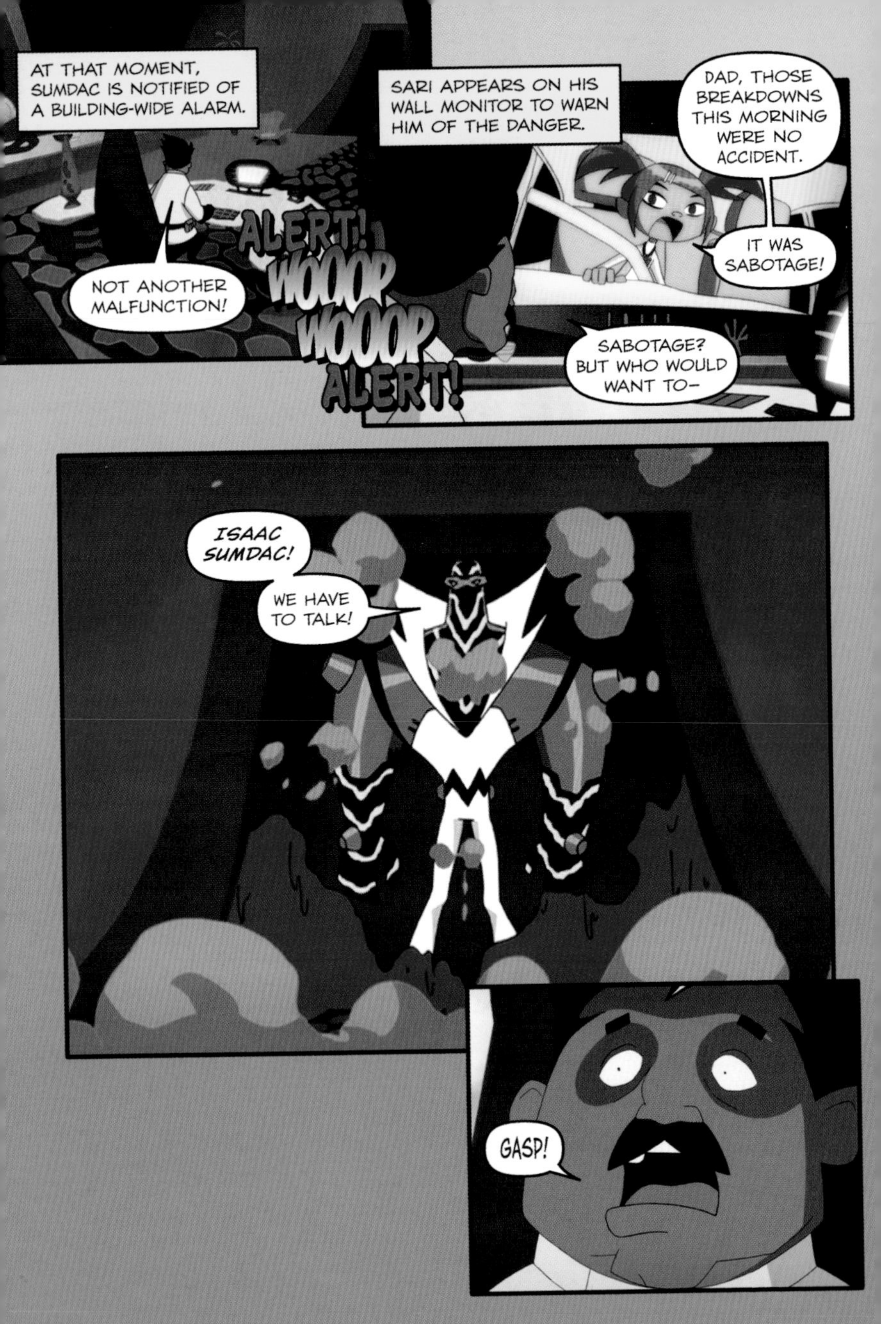
AT THAT MOMENT, SUMDAC IS NOTIFIED OF A BUILDING-WIDE ALARM.
NOT ANOTHER MALFUNCTION!
ALERT! WOOOP WOOOP ALERT!
SARI APPEARS ON HIS WALL MONITOR TO WARN HIM OF THE DANGER.
DAD, THOSE BREAKDOWNS THIS MORNING WERE NO ACCIDENT.
IT WAS SABOTAGE!
SABOTAGE? BUT WHO WOULD WANT TO–
ISAAC SUMDAC!
WE HAVE TO TALK!
GASP!

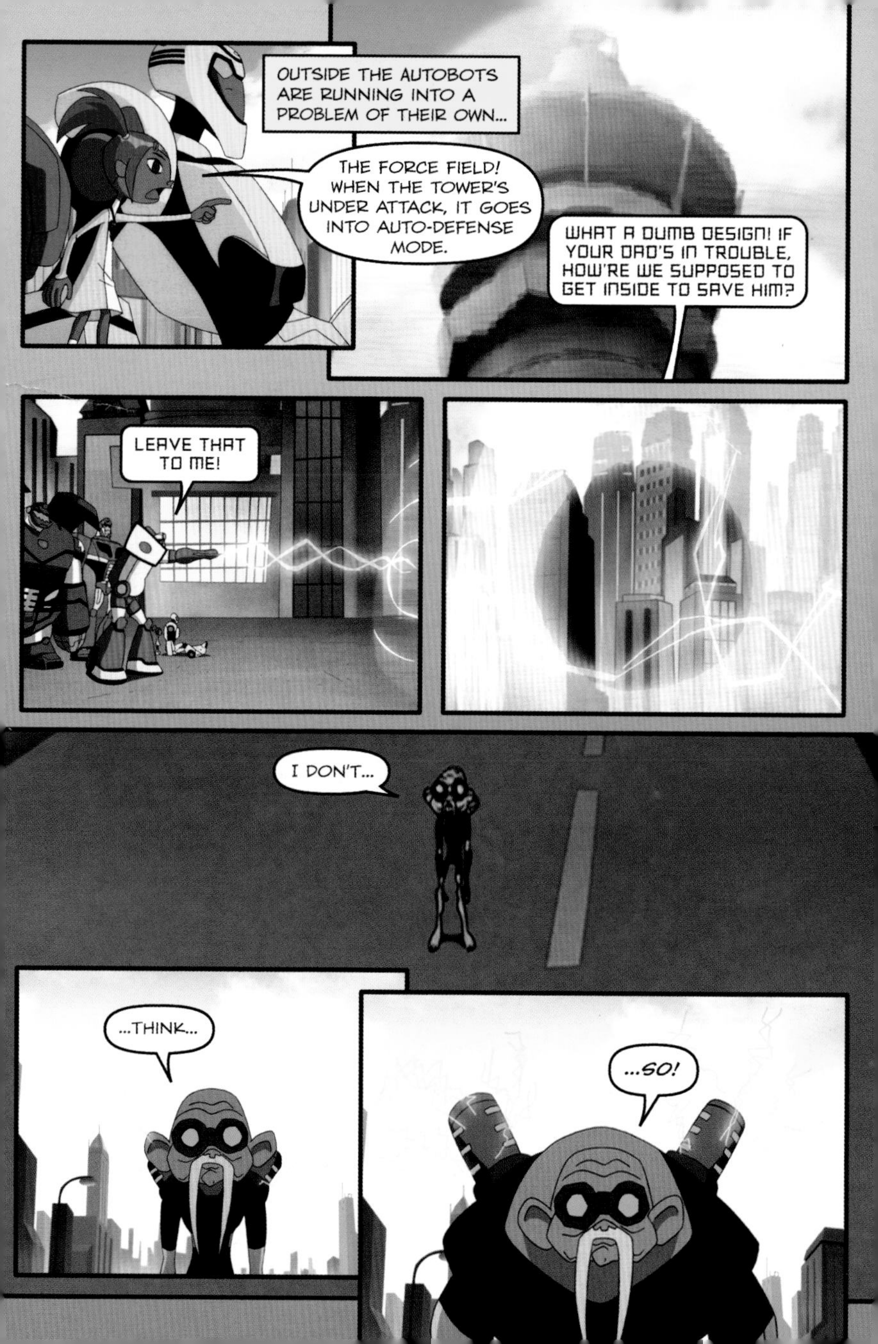
OUTSIDE THE AUTOBOTS ARE RUNNING INTO A PROBLEM OF THEIR OWN...
THE FORCE FIELD! WHEN THE TOWER'S UNDER ATTACK, IT GOES INTO AUTO-DEFENSE MODE.
WHAT A DUMB DESIGN! IF YOUR DAD'S IN TROUBLE, HOW'RE WE SUPPOSED TO GET INSIDE TO SAVE HIM?
LEAVE THAT TO ME!
I DON'T...
...THINK...
...SO!

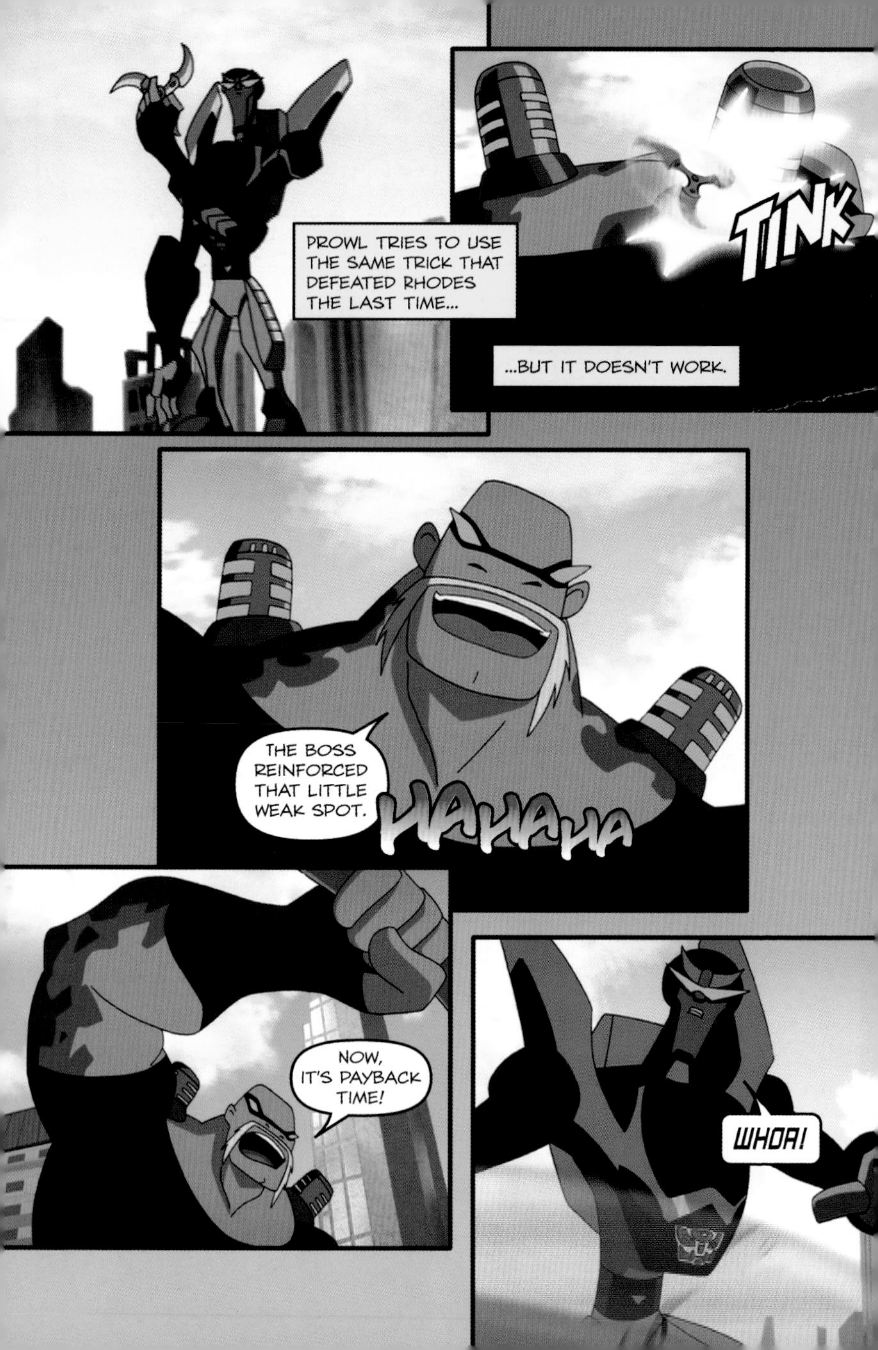
PROWL TRIES TO USE THE SAME TRICK THAT DEFEATED RHODES THE LAST TIME...
TINK
...BUT IT DOESN'T WORK.
THE BOSS REINFORCED THAT LITTLE WEAK SPOT.
HAHAHAHA
NOW, IT'S PAYBACK TIME!
WHOA!

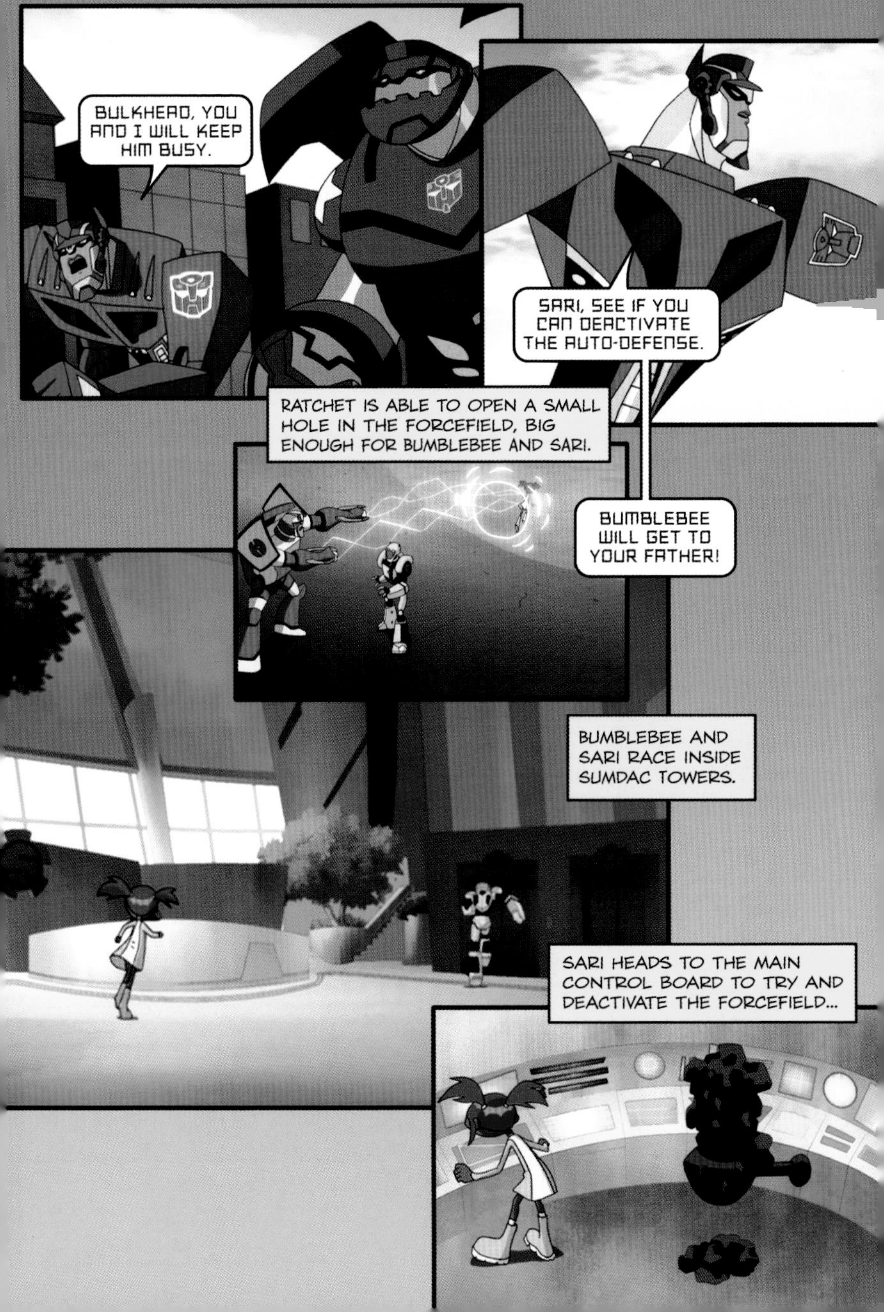
BULKHEAD, YOU AND I WILL KEEP HIM BUSY.
SARI, SEE IF YOU CAN DEACTIVATE THE AUTO-DEFENSE.
BUMBLEBEE WILL GET TO YOUR FATHER!
RATCHET IS ABLE TO OPEN A SMALL HOLE IN THE FORCEFIELD, BIG ENOUGH FOR BUMBLEBEE AND SARI.
BUMBLEBEE AND SARI RACE INSIDE SUMDAC TOWERS.
SARI HEADS TO THE MAIN CONTROL BOARD TO TRY AND DEACTIVATE THE FORCEFIELD...

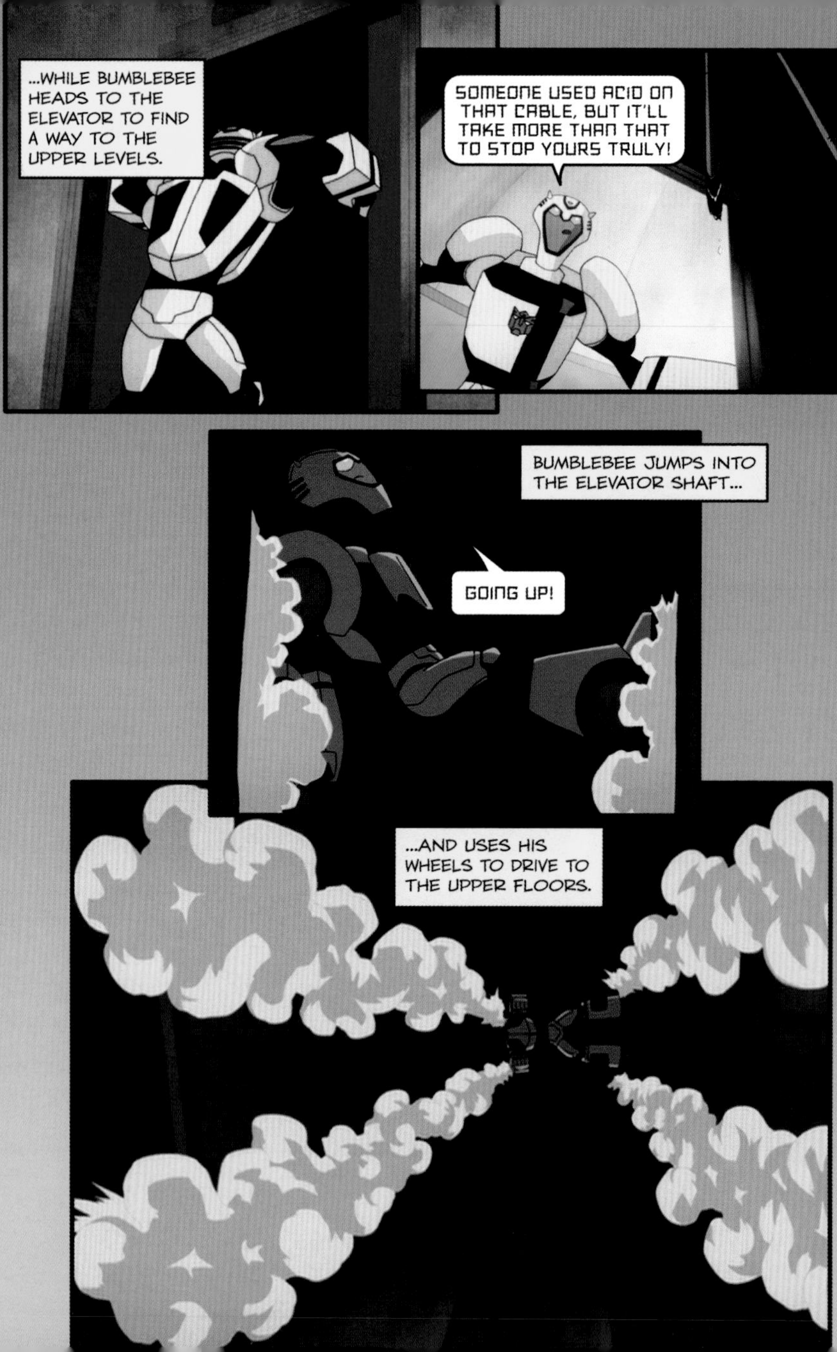
...WHILE BUMBLEBEE HEADS TO THE ELEVATOR TO FIND A WAY TO THE UPPER LEVELS.
SOMEONE USED ACID ON THAT CABLE, BUT IT'LL TAKE MORE THAN THAT TO STOP YOURS TRULY!
BUMBLEBEE JUMPS INTO THE ELEVATOR SHAFT...
GOING UP!
...AND USES HIS WHEELS TO DRIVE TO THE UPPER FLOORS.

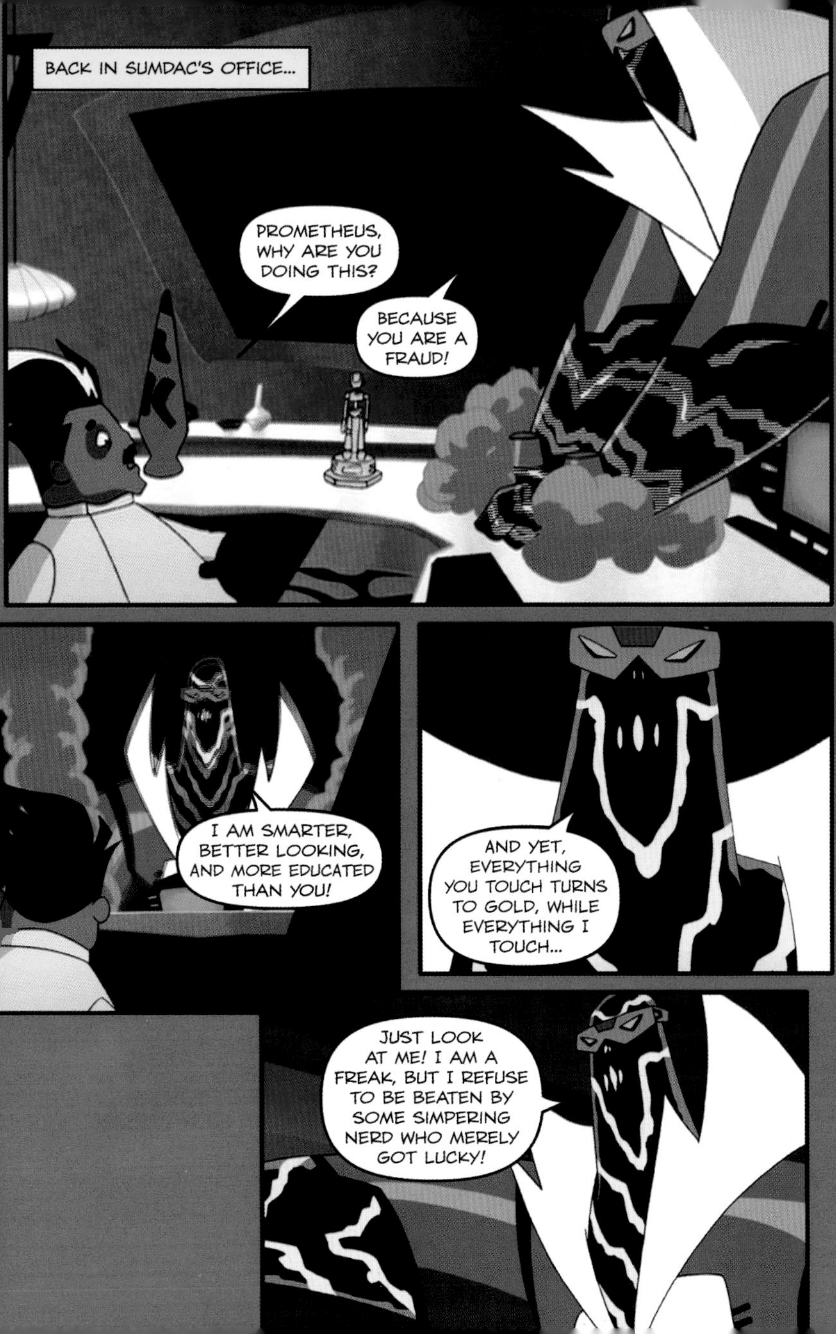
BACK IN SUMDAC'S OFFICE...
PROMETHEUS, WHY ARE YOU DOING THIS?
BECAUSE YOU ARE A FRAUD!
I AM SMARTER, BETTER LOOKING, AND MORE EDUCATED THAN YOU!
AND YET, EVERYTHING YOU TOUCH TURNS TO GOLD, WHILE EVERYTHING I TOUCH...
JUST LOOK AT ME! I AM A FREAK, BUT I REFUSE TO BE BEATEN BY SOME SIMPERING NERD WHO MERELY GOT LUCKY!

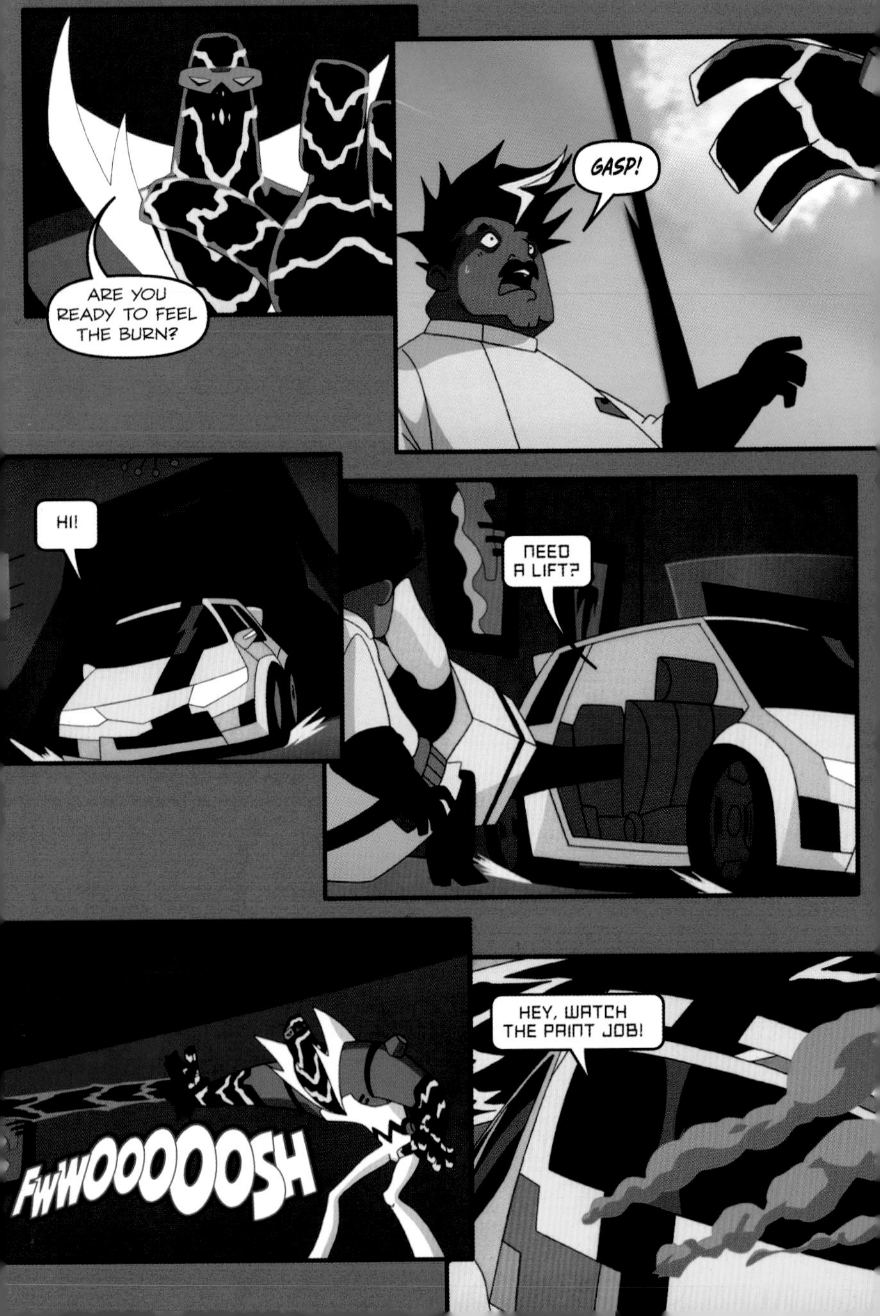
ARE YOU READY TO FEEL THE BURN?
GASP!
HI!
NEED A LIFT?
FWWOOOOOOSH
HEY, WATCH THE PAINT JOB!

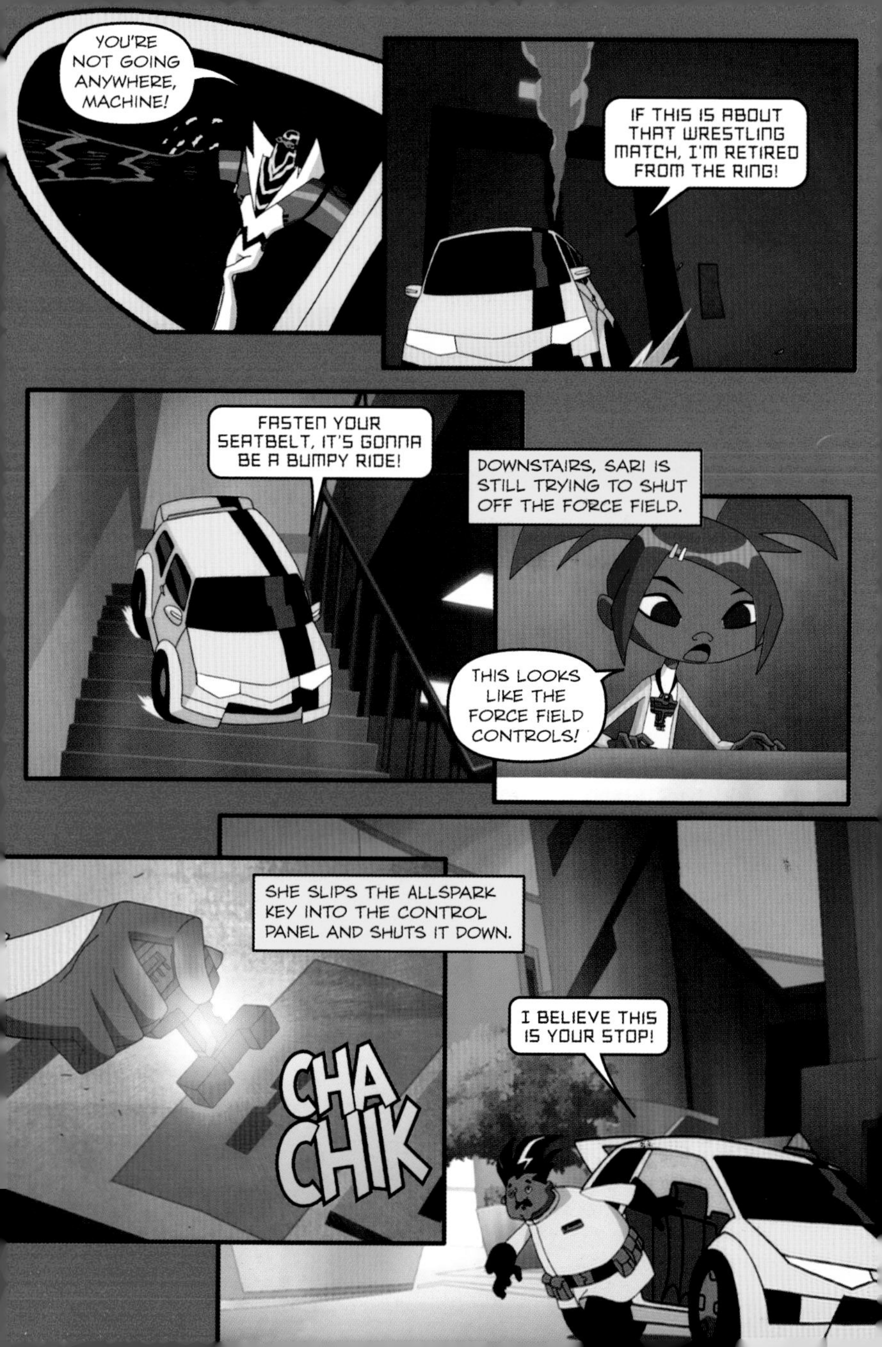
YOU'RE NOT GOING ANYWHERE, MACHINE!
IF THIS IS ABOUT THAT WRESTLING MATCH, I'M RETIRED FROM THE RING!
FASTEN YOUR SEATBELT, IT'S GONNA BE A BUMPY RIDE!
DOWNSTAIRS, SARI IS STILL TRYING TO SHUT OFF THE FORCE FIELD.
THIS LOOKS LIKE THE FORCE FIELD CONTROLS!
SHE SLIPS THE ALLSPARK KEY INTO THE CONTROL PANEL AND SHUTS IT DOWN.
CHA CHIK
I BELIEVE THIS IS YOUR STOP!

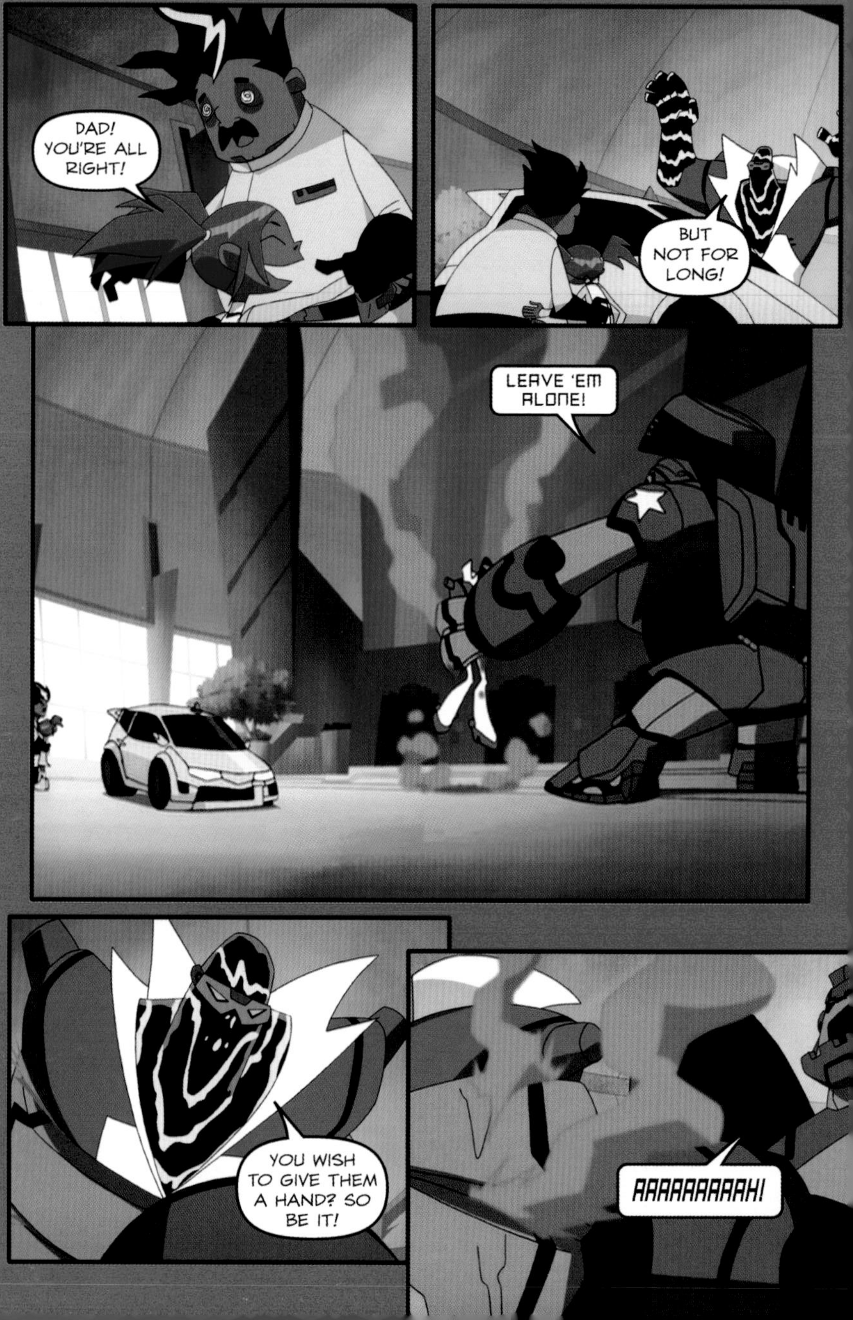
DAD! YOU'RE ALL RIGHT!
BUT NOT FOR LONG!
LEAVE 'EM ALONE!
YOU WISH TO GIVE THEM A HAND? SO BE IT!
AAAAAAAAAH!

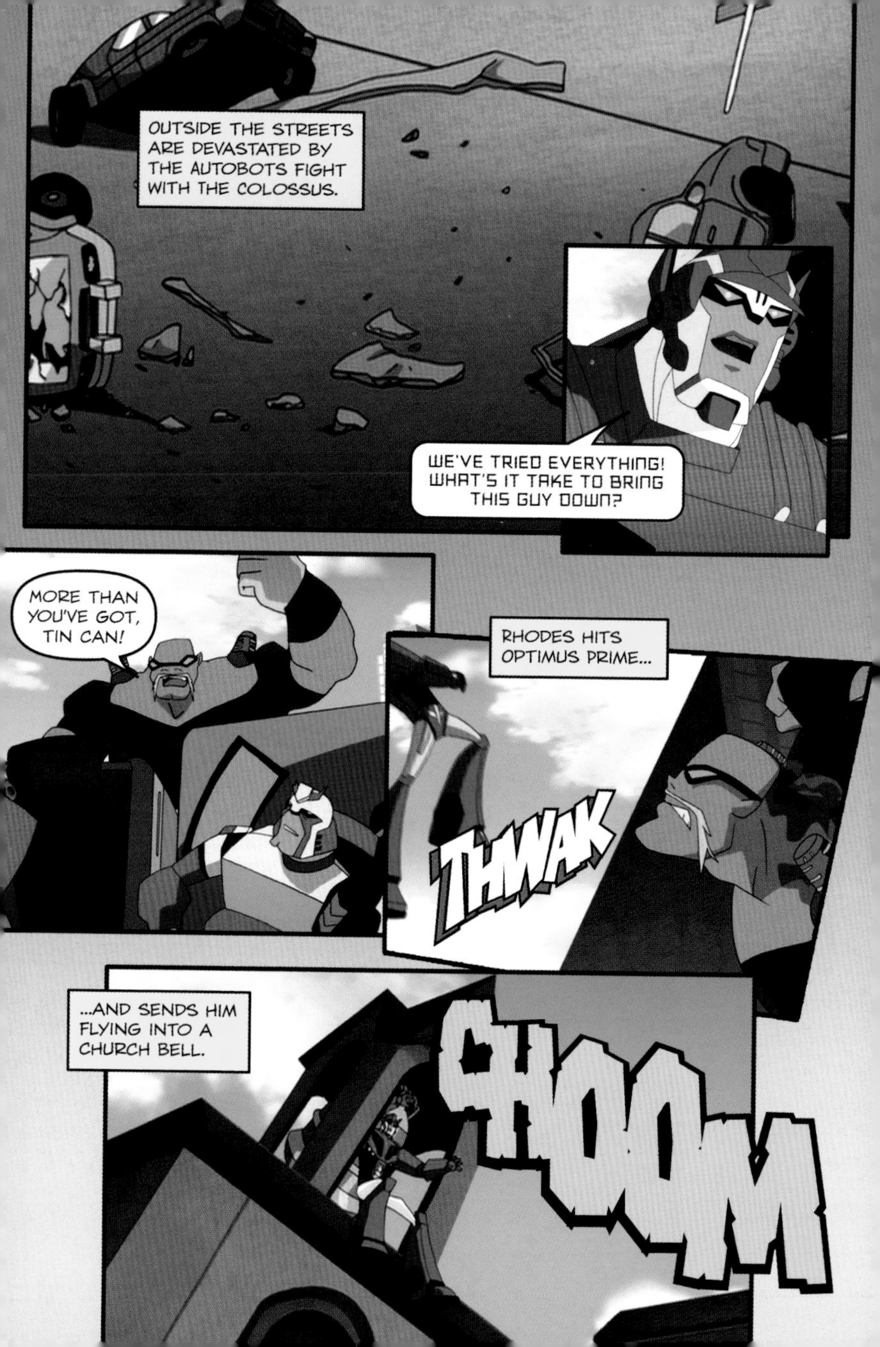
OUTSIDE THE STREETS ARE DEVASTATED BY THE AUTOBOTS FIGHT WITH THE COLOSSUS.
WE'VE TRIED EVERYTHING! WHAT'S IT TAKE TO BRING THIS GUY DOWN?
MORE THAN YOU'VE GOT, TIN CAN!
RHODES HITS OPTIMUS PRIME...
THWAK
...AND SENDS HIM FLYING INTO A CHURCH BELL.

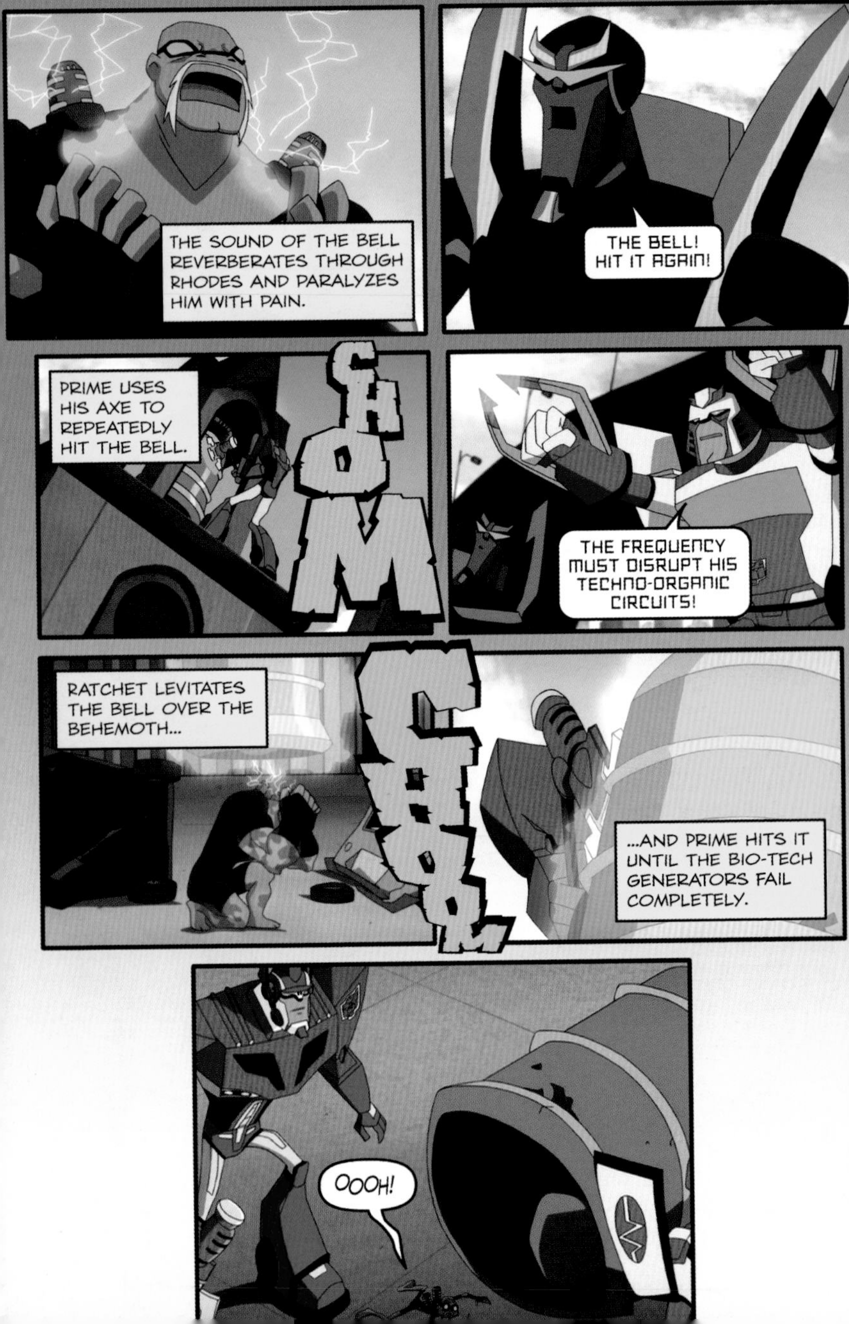
THE SOUND OF THE BELL REVERBERATES THROUGH RHODES AND PARALYZES HIM WITH PAIN.
THE BELL! HIT IT AGAIN!
PRIME USES HIS AXE TO REPEATEDLY HIT THE BELL.
CHOM
THE FREQUENCY MUST DISRUPT HIS TECHNO-ORGANIC CIRCUITS!
RATCHET LEVITATES THE BELL OVER THE BEHEMOTH...
CHOM
...AND PRIME HITS IT UNTIL THE BIO-TECH GENERATORS FAIL COMPLETELY.
OOOH!

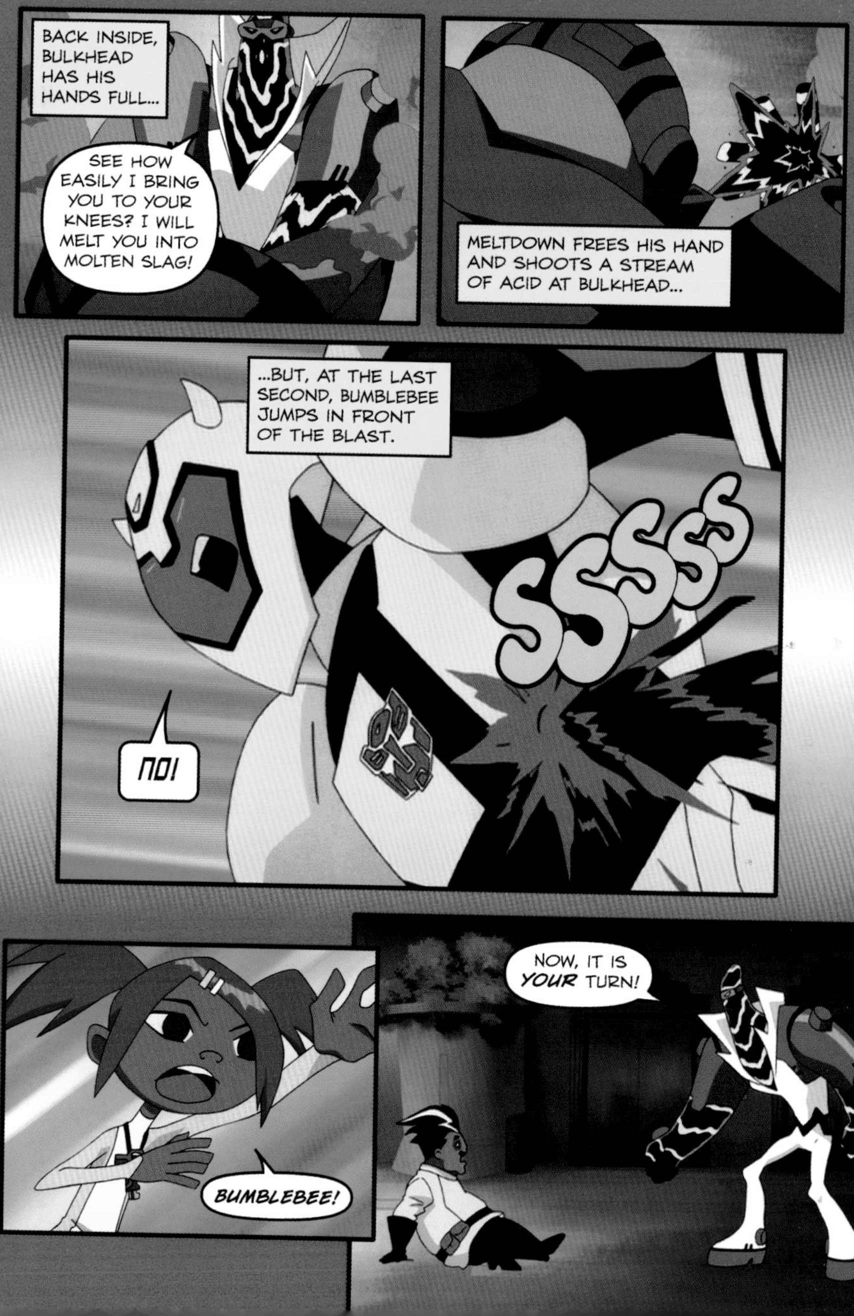
BACK INSIDE, BULKHEAD HAS HIS HANDS FULL...
SEE HOW EASILY I BRING YOU TO YOUR KNEES? I WILL MELT YOU INTO MOLTEN SLAG!
MELTDOWN FREES HIS HAND AND SHOOTS A STREAM OF ACID AT BULKHEAD...
...BUT, AT THE LAST SECOND, BUMBLEBEE JUMPS IN FRONT OF THE BLAST.
SSSSS
NO!
BUMBLEBEE!
NOW, IT IS *YOUR* TURN!

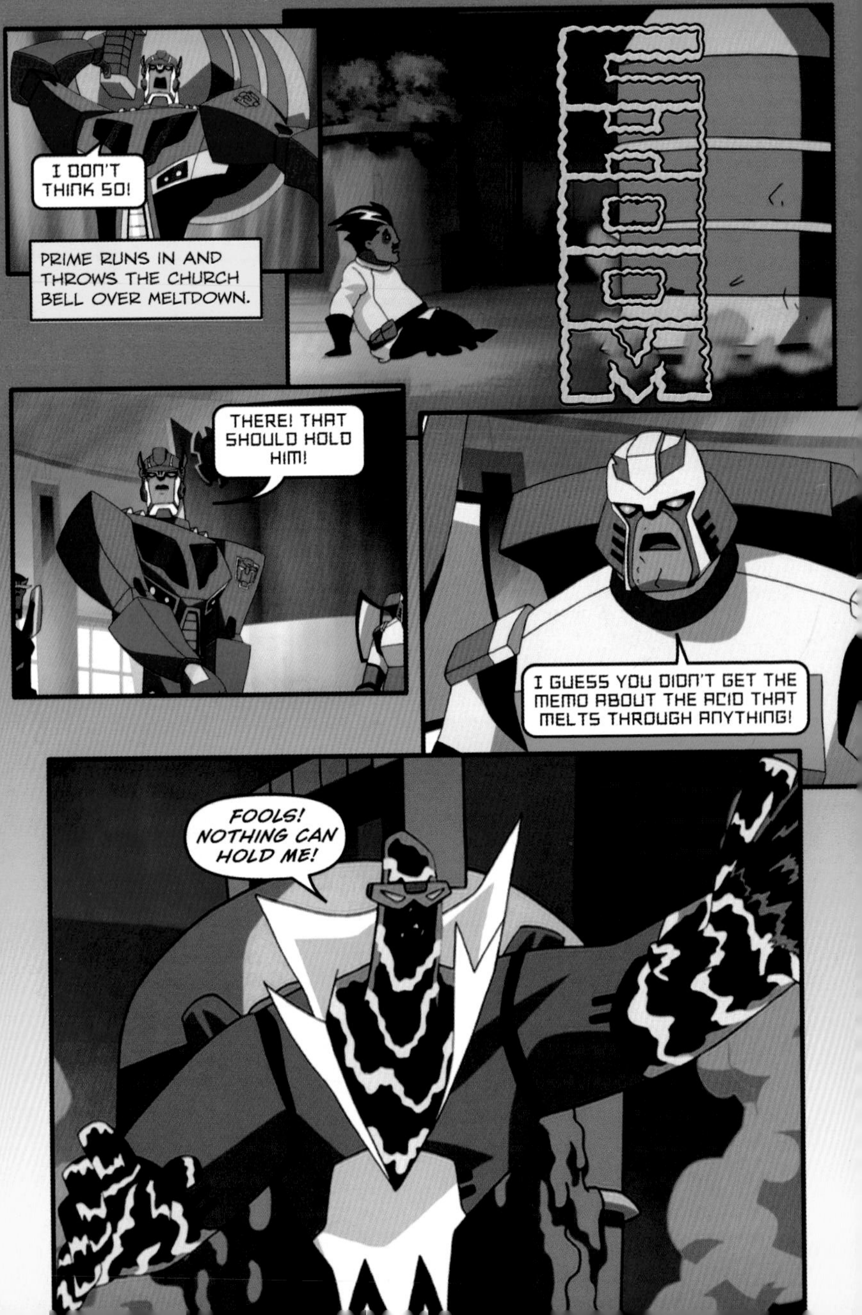
I DON'T THINK SO!
PRIME RUNS IN AND THROWS THE CHURCH BELL OVER MELTDOWN.
THERE! THAT SHOULD HOLD HIM!
I GUESS YOU DIDN'T GET THE MEMO ABOUT THE ACID THAT MELTS THROUGH ANYTHING!
FOOLS! NOTHING CAN HOLD ME!

SUGGESTIONS ON HOW TO STOP HIM!

HOW ABOUT USING THE ONE THING THAT STOPPED US!

THE AUTO-DEFENSE FIELD!

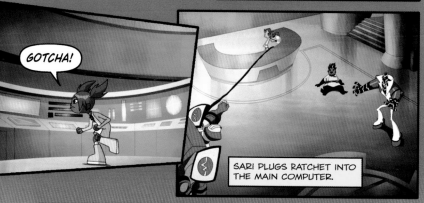

GOTCHA!

SARI PLUGS RATCHET INTO THE MAIN COMPUTER.

RATCHET THEN CREATES A FORCE FIELD AROUND MELTDOWN.

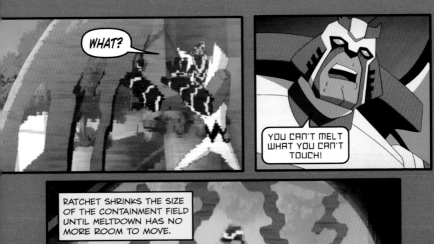

WHAT?

YOU CAN'T MELT WHAT YOU CAN'T TOUCH!

RATCHET SHRINKS THE SIZE OF THE CONTAINMENT FIELD UNTIL MELTDOWN HAS NO MORE ROOM TO MOVE.

I SAY LET HIM STEW IN HIS OWN JUICES.

BIG HELP YOU WERE, BULKHEAD. WHY DIDN'T YOU JUST DRAW A BULLS-EYE OVER THAT OVERSIZED CHESTPLATE OF YOURS?